STORM OUT OF TEXAS

Susan Yawn Tanner

Books by Susan Yawn Tanner

HISTORICAL ROMANCE
THE BELLAMYS OF TEXAS SERIES
Winds Across Texas
Fire Across Texas
Storm Out of Texas

A Warm Southern Christmas
(a historical romance novella)

SCOTTISH HIGHLANDS ROMANCES
Highland Captive
Captive to a Dream
Exiled Heart

**Praise for Susan Yawn Tanner's
Bellamys of Texas series:**
"Non-stop Western action combined with a
passionate love story. Five breathless stars!!"
–Sue's Reviews online

"I love the story line of this book. Very well written.
Author does a great job making you feel like you are in
the book!" – Lisa Armand, 5 stars, Amazon

"Great book! This book is about love; love for
family, love for your child, first love, lost love, and true
love." – SKM, 5 stars, online review

"A journey to the past … fast paced, intriguing,
action packed and romantic!"
– Carol LaGatta, 5 stars

Storm Out of Texas

The Bellamys of Texas, Book 3

Susan Yawn Tanner

Secret Staircase Books

Storm Out of Texas
Published by Secret Staircase Books, an imprint of
Columbine Publishing Group LLC
PO Box 416, Angel Fire, NM 87710

Book layout and design by Secret Staircase Books
Cover illustrations © Alanpoulson, Pictureguy66

First trade paperback edition: January 2021
ISBN 978-1649140456

First e-book edition: January 2021
ISBN 978-1649140463

*The dearest friends are those with whom
we grow and change.*

*For Lorene, for that season of innocence, when we
thought our world would never change. And for Becky, for
that age of awakening, when we realized everything would
change and we would be forced to change with it.*

Acknowledgements
First and foremost, to my publisher, Connie Shelton,
who wanted *just one more*. And for my readers who
wanted Ford in New Mexico with Slade & Katherine
and Jeb & Hannah. Without that push from both
directions, this book would never have been conceived,
much less written.

Chapter One

New Braunfels, Texas October 1860

Ford Bellamy let the peace of the place wash over him as he sank to the ground. He leaned his back against the cool stone and stretched his legs in front of him. The wind sang through the pine needles above him. For a moment, he lifted his gaze to the scattering of blue he could see through the swaying branches. It was time for him to move on. He'd known that for some time, but it was hard to do.

He never thought he'd leave Elizabeth. Never thought she'd leave him. This wasn't what he'd expected the day they'd stood in front of the preacher, wasn't what he'd wanted for either of them. He'd expected forever. He'd counted on it. But some things couldn't be undone and death was one of them. He'd come here for nearly a year, now, every day without fail, whether rain or shine, snow or suffocating heat. To talk to her. Long conversations about the unimportant bits and pieces of his day. Even longer ones about the important things.

In the first few weeks, he'd railed and cursed fate just so he could hear the soft sound of her voice in his mind chiding him for blasphemy. Anger had kept him on his feet when pain had threatened to bring him to his knees. A man should never have to know that kind of agony. He missed her every single minute of every single day and when he held their daughter in his arms each night, his heart broke all over again—for McKenna who would never know her mother's touch, for Elizabeth who'd never had the chance to hold her beautiful baby girl. And for himself, just because he loved her so damned much.

Ford closed his eyes and let the grief rip through him.

When the knot in his throat eased, he started to talk. "I guess you know I'm leaving. Never thought I would. We were going to live on this piece of ground together forever. We were supposed to have that. It hurts every damned day that I'm here alone. Me and McKenna, without you. And I just don't have the heart to work the farm anymore. This place was our dream—yours and mine." He paused. "I reckon Aunt Dee's going to be pissed. Pissed and hurt and scared for me to go, but my mind's made."

He ran his hand over the grass that had grown lush and thick through the first months of summer, but had dried and grown brittle in August's heat, a heat that September had done little to alleviate. And now it was October. He couldn't face another winter here. Not without his wife.

"I'll love you forever, Elizabeth. God knows I will and

I think you know it, too. At least I hope you do. I'll never love any woman the way I love you." He couldn't begin to imagine loving another woman. He didn't want to try.

When he finally got to his feet, he settled his hat on his head and looked at her name etched into the stone one last time. Then he turned and walked away.

"I can't believe you've done this, Ford. It's madness." His Aunt Dee was a pretty woman, but right now she was a riled one. Ford watched her warily. She wasn't past boxing his ears, even now he was grown. Maybe especially now.

They stood in her kitchen while McKenna played on the well-swept, wood plank floor with a rag doll his aunt had made for her.

"I'm sorry." He didn't know what else to say. And that was a half-truth at best. He was sorry to upset her, but he wasn't sorry over his decision. With that, he thought it best he say as little as possible.

The back door opened and Ford knew without turning that Doyle Shanley had walked in from the fields. It was that time of day. Doyle was a good man, better than most. He'd fallen in love with Dee McKenna the moment he'd laid eyes on her and never stopped, never given up. He'd given her and Shea a safe haven to call home. Ford would always be grateful to him for that.

"But you've sold the farm!" Dee said, the wound of that realization clear in her tone. "It's already done and without a word to me? How could you do that?"

He hadn't meant to hurt her. She'd raised him and Katherine after their mama—her sister—and then their father had died. Raised them alone and raised them right though Ford hadn't always acted in accord with that upbringing. "I got an offer I couldn't turn down." Ford felt Doyle's gaze between his shoulder blades.

"And what is your sister going to say about this? You just showing up on her doorstep and leaving her with no home to come back to? Have you even given a thought to that? It's as much hers as it is yours though I know she'll never come back to this town. Not to live."

Ford sighed. This was harder than he'd thought it would be and he'd never thought it would be easy. "Katherine's looking forward to seeing her niece for the first time. And seeing me, too, I guess." He hesitated. "She's good with me selling out and moving. I'd planned to split the money with her, told her so. She won't take it."

With a stricken look, Dee crossed her arms in front of her. Her gaze went from him to his daughter, her namesake. "You've known that long a time, Ford? Long enough to write to Kate and for her to write back to you?"

Ford simply nodded. Saying *I'm sorry* yet again wouldn't be nearly enough to make this right with her.

"So, then, what was this offer you couldn't turn down? Who is it that will be moving into the place I called home those many years? Where I made a home for you and your sister? For the three of us?"

Doyle cleared his throat and Ford took a breath of relief. What came next needed to come from her husband, not from Ford. "Now, Dee, you know this is your home now."

"Well, of course it is! And I love our place. But even so——." She stopped midsentence and spun to look at her husband. A strand of warm brown hair slipped free of the knot at the nape of her neck and curled over her shoulder. Ford noted for the first time that it was finely threaded with silver. "Doyle Shanley, for shame. You already knew?"

"Yes," he said cautiously.

But her eyes were still just as stormy and their almond shape narrowed at her husband. "You made the offer he couldn't refuse." It wasn't a question. His Aunt Dee was nothing if not perceptive. She'd often known what he and Katherine were thinking before they themselves knew.

"I did." Doyle answered without wavering. He'd had that steadfast way about him as long as Ford could recall.

Dee threw her hands in the air.

"Now, Dee…"

She glared a warning. "Just don't."

Wisely, Doyle didn't. Even so, he chanced a wink at Ford when Dee turned back to look at her nephew. "You know I love you like my own."

Ford stepped closer, wishing he knew how to make this easier. "And I love you, Aunt Dee. You're all I remember." That struck him with a pang. Who would McKenna remember? She'd never even seen her mother's face. Never would.

"This scares me for you and for that baby girl. That's a hard trip." She leaned into the arm that Doyle curved around her as he came close. "But you're a man with a man's choices to make. Little as I like it." With the sheen of tears in her eyes, she cupped the palm of her hand to Ford's cheek. "You won't be back, will you?"

"It may be that I won't," he said, being honest, "but never is a word I won't say. Taos is closer than it used to be."

Dee blinked back her tears and found a smile. "Well, it certainly hasn't moved!"

But Ford knew she saw the West becoming smaller just as he did, with rails going across mountains and valleys, with stagecoach routes increasing day by day. Doyle didn't have the least bit of wanderlust in him, but Ford could picture him taking Dee westward to visit the children she'd raised to adulthood.

Ford bought his tickets for the stage the next morning. He'd only been waiting until he'd told Aunt Dee, not wanting the town gossips to get to her first—and gossip traveled faster than lightning in New Braunfels. Stagecoach sure wasn't his preferred method of travel but, with McKenna, he didn't have much choice. Oh, there might be days where he could ride with her held before him and that would break the tedium of travel for him and for her, but there would be hours more that he was cooped up inside that hell on wheels Butterfield called a coach with his horse tied to the boot.

From the stage office, he walked to the Kern's, Elizabeth's childhood home, the front porch where he'd courted her, the parlor where he'd slipped his mother's ring with its sparkle of tiny diamonds and emeralds on her slender finger and asked her to marry him. Elizabeth wore that ring and his mother's gold band still, and would forever.

Martha Kern opened the door to him just as she had done so many times before. But she didn't smile at him. She hadn't smiled at him, not once, since the day her daughter had died in childbirth. "Ford. Come in."

He pulled off his hat and stepped into the front room. The curtains were closed as they always were now. She didn't ask him to sit. "I came to say good-bye."

She nodded. "I wish you well, Ford."

A sigh escaped him. He knew she did, but she blamed him as well. Him and McKenna. They'd cost her the thing she held most dear in this life.

"Are you sure you don't want to see McKenna before we go? I could bring her by tomorrow." So, she could hold the grandchild she'd never once held, look into her eyes … eyes she'd never seen.

"I'm sure."

"And Mr. Kern?"

"No," she hesitated. "We know you'll take care of the child exactly as Elizabeth would want."

And they both knew that was all that mattered to her. When she didn't say anything else, Ford moved toward the door she opened to him. He placed his hat on his head as he walked out. His boots were still on the steps when he heard the door close softly but solidly behind him.

Leaving the Kerns with a heavier heart, Ford stopped by the blacksmith. Evan Burch, whose father owned both the smithy and the livery stable next door, ran the stable while his father worked the forge. He and Evan had been friends since they were pulling girl's pigtails in school. Evan had pulled Katherine's most often until they'd reached their early teens and Katherine had quit pretending she didn't like it. The two might even have ended up married if the Comanches hadn't taken her and the friend she'd been visiting, killing the rest of the family in a murderous rampage. And if Katherine hadn't been rescued with a half-Comanche baby girl in her arms.

"Morning." Evan stepped through the door that connected the smithy to the livery. He watched as his father lifted the back leg of Ford's grullo gelding. "Thought I heard your voice. Loose shoe?"

Ford smiled. It felt funny to know this was likely the last time he'd see so many people he'd known all of his life. But he couldn't deny a prickle of excitement at the thought of getting away from a place of overwhelming grief. And that's what this town had been for him for the past year. "No, thought I'd best get this guy re-shod all around. I'm headed out, Evan. Just bought tickets for the stage out of San Antonio day after tomorrow."

Evan eyed him with a mixture of admiration and surprise. "You never could stay long in one place. Where you headed? And why are you taking the stagecoach?"

"New Mexico Territory. To Katherine and Slade's place 'til I build one of my own. Slade's filing a land claim for me, property that adjoins his. McKenna can't ride horseback that far. And the coach will add protection for her." And not just from the weather. Renegade Indians were still a risk for travelers and for settlers from time to time although not as much as they once were. On the other hand, bandits were increasing as a hazard. Every stage had at least one shot-gun rider plus a driver who could wield a weapon as handily as he could the coach lines. That was at least two guns added to Ford's.

"I'll bet your aunt isn't happy."

"You'd win that bet, but she'll be fine. She has Doyle and she has Shea." Katherine had claimed the baby for her own when the soldiers had taken her. But Shea was the daughter of a Comanche named Wolf Killer and Jeane Pearson, the girl taken with Katherine on that godforsaken day. Both Wolf Killer and Jeane were gone now. Dead. Katherine's heart had broken to leave Shea behind but Ford knew she'd recognized the child belonged more with their aunt than with her. Shea was loved and she was safe.

When Ford's horse was reshod, Evan followed him out

into the dust of the road that ran through the center of town. Ford turned to say good-bye, knowing this was a good friend he might never see again.

"Say, Ford, what if I went with you?" For a moment, Ford couldn't think what to say and Evan rushed ahead. "You know I'm a good shot and a fast rider. McKenna will be safer with both of us looking out for her."

"That's a big decision," Ford said slowly. Evan had a life mapped out for him, a comfortable one at that. And Evan had no idea how ugly life could be beyond the boundaries of civilized towns, especially if he decided to strike out for himself once they reached Taos. "Things can happen you don't expect, don't want."

"If I don't get out of here, now, I never will." Evan's voice wasn't pleading but his eyes held a quiet desperation that Ford had never seen in him before. "I'm a man grown. I can take what comes my way."

"Your pa won't be thanking me for putting ideas in your head." But Ford wouldn't be around to see or hear that displeasure and Evan was a man with a right to make up his own mind. Just as Ford had done since the day he'd turned seventeen. He'd survived his mistakes and learned enough to be a better man because of them. He reached out and shook Evan's hand. "Best get your ticket then. We'll head for San Antonio at daybreak."

* * *

McKenna had her mother's eyes, in shape if not in color, and right now they were wide with wonder. To Ford's amusement, Evan's weren't any less so.

San Antonio bustled with people and horses and wagons. Ford knew there were bigger towns and cities but not out West. Not yet. He would be among those who helped forge a path for others to follow. In any direction were places he'd never seen, and didn't know that he cared to, but he wanted every opportunity for McKenna. Everything he did from now on would be with a mind to McKenna's future.

To his relief, their coach was a Concord, made so that the body was held up with leather thoroughbraces. The rocking motion would be easier on McKenna than the jolting of a coach supported by steel springs.

With his little girl in one arm, Ford tied his horse to a post near the coach where a handful of people waited. Evan stepped up to take McKenna while Ford strode forward to greet the driver who stood with a ledger. The man wore a disgruntled expression which didn't bode well for the start of their trip. At least not in Ford's opinion.

The man thrust out a calloused hand to shake Ford's as he introduced himself then made a notation in the book with a stub of a pencil. "Name's Henry. We'll head out sharp at noon. You were told to travel light?"

Ford nodded. "Ticket clerk said you'd be carrying mail as well as passengers with limited room for baggage."

Henry nodded. "We'll be traveling fast and light. It's a small line with a new contract. Owner's eager to make a name for himself." He eyed Ford carefully, the gun at his side. "You any good with that?"

"Fair."

Whatever he saw in Ford's gaze must have resonated with him. He gave a nod and said, "Good. Ain't impressed with my shotgun rider. I'll feel better about traveling with women and a baby if I have another gun."

Ford started to explain that there was no woman

traveling with him and his daughter when he realized Henry had turned to glance toward the small gathering of fellow passengers. Two were older, not elderly, but far from spry. And a young woman, perhaps a daughter but surely not a servant. The green of her traveling cloak had the sheen of fine fabric and the tiny hat, which did nothing to cover her hair, matched the color of the cloak exactly. She was dressed far finer than the older people who stood beside her, but he supposed parents tended to do that. He could already see himself wanting more and better for McKenna than his parents had been able to afford for him and Katherine.

Perhaps feeling the looks sent their way, the girl turned. Ford caught a glimpse of her face and the desire that slid through him was as unexpected as it was unwelcome.

He turned away, forcing his attention back to the driver who spat tobacco juice into the dust between them. "Young lady was supposed to have a maid with her. Said the woman lost her nerve and refused to go on when they got off the steamer in Galveston. Supposed to have two vaqueros meet her here. No sign of them either. I would've been glad for their guns." Henry spat again.

* * *

Maria forced herself to stand quietly in place rather than pace the dusty road beside the boarding house as she longed to do. The stage coach was loaded with their bags and ready to leave. She was ready to leave as well.

"Mr. Hanson," the woman who hovered near the coach whispered loudly to her companion, "I've got a bad feeling."

The man patted the hand that rested in the crook of his arm. "Nothing to fear, Emmaline." He didn't whisper, but he sounded as if he were naturally a quiet-spoken man.

Maria thought it odd that the woman called her husband by his last name. And oddly uneven of them, that he did not do the same of her. They were not a young couple, nor were they elderly, perhaps the age of her parents.

"Where are the other passengers?" she persisted. "There should be more, shouldn't there?"

The man lifted one narrow shoulder in response to a question he could not answer.

Maria could have told her there would be no other passengers, but she remained silent as the question was not addressed to her. Her father had purchased tickets for the two vaqueros who were to wait for her here. They wouldn't have ridden in the coach but alongside it, their presence accomplishing both of her father's aims—that his daughter would not be crowded by strangers on her journey and that she would be well guarded on this last, most dangerous leg of the trip.

But her father's men had not been here to meet the coach. The driver, or whip as she'd heard Mr. Hanson refer to him earlier, believed they'd been slain by banditos. Maria supposed it possible but thought it just as possible that— once away from the confines of the ranch—they'd been hit by a wanderlust to see more of the world. Just as she had. But they were men and had the wherewithal to make their own way in the world. Maria did not.

Nor did she agree with Mr. Hanson that there was nothing to fear. Maria wasn't frightened but she was wise enough to realize there could, and likely would, be danger on the road ahead. The first half of her journey had been by ship, uneventful and not too uncomfortable as she was not plagued with seasickness as her maid had been. The private carriage from the coast inland to San Antonio had been tiresome and the route dusty, but still not intimidating. This morning, however, she could almost feel the tension emanating from the coach driver. And, clearly, she was not the only one.

Two men approached with the coach driver and Maria watched, curious because one carried a young child, little more than a baby. She glanced around for the mother for, surely, the child would not be journeying without her.

The baby patted the cheeks of the man who carried her and Maria's breath caught at the flash of a smile the action brought. He was the child's father if Maria were to judge by the rich copper hair and dark eyes of the man, which were reflected more subtly in the child. Whipcord muscles rippled beneath his clothing and Maria turned her eyes away. He was wed and she was betrothed.

* * *

Their driver, who seemed to have no last name—at least not one he'd shared with them—was a rough sort of gentleman, but a gentleman just the same. At least to Ford's mind. He'd introduced his passengers to one another, then—with his jaw bulging around a wad of tobacco—he'd handed each of the women into the coach. He assisted the youngest woman first, gesturing her toward the space just behind the driver. Ford knew that was the seat which would receive the least jolting along the way. He directed the Hansons to the middle seat.

Ford cast a glance inside and grimaced. "Evan and I will take the middle."

Henry squinted one eye at him. "Least comfortable.

No back to it," he pointed out needlessly. "Just that strap hanging over."

"I'm aware."

"Mr. Bellamy, you paid for first class. Third class is the seat that'll get out and help push if'n I need it."

"The name's Ford. We'll take the middle and what goes with it."

Mr. Hanson gave Ford a grateful look. "Much obliged, Mister."

Ford thought Henry's expression held a touch of gratitude as well. The Hansons were unlikely to have been much help to the driver even if they gave it their best effort. But when Henry had the older couple settled in the rear of the coach, "Obliged," was all he said to Ford and that was enough.

Ford tossed McKenna's bag under the seat and stepped inside with her. He wedged his back against the wall of the coach so that he could brace himself and better protect her from the jostling. He felt the stare of the young woman from her place at the front. He'd deduced by now that she wasn't part of the Hanson's small party, but couldn't fathom her parents—or a husband—allowing her to travel alone. He supposed he was as much an oddity to her as she was to him.

McKenna had been wide-eyed on the horseback ride into San Antonio so was content to eat the biscuit he unwrapped for her and sip from his canteen before nestling against his chest.

* * *

Maria fought her curiosity at the realization that the two men did, indeed, travel alone with a baby. She fought, also, the urge to tell Mr. Bellamy that she would hold the child should it become necessary for him to help push the wagon. Perhaps it would not come to that and there would be no need to make that offer. A lady did not speak to a man who had not been properly introduced to her. The quick sharing of names by their driver could hardly be called a proper introduction.

She sighed and glanced out the window as the coach lurched forward.

Chapter Two

By the end of the third day, Maria was heartily sick of the view of the plains outside her window. Their last stop came long past dark. The blast of a horn from atop the coach startled her and she realized she'd been close to drowsing. The second blast of the horn came several minutes later. She'd gleaned by now that the horn signaled their arrival, giving time for the station keep to prepare for the coach to roll in with hungry passengers and weary animals that needed to be swapped for fresh.

She'd also gathered that the lateness of the hour was customary and a matter of pride for their whip who seemed to be in competition with another driver on this route. The food was decent and she was hungry so she ate, but the common room smelled of old food and old sweat so she stepped out to walk as soon as she had thanked the boy who'd set platters of food on the rough board table.

Henry stood just outside the door. "Don't wander."

She didn't need a more explicit warning than that and gave him a nod. She did not plan to go any farther than the low fence which served no purpose that she could see. It would keep nothing in nor out of the small clearing, but it was close to the building and marked a boundary for her to heed.

Maria had been spoiled from the moment she was born and she knew it. She had never, however, taken that for granted or taken advantage of the fact. At twenty-two, she'd been given far more latitude than any girl she knew, certainly more than any of her friends. For the past five years, she'd been allowed to stay with her mother's brother in Boston and study. Not, of course, in any public venue but she'd had her own tutor and access to some of the finest literature and mathematical books available in the East. She'd traveled frequently with her aunt and an array of servants to various towns, staying with friends as wealthy as they and seeing more of the world—at least the new country—than she ever could from the windows of the New Mexico territory that was her home.

A few weeks ago, her father had bidden her home to wed and she'd veiled her disappointment behind a pleasant response to his missive and packed her belongings. She wasn't looking forward to marriage but she wasn't dreading it. No one in Boston or the surrounding towns had caught her interest and she could never imagine herself living there. The New Mexico Territory was wild and beautiful and she had always expected to return. And marriage was inevitable if she were to have a home of her own. She could hardly expect her father to establish a residence for her as a single woman.

Still, the sigh that escaped her was heartfelt. A deliberately cleared throat from close behind caused her to whirl.

Maria touched a hand to her throat. "Mr. Burch."

"I didn't mean to startle you, ma'am." He seemed to hesitate. "Probably best you keep your mind on your whereabouts when you're away from the group."

"You are correct in that," she said carefully. "Thank you." She glanced back at the log exterior of the station where there was no evidence of their driver. She would indeed need to pay more attention to her surroundings. Still, she felt no fear of Mr. Burch though they had done no more than exchange nods until now. She'd guessed him to be close in age to Mr. Bellamy, perhaps a bit older than him by his face, but he'd seemed far less self-assured. Or perhaps it was just that he had the tall and gangly build of someone who'd yet to grow into manhood although he clearly was a man full grown.

"Henry says we'll cross into New Mexico in the morning. That's home for you, isn't it?"

Maria nodded. "It is, yes."

"Have you traveled by coach before?"

"I have but it was long ago." She turned to walk and he fell into step beside her. "My parents took me to Boston five years ago, but it was different then. There were two coaches and my father owned them. We had more than a dozen vaqueros on horseback to guard us from Indian attack."

"Were you? Attacked, I mean."

"No, we traveled in safety. Such a long journey, though, and so tiring."

"And now another long journey home."

She laughed. "Far shorter. My maid and I traveled from Boston to Galveston by steamer. It was not pleasant and poor Trella did not fare well. She refused to travel farther with me. I think she did not choose wisely as the private coach to San Antonio proved quite comfortable. Now she must travel inland by stage or take the steamer again."

"Maybe she'll choose to stay in Galveston?"

Maria thought that unlikely but all she said was, "Perhaps. I left her with money to return, but it would be enough to live for a good while until she finds another position." Or enough to return her to Boston which was much more likely. Trella had not been happy to leave and Maria suspected she had a beau.

* * *

Ford stood in the open doorway of the station, one ear listening for McKenna who'd settled onto a cot in the common area. He'd sleep there as well, although he'd been shown a tight niche with an oilskin covering for a door. He preferred an open space where a man could move.

He'd meant to step out into the night air for a few peaceful moments, but the sight of Evan and the woman, not touching but side by side as they walked the perimeter of the clearing, stopped him. Her name was Maria, he reminded himself, Maria Cordova. He couldn't hear their conversation, but he heard her laugh. The sound arrowed through him, bringing an unwanted awareness of her. Much as his first glimpse of her had done.

Deliberately, he brought memories of Elizabeth to mind. Blue eyes that sparkled with joy at the sight of him walking in the back door after a hard day. Hair so dark it reflected the purple of the sky in the evening light. He remembered those evening light moments, the moonbeams streaming through their bedroom window. He remembered Elizabeth. And the remembering crushed every thought of the pretty Spanish girl from his mind.

Ford turned and went back inside to his daughter.

The next morning, Henry stood waiting at the coach as his passengers filed out of the station after breakfast. Lem, his shotgun rider, had already climbed to the box of the coach. The station keeper stood next to Henry, the two of them deep in conversation.

As the other passengers climbed into the coach, including Evan with McKenna, Henry waved Ford over.

Ford read their expressions as he walked their way. "Something wrong?"

Henry gave him an abrupt nod. "You'll be mounted today?"

"Planned on it for the morning. Evan will have McKenna."

Henry nodded at the station keeper. "Tell 'im what we got, Cleve."

"Rider came through a while ago. Rode all night giving warnings. Homestead burned out close to your midday station stop."

"Dead?"

Cleve gave him a somber look. "Family of seven. Five kids caught in the loft when the fire was set just after dark. Parents gunned down in the yard."

"Indians?"

Cleve shook his head. "Comancheros, more like."

Ford knew that most Comancheros wouldn't go out

of their way to burn a homestead. They were mercenaries more than anything, making their living by trading with the Comanches. Even so, they could be ruthless with anyone who got in the way of that trade. For decades, their wares had been legitimate goods, like cloth and metal and beads. More recently, they'd begun to trade in stolen cattle and horses and whiskey. He thought of the kids caught in that fire, then he thought of McKenna and took a deep breath before turning to Henry. "What's your plan?"

Henry scratched the side of his jaw. "Don't know that they'll be watching the stage route, waiting for us to come through. Don't know that they won't. Not much we can do but be ready." He scratched his jaw again. "Maybe you'd give some thought to Mrs. Hanson watching that little girl of yours so's Mr. Burch can ride. The more guns the better."

The driver didn't look away when Ford searched his gaze. Ford didn't read fear, but the man clearly wasn't a fool and he was worried. Taking a deep breath, Ford nodded and turned toward the coach. He tried to convince himself that Mrs. Hanson could manage keeping his daughter comfortable. But the image he had in his mind was the one he carried from yesterday's long afternoon hours. The woman sitting, hands clasped together, periodically twisting and untwisting. Her worried whispers to her husband. How would she react if shots were fired and Henry had to put the mules to flight? Would she protect McKenna with her life or would she panic?

By the time Ford reached the Concord, his mind was made. "Evan, can you talk a minute?"

When Evan stepped out, Ford took McKenna and gave Evan a quick recap of the conversation and what he planned to do. Then he climbed in and faced Ms. Cordova.

She watched him gravely. She was young, but not as young as he'd first thought, not a silly girl but a woman grown.

He could tell from her expression that she'd watched his conversation with the station keeper and their driver and had already sensed something was wrong. As had Mrs. Hanson. He could hear the woman's stressed breathing from the back of the coach, the shuddering way she caught her breath.

Ford didn't waste time with pleasantries. "Ms. Cordova, will you take care of McKenna for me? Me or Evan—we'll take her as soon as it's…" he hesitated thinking of the older woman listening anxiously, "as soon as we can."

Maria Cordova nodded gravely and reached for McKenna who gurgled at her, a happy sound that wrenched Ford's heart as he let her go to the woman's arms. "Of course." She glanced back at their other passengers and said more quietly, "Should it be necessary, I'll sit in the floor with her. Away from the window."

"Much obliged." Ford backed out and closed the door of the coach securely before mounting up. He nodded at Evan who rode on the opposite side of the coach, near the rear as he did. Henry and Lem would see anything coming at them. It was up to Evan and Ford to watch for an attack from behind.

They reached the swing station by midmorning. Within minutes, their mule team was replaced with a fresh one by the stock tenders without incident. Ford would've liked to relax, but that itchy spot between his shoulder blades hadn't left him. He contented himself with looking into the coach at his baby girl. Asleep, she nestled against Maria Cordova who gave him a small smile of reassurance. Ms. Cordova had removed the fancy jacket she'd worn in the chill of morning. The bodice of the pale gray gown beneath was plain but fitted. McKenna's cheek lay against the curve of her breast. Ford looked quickly away.

He remounted and reminded himself it didn't do any good to wish that McKenna snuggled against her mother instead of a stranger. If Elizabeth were alive, they'd be home, the three of them, safe on their farm in New Braunfels.

The next leg of the journey and team swap were equally eventless. Ford calculated they were near their midday stop when the itch between his shoulder blades became a burning. His gut tightened as he looked around them.

He glanced toward the box. Henry stretched the muscles across his broad back, looking first to the right and then to the left. Ford knew he felt it as well. Lem slouched in his seat, grunting when Henry nudged him. He straightened reluctantly, looking around.

The first bullet went low, just over the backs of the mules, but Henry was ready and kept the two leads in steady control as he urged them to a gallop. From inside the coach came Ms. Hanson's shriek of terror. Ford ignored her as he judged the path of the bullet by the sound it made and carefully returned fire. Evan followed suit.

Another shot came across the traces and Lem took aim. Ford held his, trying to gauge the number of horses that came after them by the drumming of hooves on hard ground. At least three, but no more than four or five.

Ford knew the goal would be to send the mules careening out of control, the coach bouncing against boulders or scrub trees until it came apart. The fate of the passengers wasn't of concern, only the possessions they might carry.

The next bullet ripped into the wood of the carriage near the rear. Ford prayed that Maria Cordova had kept her promise and was on the floor with McKenna.

He caught Evan's attention and made a circling motion with his hand as he veered his horse to the side and made for a stand of cottonwood trees on low ridge. Evan nodded and fired another shot to give Ford some cover but continued on, keeping pace with the coach.

Moments later, four riders crested the slope behind the coach. Picking his target, Ford sighted along the barrel of the Spencer, ignoring the trickle of sweat sliding down between his shoulder blades. Aiming for a horse would be more of a sure stop but he couldn't bring himself to do that. He squeezed the trigger and a heartbeat later the rider on the last horse toppled from the saddle, arms outflung, gun tumbling.

Ford slid his rifle back into the saddle sling and pulled his revolver. As he'd hoped, the other three seemed not to realize they were now a man short. With a squeeze of his knees against his mount's side, Ford moved in behind them. The animal beneath him fell into a willing run, eager to catch up with the horses ahead.

In the few moments that it took for Ford to make a plan, he was aware of the blaze of the sun overhead, the brilliant blue of the sky—and that he might never see his baby girl again. He took his time making the first shot, taking another man to the ground, but was forced to make the next too quickly after the first. The rider jerked. He was hit, but managed to keep his seat and spin his horse around, returning fire rapidly. The fourth man wheeled his horse about as well, both of them riding hard toward Ford, sending bullets ahead of them.

The rider that Ford had injured swayed in the saddle before slipping to flop helplessly against the saddle. His horse veered at the weight shifting to one side and rammed the horse beside him. Ford could hear the vicious curse in response. Then there was the sharp report of a shot and the final man slumped in the saddle as his horse raced past Ford.

Evan met Ford's gaze across the distance then wheeled his horse back the way he'd come, to catch up with the coach. Ford followed, urging his horse on, anxious to get to McKenna, afraid of what he'd find on the other side of the rise.

Maria sat on the ground beside the coach that their driver had finally, blessedly stopped. She cradled the little girl close against her chest. McKenna, her father had called her. An odd and grown-up sort of name for such a little girl, but she'd grow into it no doubt. Her terrified screams had faded to sobs and then shuddering breaths interspersed with hiccups.

Every inch of Maria's body ached from taking the brunt of the jolts as she was flung about the inside of the coach. With her arms wrapped around McKenna, she hadn't been able to brace herself but the little child's protection had come first. Maria didn't think anything was broken although her lip had split when the side of her face hit the seat and she suspected the shirtwaist of her gown was ruined by the bloodstains. But that was the least of her worries.

Henry sat on the ground beside her, a shotgun across his knees. Neither one of them knew who would be riding toward them. Friend or foe. The shotgun rider, as she'd heard him called, was dead, still in his seat atop the coach. Mrs. Hanson had quit screaming and now sat in her seat staring straight ahead. Mr. Hanson patted her hand continually and murmured to her but Maria didn't think the woman heard him.

Maria saw them first, recognized the grullo that Ford Bellamy rode and let the tension slip from her. Henry scrambled to his feet and waited. She could only imagine what he was thinking. Were it not for the courage and quick-thinking of Ford Bellamy, they'd all be dead. She'd watched from the window as McKenna's father had faded into the trees, putting himself at greater risk as he was left separated from the rest of them. He'd done it for his child, of course, but—in the doing—he'd saved them all. All except for the shotgun rider.

When she could no longer see him, she'd moved with McKenna to the safety of the floor and began praying in earnest.

As the two men came closer, her gaze searched them for injuries but she saw none. What she did see was the horror on Ford's face as he saw his baby cradled in her arms. She glanced down, remembered the blood on her gown, and began shaking her head. "She's fine," Maria called to him as he slid from his horse and stumbled toward them. "McKenna's not hurt."

Ford lifted his daughter and tucked her head under his chin for a brief moment. He pressed a kiss to the top of her head then passed her to Evan, before kneeling beside Maria. "The bleeding ... where are you hurt?"

She tilted her face to him. "My lip hit the coach seat."

Ford winced and she suspected it looked as bad as it

felt. "Looks like the whole side of your face hit."

The smile she attempted faded in the wave of pain that followed the small movement. "And it feels that way as well."

Maria made an effort to stand and he slipped an arm around her waist, helping her to her feet. The polite touch—and that's all it was—drew a flush to her cheek. She could feel the heat of it, just as she felt the heat of his hand through the thin material of her dress.

"Not much we can do here," Henry said. "The midday station's not much farther. There'll be cold well water. That'll help about as much as anything can."

"I'll be fine," Maria assured him. "What about…?" She hesitated and glanced at the coach where the shotgun rider still slumped half-on, half-off the seat where he'd died.

The lines on Henry's forehead deepened. "We're close enough we'll take him on, give him a decent burial."

McKenna woke as Henry and Ford were wrapping Lem's body in a blanket. The little girl looked at Evan who held her, then held out her arms to Maria who took her without hesitation. McKenna touched the place where Maria's face was most tender, and likely most discolored, then laid her hand there as if to soothe.

The little girl's face crumpled when Mrs. Hanson began to shriek. "No, no. He can't go with us! Leave him here!"

The woman rushed toward the driver, arms extended, hands curled into claws. Maria took one look at the wildness in her eyes and turned McKenna in her arms shielding her from the scene. She put several more steps between them and the hysteria unfolding.

"Ma'am, Lemuel may have been a piss-poor shot, but he was a Christian man and he'll get a Christian burial."

"You won't take him. I won't have it."

Henry spoke sharply to her husband. "You'll want to get her calmed down, sir. People die on the trail for a lot of reasons. One of them is the inability to control their mind."

Evan moved to stand between the frantic woman and the corpse. When she rushed at him, he took her by the forearms and said gently, "Ma'am, you won't even see him. I promise. What if this was your kin, your husband, lying there? You'd want us to take care of him, wouldn't you?"

Mrs. Hanson closed her eyes and swayed and her husband stepped forward. Maria saw the grateful look he gave Evan Burch as his wife allowed him to lead her toward the coach.

"Let's sit down, Emmaline. I'll get you a swallow of water from our canteen. Maybe dampen my handkerchief and cool your face."

Henry gave the couple one last look of distaste and turned back to help Ford tie the blanket around the dead man. They hoisted him above the luggage stowed in the boot and secured him with rope.

Maria watched as Ford climbed down and walked toward her. When he would have reached for his daughter, she stopped him. "I would much rather you and Mr. Burch, both of you, were on horseback, watching for trouble." She hesitated. "I promise I'll put her life before mine."

Ford's gaze skimmed her face, her battered cheek and lip, before returning to meet her own direct look. "Yes, ma'am."

It was all he said. He held McKenna in one arm and helped Maria step up into the coach with the other before handing his daughter in to her and turning to walk back to his ground-tied grullo. He and Evan Burch mounted and Henry urged the team forward.

Chapter Three

Taos, New Mexico Territory

Katherine waited as Slade walked through the back door into the kitchen. Jeb was a step or two behind. She could tell by their expressions that what they'd found wasn't good. "You found him? The bull?"

"Dead."

"Not just dead," Jeb added. "Slaughtered and left for carrion. Like the first one."

Katherine felt sick. It was the second bull in a week. They'd bought four beautiful Durham shorthorns, placing one in each of the four quadrants of their combined properties. Each quadrant had a lead vaquero assigned to oversee the herd. Those leads directed the branding and castration, the movement of the cattle from one grazing section to another, and selected the men who worked for them.

As soon as the first bull had been reported missing by that quadrant's lead, every available hand was assigned to comb the hills. The animal had been found a day later. And now this. They lost cattle now and again, every rancher did. A cow birthing, a calf lost to predators, a heifer to lightning or some freak accident but not this senseless butchery.

"Apache?" Katherine hated the thought, hated the possibility.

One small band made their home at the northern edge of their property. The first year they'd made Katherine wary with their presence, but they'd remained peaceful though watchful. From time to time, a solitary rider would follow the stream through the center of their property and stand his pony on a small rise where he would observe the comings and goings of their ranch life before turning back the way he'd come. But now this.

Slade shook his head at her question. "I can't see it. They know we don't mind a missing cow or two, that we turn a blind eye when game is scarce and babies are hungry. Jishnu has more wisdom than to cause trouble or allow his braves to cause trouble."

"He keeps a strong, steady hand over his people," Jeb agreed with Slade. "I'm going to check on Hannah then head out to talk with Mateo." He crossed the wide space to the door that opened onto a dog trot. Two open breezeways connected their individual homes with the common kitchen.

During their first months in New Mexico, Katherine and Slade had lived in a loft over the barn. When Jeb had arrived with an unexpected bride, the men had begun the arduous task of splitting timber for lumber. The structure, already weathering to silver, wasn't finished but they'd made a good start. What mattered most was that it was home and a good place to welcome a baby.

Slade frowned as Jeb disappeared from sight. "Is Hannah alright?"

"She's fine, just tired and I'm pretty sure that's normal in every stage of pregnancy," Katherine reassured him. "She's not worried, nor am I."

"Jeb is."

"She won't lose this baby like she did her first with that preacher man. She was slung to the ground by men intent on raping her. That's what killed her baby." Katherine's tone was fierce at the thought. "I wish I could kill them."

"Too late." Slade drew her close, lifted his hands and began pulling pins from her hair.

Too late for others to take retribution. Hannah had pulled that trigger to save Jeb's life, but Wilkins' death had delivered justice for Hannah's tiny son who'd never had a chance to draw a breath. Katherine knew she would do the same if Slade's life or a life they had conceived was ever at stake.

Her fierce thoughts faded as Slade's Ranger-tough hands slid through her hair, caressed her neck. He and Jeb had resigned, true enough, but they would both always be on the side of law and order, both would always be willing to give their lives to save another, willing to take a life that needed taking.

Slade skimmed his palms down her arms and captured one of her hands in his. He led her to the opposite end of their breezeway and laid her down on their marriage bed where she welcomed him into her arms.

* * *

Slade woke to afternoon light streaming through their bedroom window. Katherine had insisted on glass and he had obliged, if only because the woman asked for so damned little in life. And because she made life good and worth living.

Murmuring, she rolled, shifted closer. He laughed, then growled low in her ear. "I've work to do. You're keeping me from it."

"Not often enough," she murmured drowsily then gave a chuckle. "Or long enough."

"Damn, woman."

"I'd best get up, too, as I suppose you'll be wanting food when you're done."

He rose from the bed, found his pants and shirt, then stood looking down at the beauty of her. "Lie here a bit. Given the choice between you and food or anything else, Kate, I'll always choose you."

They weren't just pretty words. She was his life, his to love, his to protect. And something nagged at him about the two slain bulls, nagged and warned of trouble to come. Even so—whatever came their way—he would protect what was his.

Katherine always felt that she and Hannah worked well together. Neither cared for cooking, but they'd developed a rhythm that served them well. Lately, since Hannah had begun increasing with her child, Katherine made sure she had tasks that kept her off her feet. At the moment, Hannah was seated at the large table, grinding dried herbs with a mortar and pestle while Katherine churned butter from the cream she'd separated earlier in the day from the milk.

From time to time, Katherine glanced at Hannah whose normally creamy complexion gave an illusion of delicacy in a woman who was as strong inside as an oak tree. It was also a quick giveaway with flushed cheeks or shadows under her eyes when she became overheated or overtired. Even with the sun sinking, Katherine could feel the kitchen grow increasingly warm from the mutton leg she turned periodically on the spit.

"Quit watching me," Hannah told her.

"I wasn't."

"Liar."

Katherine chuckled in response but the sound was cut short by Bartolome calling her name from the door that stood open to the breeze. The older gentleman tended their barnyard animals, the pigs and sheep and poultry. Katherine stepped to the door to greet him.

"Mrs. Katherine, Señor Arellano approaches." Bartolome twisted and untwisted his hat as he spoke.

"How many ride with him?"

"A dozen, at least, maybe more."

At his words, Hannah rose to her feet, still graceful in her pregnancy. She took the shotgun from its rack beside the door, placed it on the table beside her, and gave Katherine a look as she sat and reached for the mortar and pestle once more. Katherine took a deep breath. The visit with so many men could mean nothing but, like Hannah, she wasn't entirely comfortable. She patted the pocket of her gown, reassuring herself the revolver was there then stepped out onto the porch and waited.

She didn't dislike the man, barely knew him, but a visit

with a dozen or so riders could have all kinds of meanings, none of them good.

Recently arrived from Spain, Arellano was the sole heir to an uncle who had died childless. The Spaniard now owned land that adjoined theirs and had made a courtesy visit a few weeks earlier. Katherine had paid him little attention until he'd enquired smoothly if Slade and Jeb had made any attempt to dislodge the Apache tribe to the north. Slade had been quick to answer that they had not and would not because the Apache had given them no cause. Although Arellano had nodded agreeably, Katherine hadn't missed the narrowing of his lips in displeasure at the response.

Katherine could understand his concern—to a point. She, more than most, had little reason to trust any of the tribes. But she, more than most, understood the lack of trust was on both sides and with good reason. What reason had the Indian nations to trust settlers who encroached more and more on land that had once belonged solely to the natives? Arellano did not have that knowledge but he needed to learn and learn swiftly.

The Spaniard rode unerringly to where Katherine waited. Bartolome stood at her side. She knew he was armed but could feel his tension. Several yards away, Arellano lifted one hand and his men halted their horses while Arellano continued closer. He and one more, a younger man, much younger. The resemblance between them was clear but the beaked nose that looked strong with Arellano's high cheekbones and chiseled jaw was less fortunate paired with the flat cheeks and weak chin of the younger.

Arellano tipped his hat to Katherine. "Señora, *buenas tardes.*"

"Good afternoon, Señor Arellano."

"Señor Slade ... is he at home?"

"He's on our property," she said, giving nothing away.

"But not here?" Arellano made a show of looking about. "He takes great risk leaving his beautiful wife unprotected." Clearly, he thought the servant by her side little protection—as both of them knew he would be when outnumbered by so many.

Katherine heard the door open behind her as Hannah stepped out with the shotgun. "She's not without protection," Hannah spoke in the cool, clear voice that Katherine always thought ready-made for a church choir. "I protect her and she protects me."

With a grunt of unpleasant laughter, the young man who'd come close with Arellano tossed his reins to his horse's neck and threw his leg over the saddle, landing lightly on his feet as he leapt to the ground. Throwing his chest out, he started toward the porch.

In one smooth motion, Hannah swung the shotgun up level with his face, which blanched then tightened with fury.

Arellano spoke one word, sharply, and the young man stopped in his tracks. They exchanged words in angry tones before the younger returned to his horse and remounted.

"Forgive me, ladies. I present to you my nephew, Javier. He is impetuous."

Katherine looked from Arellano to Javier, fixing him with her stare. "And perhaps unwise as well."

Her words were a warning to Javier, but it was Arellano who answered. "Perhaps so, but the young must have time to grow and learn."

Several comments came to mind but Katherine simply nodded. A war of words would gain nothing for either of them. "Would you care to dismount and wait for Slade and Jeb to return? Our well water is cool."

"Thank you for your generosity, Señora, but it grows late. Javier and I shall return to our ranch. Once I am confident my holdings are secure, I must go to Spain, to my properties there, and Javier will manage the ranch in my absence, which could be lengthy. It will be good for him to know his neighbors."

"Secure?"

Arellano shrugged. "My uncle ruled with an iron hand. The Indians, no doubt, respected that. I must ensure they retain that respect."

Katherine could no longer hold her comments. "I suspect the Apache, like the Comanche, return what is given to them. Respect for respect."

Arellano regarded her with the slightest tilt of his head. "You sound very certain of that."

"I am."

After another moment or so of silence, he nodded. "I will bid you good day, Señora Slade."

"Good day, Señor Arellano." She intentionally excluded his nephew from her comment. She could have furthered the insult by including him by his first name only, but it seemed small-minded so she didn't.

Hannah stepped closer as the Spaniards wheeled their horses about in an almost synchronous motion. "I don't have a good feeling about Mr. Arellano or his nephew."

"No," Katherine said on a sigh. "Nor do I."

Nor, she was afraid, would Slade.

Chapter Four

The men took turns digging a grave for the shotgun rider at the edge of the clearing behind the station. Ford set his jaw as he thrust the shovel into the heavy, clay-filled soil. Not because the ground was hard, although it was, but because of all the thoughts tangling in his mind. He had no qualms about leaving the bodies of their attackers behind for the carrion eaters. He had no qualms about taking their lives. What he did have was a gut-wrenching realization that he had brought his daughter into a danger from which his gun and his fist might not have been enough to protect her. He couldn't rid himself of that first glimpse of the blood staining Maria Cordova's gown, his devasting fear that it might be McKenna's.

For now, his baby girl was safe with Evan who'd taken first turn with the shovel. When Ford's arms tired, the station master would take the shovel, then Henry. Mr. Hanson had offered to take a turn, but Henry had quickly suggested he prepare a few words to say over the grave. Ford considered that a wise move on Henry's part since, despite the delay, the driver wanted to push on. He doubted Mr. Hanson would make much progress against the stubborn earth. As it was, they'd be after dark reaching their final stop for the night.

Miss Cordova, who'd changed into a fresh gown, sat with Mrs. Hanson on a blanket on the ground near the coach while Mr. Hanson, Bible in hand, walked back and forth nearby. Ford couldn't blame them for not choosing to sit inside the station. The food had been decent, but the roof was low and there were only two narrow slits for windows. With just the one door to let fresh air inside, the station smelled of the many unwashed bodies who traveled the coach lines.

When Henry deemed the hole sufficiently deep, he and Ford lowered Lemuel to his rest. Mr. Hanson stepped forward and the women got to their feet. Miss Cordova walked close to the grave but Mrs. Hanson hung back. Ford suspected it wouldn't take much for the woman to dissolve into hysteria once more.

At Henry's nod, Mr. Hanson began to read from his Bible. Ford took McKenna from Evan and steeled his spine as recognized words from the Book of Psalms unfolded. Elizabeth's service had been from the Book of Psalms because it was one of her favorite books of the Bible. The pain of remembering was less sharp than he expected. But, as much as that helped, it also stung. He knew a body couldn't live with unending grief, but he didn't want to forget Elizabeth ever; he didn't want to get over the pain of losing her.

McKenna's babble merged with Mr. Hanson's drone. The little girl in Ford's arms had given him his first reason to continue once he accepted Elizabeth was gone. She gave him that same purpose each day, and each day his heart grew a little easier and the burden of grief a little lighter. Their pastor had told Ford it would happen but Ford hadn't believed him, hadn't wanted to believe him.

He took a deep breath and bowed his head as Mr. Hanson led them in the Lord's Prayer. He could almost feel Elizabeth's arm brushing his, as if they stood side by side in church just as they'd done so many times. That brought him comfort as did the feel of their little girl, safe in his arms.

"I want his weapon, please."

Henry blinked and stared at the young woman facing him down. "You want what?"

"Mr. Lemuel's gun. I want it."

Ford propped his shoulder against the doorpost of the station, curious.

"What the blazes you going to do with that?"

"Shoot, if I have to. Unless you can assure we won't be attacked again."

Ford wouldn't take that bet and he doubted the coach driver would either.

Henry grunted, rubbing his jaw in thought. "How much do you know about guns?"

"More than Mr. Lemuel." She crossed herself quickly and Ford stifled a grin. Being honest wasn't really speaking ill of the dead to his way of thinking. "When I pull the trigger, I hit where I aim."

"I don't know. It ain't mine to give. Exactly."

The driver still looked dubious and Ford suspected the man had serious doubts about Maria Cordova's claim of skill. He hadn't planned to voice an opinion, but he couldn't see the harm in her request. "Why don't you let her take a shot or two. Just to see how she feels with it?" he suggested.

Henry shot Ford a scowl, but Miss Cordova sent him a quick look of gratitude and he found himself noticing the way the sunlight sparkled in the golden flecks of her green eyes. Her hair was odd-colored as well, halfway between blonde and brown with streaks of both.

Evan stepped out from behind Ford and walked toward a tree on the far side of the clearing. He unwrapped his bandana from around his neck and tied it to a low hanging tree branch that swayed with a steady breeze. He walked back and looked at Henry. "If she can hit that, she's a better shot than most." Then he gave an encouraging nod to the girl.

Henry gave a harrumph in answer but retrieved Lemuel's firearm from the box of the coach. He walked back with the rifle and handed it to Miss Cordova along with a cartridge. Ford wasn't surprised when she took both from the man and loaded the cartridge without hesitation. He glanced at Henry's face, knowing she'd passed the first test.

When she swung the rifle to her shoulder, Ford stepped back a few feet to distance McKenna from the sound of the blast but watched Miss Cordova's face as she focused on Evan's dust cloth swirling in the breeze. He knew the moment she pulled the trigger by the narrowing of her eyes and, a heartbeat later, the bullet ripped the cloth from the branch. The spark of pride he felt took him by surprise.

Evan grinned at Henry. "I'd say the lady wins."

Henry didn't smile, but his face relaxed as he nodded. "I reckon she does, at that."

As Evan praised her shot, Maria found herself casting a glance toward Ford Bellamy who watched from a little farther away. She shouldn't, she knew that. He might be widowed but she was still betrothed. Nor had he shown any interest in her other than as a fellow passenger. One to whom he'd trusted his child, certainly, but what choice had he?

She smiled politely at Evan and murmured an excuse as she put some space between them. Mr. Burch was nice and she'd never intentionally hurt his feelings nor would she encourage his interest.

Maria tried to imagine the man to whom her father had betrothed her but knew little more than that he was twenty-three, close to the same age as she, and heir to significant property. She was glad he was not an old man. Surely, they would learn to like each other, to share laughter and dreams for the future as young people do. And, of course, she had wanted to marry someday, not now, but someday.

She sighed and the sound seemed swallowed up by the wind that never seemed to stop in this Texas.

"You did well."

She whirled at the voice behind her. "Mr. Bellamy, I didn't hear you before you spoke. But … I thank you for the compliment. It was not too difficult a shot."

"You were so deep in thought, I hesitated to speak." He seemed to hesitate again. "And I'd just as soon be called Ford."

"Very well. And I am Maria."

"Maria," he repeated, as if testing the sound of her name on his lips. "Who taught you to handle a gun?"

"My father. I think it's what fathers do when they do not have a son."

"If I had ten sons, I'd still teach McKenna."

"That is a good thing. And, McKenna, where is she now?"

He smiled and his dark eyes lit with affection. "Evan has her horseback, riding around the station yard. Henry said we'll leave within a few moments. The tenders are hitching up the team now."

"I'm ready," she said simply.

"I think we all are."

"I'm truly sorry for the news that Mr. Lemuel's family will receive."

"Henry says there was no one who was close to him."

"And that is even sadder, that there is no one to mourn him."

A shadow chased across Ford's face and Maria would have recalled her words if she could. Of course, Ford still mourned his wife. Fortunately, Henry gave a shout to gather them for the journey and the moment disappeared in the activity of loading.

As she neared the coach, Maria realized that Lemuel's death had left them short of protection. Taking a breath to nerve herself, she placed her hand on Ford's arm. "Please, I know you would rather be horseback," as would she, if it were possible, "and Mr. Henry has no one to guard the coach but you and Mr. Burch. If you'll trust me again with McKenna, I'll be more than happy to care for her." It would, she thought, make the long hours ahead of them not so dreary. Still, she was, after all, little more than a stranger to him. He'd called on her during a moment of intense danger, but she could not discount that he might consider her offer an intrusion.

His brow furrowed. "Are you certain? I'd feel better if both Evan and I were able to watch for danger, but I don't want McKenna to be a burden."

"Oh, she wouldn't be a burden. She will make the tedium of travel less ... tedious." She hoped his soft sigh was one of relief at her offer and not one of frustration at her insistence.

"If you're sure, I'll appreciate it. If you need me, all you have to do is wave a hand out the window. I'll have Henry stop the coach."

Maria climbed up into the coach and watched as Ford took McKenna from his friend then stepped up to hand the child in to her. He waited a moment as if to be sure that his daughter wasn't going to complain before he strode toward his horse. Realizing she was staring at his broad shoulders, Maria settled back against the coach seat and shifted the little girl to a position that was more comfortable.

Clean and dry in a fresh diaper, McKenna laid her cheek on Maria's shoulder and dropped into a nap as the stage coach rolled away from the station.

"That Miss Cordova's a pretty girl."

Ford nodded. He wouldn't lie and say he hadn't noticed but he wouldn't tell Evan he had either.

"Never seen eyes quite that color. All that gold in with the green."

Like autumn leaves, Ford thought, the green mixing with the first touch of gold. He could feel Evan watching him. Evan was a couple years older than Ford, but he'd seen and experienced far less. He looked up to Ford which made Ford uncomfortable. He knew he could say something to discourage Evan, to express his own interest, and the other man would back away immediately. She was pretty. In fact, she was beautiful. But Ford didn't plan to marry again. He wouldn't do anything to attract Maria Cordova's interest so there was no reason for him to discourage Evan's interest in her.

"Never was a girl prettier than Elizabeth," Evan said more quietly.

"No," Ford agreed softly. "Never was."

"It's been a year."

Ford just looked at him and Evan fell silent for which Ford was grateful.

Chapter Five

Jeb sat on the bed, legs stretched out in front of him and watched as Hannah plaited her hair. He never tired of watching her even though he wished she could leave her curls loose at night. Seeing her pick painfully through the tangles one morning was all it had taken to make him quit asking.

She gave him a glance. "You're looking at me like I'm not nearly seven months pregnant."

"I'm looking at you like you're the most beautiful woman in the world." To this day, he knew she didn't believe him, but she didn't mind him saying it.

Once upon a time, Jeb thought he didn't care for blue eyes in a woman, particularly if they were the crystalline blue of a hot summer sky. He'd thought her shoulders too slender, her face too pale against the dark red of her hair.

He'd learned since that slender didn't mean fragile and that her pretty cheeks could bloom with color just by him looking at her.

It seemed to take forever before she rose from her dressing table and walked toward him. She heard the sound a heartbeat before he did. Hooves thundering somewhere between the house and the barn and the sound of a horse screaming followed by gunfire.

Heart pounding, Jeb grabbed the pants he'd laid over the chair beside the bed, not bothering with his shirt as he thrust his feet into his boots and grabbed his gun. "Stay inside, Hannah." And glancing at her face, he added, "Please," knowing she might or might not do as he'd asked. His wife had a mind of her own. Sometimes that was a good thing. Sometimes it wasn't.

Slade was already in the breezeway when Jeb rushed out, they stepped to the ground in sync, guns drawn. Jeb recognized Lorenzo's voice shouting from the corral by the barn. As they reached the corral, several of the vaqueros were gathering. One held a kerosene lantern behind Lorenzo who had slipped a rope halter over the head of a pretty mare. An arrow had pierced her underbelly. There was no possibility it had missed the animal's intestines.

Fury bubbled up from Jeb's gut. The mare was Hannah's.

"Did anyone see anything?" Slade asked.

The glum shaking of heads confirmed what Jeb had expected. The hour was late, chores had long since been done. It would have been no more than happenstance for any of their vaqueros to be outside at that hour. Morning came early and sleep was a commodity not wasted unless the reason was good.

"Can you save the mare?" Jeb knew the answer before

he asked.

"No, Señor." Lorenzo's face held sorrow and regret. "The belly, it is pierced. This sweet girl, hopefully, will live only a few hours. That would be a blessing. If she lives longer, the dying will be ugly."

Jeb looked away, sick at heart. And as angry as he'd ever been in his life.

Carlos and Mateo walked out of the barn, each leading two saddled horses. Jeb glanced at Slade and said, "I'll get our rifles."

Katherine and Hannah were both in the kitchen. His rifle and Slade's and their shot pouches were already on the table. Hannah handed him his shirt as he walked in. Katherine was rolling food into a thick cloth. "How many canteens?" she asked quietly.

"Four."

Katherine gave him a concerned look and Hannah bit her lower lip.

"If we go with more, we'll be in a fight before we know if a fight is needed." And they wouldn't win. Not against Jishnu's warriors, if that was who it had been. His mind struggled with that possibility. All of their dealings with the chief had been peaceful.

He folded Hannah into his arms and kissed her forehead. "I'll be back." And then he'd have to tell her about her mare.

He took the knapsack of food and water from Katherine and picked up the rifles. He looked at both of the women. "Keep your guns close and stay inside as much as you can stand. We won't be gone any longer than we have to be."

Lips pressed firm, Hannah nodded at him. Jeb knew

how hard that was for her and he was proud of her. Hannah wasn't a weeper or a worrier.

He walked out and found Slade dividing up the hands, half to sleep, half to stand watch, and a few to bury the mare. Jeb went to Lorenzo who still stood at her head, hung low now with the pain that wracked her. As carefully as he could, Jeb broke the arrow in half, putting the feathered end into his saddlebag.

He placed a hand on Lorenzo's shoulder. "When the grave is ready, do what needs to be done, my friend. I don't want her to suffer."

"I understand, Señor. The bullet, she is fast. This lady will feel nothing in that moment."

Jeb stepped into the stirrup and swung a leg over the saddle. "Let's ride." He let Slade set the pace, mostly a walk and a trot to keep the horses fresh if and when they asked for more. There was no need to rush. They knew where they were headed and Jishnu's Apaches would be there when they arrived. Soon, once winter brought the snow and game became scarce, the tribe would drift far lower, perhaps even into Mexico.

Just before daybreak, they stopped at a stream to wait for daylight. They were too smart to approach the tribe in the dark. Slade walked down to the sandy bank of the creek to refill their canteens while Jeb unrolled the food that Katherine had wrapped for them. He watched as Slade returned and settled beside him.

"What are the odds that the arrow belongs to one of Jishnu's warriors?"

"Low to none. And if it does, I don't believe Jishnu knows."

"Still could get ugly."

"Could."

But, if not Jishnu's braves, if not the Jicarilla Apache, then who?

Jishnu's winter camp was in a valley, bordered by steep rocks on two sides and a river bed that had been cut deep into the slopes on the other two. The chief had chosen well. His people could only be reached by fording the river. Jeb and Slade dismounted on the far side and waited patiently. The tribe had already begun to stir and they hadn't long to wait before a warrior neared the bank across from them. After a moment's study, they were gestured forward in welcome.

They mounted and followed the man back to Jishnu's teepee where the chief sat cross-legged and patient before it. Several of his braves stood behind him. Their faces were impassive, but Jeb could see curiosity in their gazes. Curiosity but not guilt. With a gesture, the chief invited his visitors to sit and they did after releasing their horses to two young boys to hold. They could have left them ground-tied but the youngsters holding them were Jishnu's gesture of honor toward the white men and their relinquishment of the animals was a show of trust in the Apache leader.

Jishnu took one look at their faces and said, "Speak."

Although Jeb knew the chief understood more English than he spoke, he was still careful to talk slowly and choose his words with care. "In the night, a man rode onto our land. He shot an arrow that struck my woman's horse."

"You have?"

"The arrow? Yes." Jeb got to his feet and walked back to his horse. The young boys, probably no older than seven or eight, had been conversing quietly together. When Jeb approached, they fell silent and puffed their chests with pride at their task. Jeb nodded solemnly to show his approval of their care of the animals then he stepped to his saddlebag and withdrew the arrow he'd broken from the horse's side.

He took it back to the Apache leader who examined it carefully.

"The horse?"

"Dead." Jeb knew the shot to end her suffering would have been fired by now.

Jishnu spoke to one of the braves standing behind him and the man strode away. Then the chief returned his attention to the men before him. "Your women unharmed?"

Slade nodded. "Both are safe."

Jishnu nodded, his expression relieved. Within moments, the first of his warriors arrived. Jishnu stood, holding the broken arrow as dozens of them filed past. Jeb studied the expression of each as he was sure Slade was doing as well. There was no reaction from any of them, not so much as a flicker of an eyelid until the braves grew younger in age, more boys, now, than men. One cast a glance, then stopped in disbelief, a look of dismay clear upon his face.

Jeb wasn't sure what symbol or shape or color marked the arrow as his, but Jeb knew it was there. He judged the boy to be in his early teens. His features were even and handsome, his chest and forearms muscular. He, and others like him, were the strength and the future of the Apache nation.

The Apache chief rose to his feet, his expression dark

and immediately forbidding. The dismay on the boy's face turned to dread. Jishnu spoke sharply to one of the braves who stood behind him. The man stepped forward and laid a heavy hand on the boy's shoulder. Jeb could see the resemblance between them, brother and brother, perhaps, but more likely father and son by the difference in age between them.

Before more could be said or done, Slade shook his head and got to his feet. He looked the boy in the eye. "Is the arrow yours?"

The youngster looked at Jishnu who interpreted. When Jishnu finished, the boy met Slade's piercing regard without flinching and nodded. Slade looked at his chief. "Ask him if he rode last night."

At the question, the boy shook his head.

Slade thought for a moment then asked, "When did he lose the arrow?"

The boy listened to his chief then answered in a rush.

"Three days ago," Jishnu interpreted. "Hunting for jackrabbit across the river. He lost two."

The older brave, who still had his hand upon the boy's shoulder, had watched warily as Slade got to his feet. Jeb watched the worry in the man's eyes fade as Slade gave him a brief nod in acceptance of the boy's answer.

Slade turned from them to their chief. "Jishnu, I think we share an enemy. You are not my enemy. I am not yours. Be wary."

Jishnu rose gracefully and touched a hand to his chest. Slade returned the gesture of good will. Jeb turned toward the warrior standing with the young brave and nodded respectfully. The warrior nodded. He kept his stance formal and his face impassive, but his eyes filled with relief and with gratitude. Jeb tried to imagine how he would have felt in that situation, thought of the dangers a son would face as he grew to manhood, and again wished for a girl who looked like Hannah. But, then again, maybe not.

They reached the ranch well before dark. Hannah and Katherine were on the porch when he and Slade rode up. A shotgun leaned on the wall behind each of them.

Jeb had dreaded telling Hannah about her mare. One look at her, at the smile that didn't quite reach her eyes, and he knew she already knew. He'd seen that same look the first time he'd laid eyes on her, that same stoicism that said she'd get through this, too. The difference between then and now was that Hannah would never again have to *get through* anything alone. Not until he was cold in his grave and he didn't plan on that happening anytime soon.

She stood and walked straight into the arms he wrapped around her.

Slade and Katherine walked into the kitchen which gave them a moment alone before Hannah drew back with a sigh. "You'll be hungry, both of you."

"I'm hungry for you, right now."

This time her smile reached her eyes. "Later, cowboy." And she led him into the kitchen where Slade was putting plates on the table.

The food was good as it always was. Simple but good. He knew the biscuits were Hannah's just as he always knew the cornbread was Katherine's.

And over the food, they talked.

Katherine frowned. "There were two arrows?"

"I wonder where the second will land." Hannah voiced

the question that Jeb had been asking himself during the ride home.

"I have a feeling we'll know soon enough." Slade's tone was as grim as his expression.

Jeb nodded. Slade was more likely right than wrong on that. "Someone wants trouble for Jishnu's tribe."

"And maybe for us as well," Slade agreed.

Chapter Six

Maria closed her eyes and pretended to sleep. She could feel Mr. Hanson's discomfort at his wife's murmurings and would spare him thinking she was a witness to it. There was, however, no way to spare herself. She could hear every quiet word much too clearly in the confines of the coach.

"You must take me home," the woman said for the dozenth or so time.

Mr. Hanson had been patient in simply patting her hand comfortingly and declining to answer, but he finally told her, "There is nothing to go home to, Emmaline. We sold everything to come. The store, the house, our furnishings."

"We were wrong. We must go back. We'll die in this godforsaken land."

Maria supposed to some it did appear as a land that

God himself had forsaken. At times, they traveled through valleys and alongside streams that kept the grass lush and green. But in the hills, amongst the rocky crags and rock-strewn slopes, the brush had long since dried to brown after the long summer. Heat still shimmered with a life of its own in the late afternoon sun. When winter came—and that would be soon—it would be an abrupt falling from one season to the next. For now, the nights were chill and the mornings stayed cool until the sun was full in the sky, but during the midday, the air continued heavy and languid with the last moments of summer.

She'd missed the land, she realized with faint surprise. She hadn't been homesick while in Boston. There'd been so much to learn, so much to see and to do. But this was home to her.

Despite that, she could understand Mrs. Hanson's dismay at the landscape where violence and death had played out before them just hours ago.

"Let's just get to Albuquerque. Things will be different there, Emmaline. You'll feel better once we're in a real town. Almost like back home in Cambridge."

Maria winced at the comparison. The towns of New Mexico Territory had their appeal, but none held the sophistication of towns back East, certainly not ones like Boston or Cambridge.

"I don't want to go to Albuquerque. I want to go home. Make the coachman turn around immediately."

That startled Maria who began to wonder if Mrs. Hanson had not been overly affected by the fierceness of the morning's attack. Otherwise, surely the woman would realize her demand was not a possibility. Henry would doubtless lose his position were he to turn back, nor could he favor one passenger over others in order to do that.

Maria was almost grateful when McKenna began to stir restlessly in her arms, indicating an end to her nap. Fortunately, the little girl woke without drama, not cheerfully nor did she fret. Maria busied herself with pulling a dry diaper from the bag at her feet. McKenna was certain to be in need of a change.

A quick check proved Maria's suspicions. Before removing the damp cloth, she was careful to examine the folds in order to be able to duplicate them.

"She's not yours." Maria froze as the words cut through the coach. "Where's her mother?"

"Emmaline!" Mr. Hanson sounded as shocked as Maria felt.

"Well, it's a decent question to ask a decent woman. Where's the child's mother," the woman insisted.

Maria pressed her lips together and took a deep breath before answering. "I don't know. I offered to help so that her father could guard the coach." Her answer came more from sympathy for Mr. Hanson. She owed the woman no explanation.

"Because we'll likely be attacked again. That's the reason more guards are needed." Her voice turned querulous again and her attention shifted. "This is your fault, Mr. Hanson. I want to go home."

Mr. Hanson patted her hand again, his face filled with sadness.

It was best, Maria decided, for her to focus solely on McKenna who reached up to touch her face as Maria leaned over to replace the soiled diaper with a fresh one.

The sun dipped in the sky and the coach slowed as visibility decreased. Ford moved ahead to help Henry keep to the road, warning of abrupt curves around boulders in their path. He didn't much blame the whip for wanting to reach their next station. He did as well but their reasons were different. For Henry, it was no doubt due to schedule, particularly in regard to the mail contract. Ford preferred a safer place to rest with McKenna than a campfire along the trail.

He wondered how she and Maria had fared. He'd watched the coach window but not once had Maria signaled a need for assistance. Nor had he heard any wails from the coach and a mad or sad McKenna could make noise aplenty.

Ford breathed easier when the first signs of settlement appeared. Not long after, the coach road merged with the main street of the town, such as it was. The coach rolled to a stop in front of a boarding house dimly lit by the lantern left burning in the window. Ford and Evan dismounted to give Henry a hand with retrieving bags from the boot.

Ford set the last one on the porch of the boarding house and turned to see Evan helping Maria and McKenna from the coach. Maria smiled her thanks at Evan, then turned that smile on Ford. Even the dim light that spilled through the thick glass windows of the boarding house couldn't hide her beauty.

With a deep breath, Ford walked back to take McKenna from her arms. "Thank you. My mind was easy knowing you had her." They weren't just polite words, he realized, they were true and that was odd, because he barely knew her.

When he turned with McKenna in his arms, he glanced at the more brightly lit business next door to the boarding house. A quick grin caught him by surprise and he ducked his head, glad his back was to Maria. If the sign that hung above the door wasn't advertisement enough, the girls draped across the porch rail watching the coach's arrival would have been. Celeste's was the only word upon the sign. That one word above an elegantly curled feather in vivid red.

There were three of what he presumed to be Celeste's ladies eyeing him much more openly than he'd looked at them. All three wore simple dresses that almost looked like those in Elizabeth's clothes press. A second quick glance caught the subtle differences. The skirts of Elizabeth's gowns had all been full, billowing out from her waist. There were few gathers in these skirts. As a result, they draped enticingly against shapely hips. The greatest difference lay in the bodices which weren't cut as low as those in some bawdy houses he'd visited, but were still far lower than anything his wife would ever have worn. Ford's gaze found the swell of curves above those bodices tempting. That fact surprised him but he took a deep breath of acceptance. A man had needs that had nothing to do with love.

A bell above the door tinkled as he walked into the boarding house. The scowling woman who emerged from the doorway behind the counter proved a good antidote to temptations of the flesh. She was neither young nor old and could have been passing attractive without the scowl.

She looked over her spectacles at Ford and the travel-worn group who trailed in behind him. "The coach is late."

"Yes, ma'am." She hadn't asked a question and Ford wasn't inclined to give explanations that hadn't been requested.

"Where's Henry?"

"I'm here, Ida," their driver said from the back of the

small room as he entered last and closed the door behind him. "Ran into a little trouble."

As Henry made his way forward, Ford watched the softening in the woman's face with interest. "The hour had me worried," she admitted.

"I'm fine. Lost my shotgun rider, though."

"Don't know as you'll be able to replace him. Not much to choose from in this town."

Henry shrugged at that. "Any chance of a meal tonight?"

"You ever gone hungry here?" she asked tartly before sweeping a quick glance over the rest of them. Her gaze lingered on the little girl in Ford's arms then swept the Hansons as she said, "My name's Ida. Dining is at the end of the hallway. Rooms upstairs are full. Rooms downstairs are on each side as you go down the hall. Pick your own. No special accommodations for married folks. I don't have many come this way. There's a token for the bath house on each bed and there's an ewer of water on each dresser. Make sure you use one or the other. I don't tolerate filth on my sheets."

As the others picked up their bags and moved toward the hall, Ford hung back, letting them open and close doors and thrust bags inside. He watched to see what rooms were left, doubting there would be much difference in any of them. Tossing his bag and McKenna's into the first available, he moved on to the dining area, pausing in the doorway. The Hansons huddled together at one end of the long table. Maria sat close to the center and Evan was just taking a seat across from her. Henry also sat near the middle, leaving one chair between himself and Maria. Ford took the seat opposite Henry.

There was a setting of dinnerware and utensils in front

of every chair and Ida had already begun placing large platters of food the length of the table. Ford's mouth watered at the aromas drifting his way. Stewed meat with chunks of vegetables. Greens swimming in the fat rendered from salt meat. Biscuits with a bowl of soft butter placed in the center of the platter.

When the woman took her place at the seat closest to the kitchen door, she glanced once around the room and said, "Henry?"

Henry bowed his head and said a short—very short—blessing of the food then looked at Ida. "Will you marry me?"

"Not today."

"It's nigh on midnight," he observed.

"Not tomorrow, either." And she picked up her spoon and began to eat.

Ford began to eat as well, placing finger sized bits on the table for McKenna to pick up or mash with her fingers but she only opened her mouth when Ford lifted a spoon to her lips. Ford knew she enjoyed the activity of playing with what he put on the table but she didn't yet recognize it as food. Evan had Maria engaged in a conversation about her time in Boston which he'd never seen. Ford tried not to listen in. It wasn't his business, the people she'd met, the things she'd seen. But her voice drew his attention, again and again.

"Any additional passengers in the morning?" Henry asked Ida. "I sent a telegraph from San Antonio that I had two spaces."

"It came through. Sold two tickets. One to a preacher man, but he's only going as far as Socorro, aims to take salvation to the soldiers stationed at Fort Craig. The other looks to be salesman or a gambler. Fancy dresser. Said he'd get off when a place 'looked right' to him."

Henry gave a snort and looked around. "They here?"

"Upstairs snoring, I expect. They supped on time."

Henry chuckled at her pointed jab. "Now, Ida, no reason for you to be persnickety. You know I'd never be late for one of your meals if it could be helped."

Her gaze softened. "Reckon I'm glad you're not dead on the trail someplace at that."

A gasp from the end of the table pulled Ford's attention from their humorous exchange. Judging by her expression, Mrs. Hanson hadn't found it entertaining. Ford couldn't hazard a guess as to why the older couple had thought it a good idea to traipse out West, but it was clear that Mrs. Hanson, at least, bitterly regretted the decision.

By the time McKenna had her fill, Ford was done as well. He thanked Ms. Ida for the meal and took his sleepy little girl to their room where he bathed her from the pitcher of water and changed her clothes for sleep. After turning down the kerosene lantern, he tucked McKenna into the bed and, mindful of Ms. Ida's warning about no filth on her sheets, sat on the floor to wait. He and Evan had agreed that Evan would find the bath house first, then sit with McKenna while Ford took his turn.

With his head against the wall behind him, Ford was drifting into sleep when Evan pushed the door open. He got to his feet as Evan walked into the room. Evan's hair was still wet and he smelled of soap. And something else.

"Which direction is the bath house."

Evan grinned. "Next door."

Ford just looked at him for a moment then realized Evan was serious. "Next door?"

"Well, there's another down the street, but Celeste's—

hell, it's right here close."

That wasn't the only advantage, Ford realized as his brain identified the other scent that clung to Evan. All he said was, "I'll be back." He had every intention of heading down the street but his steps slowed when he reached the porch of the boarding house. The soft light from Celeste's windows beckoned as did the dark eyes watching him from the steps next door.

"Come see me, cowboy." Her voice was low but clear and pretty as an evening sky. "It's been a long, slow afternoon. I could use some company."

As his boots hit the dusty street, Ford found himself turning and walking her way. He stopped in front of her. She was pretty in a quiet kind of way, not flashy at all, with dark hair to match her eyes. Her gown was plain, scooped low in the front so that most of her breasts were exposed. Not the dark tips. Those were hidden so that a man craved to uncover them.

He put down a hand to her and she took it, letting him pull her to her feet. "What's your name, sweetheart?"

She tilted her head. "Bella."

Ford smiled. "It suits you. I'm dusty, Bella."

"You could use a shave, too." Her laugh was as light and enticing as her voice. "I can take care of both, cowboy." She gave him a backward glance as she tugged at his hand, urging him up the steps with her. "And more besides."

Bella nodded at a boy who stood just inside the door of the small front parlor. "Johnny, we'll be needing some fresh water hauled to my room. Fill both tubs please."

Her room was up two flights of stairs and at the very end of the long hallway. The windows of her room were open to the evening air. The room wasn't large but it was free of clutter so that a man wouldn't feel confined. She left the door open and held out her hands for the clean clothes he carried. "Let me lay those out for you proper." And she did, draping first the pants and then the shirt over the back of a chair near the bed.

"Take off your boots, hon. Just set them by the chair."

"Ford." He didn't want to be called by an endearment that didn't belong to him. "The name's Ford."

She smiled. "Ford. That's a good, strong name."

He couldn't keep his eyes from drifting to that bed. It was neatly made, as if she hadn't touched it since rising that morning. With Johnny scurrying back and forth behind them, Bella began undressing Ford. She touched him lightly, here and there. Not suggestively but more admiringly, trailing her fingers down the hard muscles of his arms. Gliding one light fingernail down one side of his chest but stopping at his hip.

"Johnny has the first tub full, why don't you step in?"

Taking a shuddering breath, Ford eased into the steaming water. The cool night air that filled the room made it seem even hotter. Bella eased a pillow behind his head and he lay looking up at her as she sank to her knees beside the tub. Her lips curved in a smile at whatever she read in his face.

She took a piece of soap in her hands and lathered it into his hair. Her fingers worked his scalp and his neck soothingly, then his face. He was almost disappointed when she lifted a dipper of water and let it run through his hair and sluice over his face then dried both with a small towel. Disappointment faded when she lowered both hands into the water and moved them along first one leg, then the other. Then his arms. By the time she'd reached his chest, his body was more ready than his mind for what was to come.

The bodice of her gown was close to his face, so close he could have shifted position to nip the peaks that pushed against the thin fabric.

"Sit up, cowboy, and lean forward." He did and felt her hands work the knots in his shoulders, washing and rubbing and digging lightly into the muscles with every stroke. "You're a strong man, Ford. I like that."

He closed his eyes and fought memories of Elizabeth rubbing his back at night when he came in tired from the field. He wasn't meant to be a farmer. He'd known that all along, but he'd have done anything for Elizabeth. Anything.

"Stand up, now." Bella's voice pulled him back to her.

Bella's touch, his own need had made him rigid and she placed her hand on the length of him, stroked lightly, once. "The next tub is for rinsing," she murmured as she dropped her hand from him.

He realized he hadn't even been aware of the boy filling the second tub. Hadn't been aware of anything except Bella's hands on his body. He stood and stepped on the towels she'd dropped onto the floor between the tubs. When he sank into the clean, hot water, she began pouring dipper after dipper of water over his head and face and back and shoulders.

"Want a shave, too?"

"Yeah," he stood up and pulled her against his wet body. "But not just yet."

Laughing, she handed him a towel and moved her hands to unfasten the bodice of her dress.

"Wait," he said quietly. "Let me."

And her hands stilled, fell to her side. He didn't want

to know what was behind the look she gave him. Didn't want to know what she felt or what she was thinking. That was selfish, he knew, but this was all he had to give and he would make it good for her. He'd be gone and he wouldn't think about her again, but tonight would be good.

He stepped from the tub and dried himself with the towel she handed to him then reached for the hooks that fastened her gown together. He loosened the gown, sliding the fabric from her shoulders, easing the sleeves from her arms. Her breasts were full and good to look at and better to touch. When he scraped his teeth lightly against one, she murmured in surprise, and he knew she hadn't been given half as much as he planned to give her in the hour or so. He kissed and nipped his way from one breast to the other, then down her ribs to her belly. He bit the flesh against her hipbone and she moaned.

He eased her onto the bed with her feet touching the floor and pushed her backward then sank to his knees between her thighs. When his tongue touched her, she drew a shuddering breath and he felt her relax, finally, and he made her cry out when she came against his mouth.

He'd been with whores since Elizabeth. A man had needs. But this was the first time since Elizabeth's death, the very first, that he hadn't thought of his wife when he sank into hot, willing flesh, the first time he hadn't seen Elizabeth's beautiful blue eyes looking up into his. Nor did he see the brown of Bella's dark gaze holding his. When he closed his eyes and thrust, when his seed spilled, he saw the intriguing mix of gold and green that was Maria's.

Later when the guilt hit, he told himself it was alright. It had been a year. It was okay for him to move on, but it didn't feel okay. Not when he'd been imagining it was Maria beneath him.

Chapter Seven

Maria watched through the coach window as Ford and Evan stepped out of the boarding house followed by two men who were better dressed and looked older than either of the cowboys. Their driver leaned against a post. She didn't see the Hansons.

A movement on the porch next to the boarding house caught her eye. One of the ladies she'd seen the night before stepped out. Her gown, like the one the night before, clung to her hips but this morning her breasts were not on display. A shawl wrapped around her shoulders, discreetly covered her upper body.

Maria felt a pang as Ford handed his daughter to Evan then crossed the distance between the two buildings as the lady walked down the steps to meet him in the street.

For a moment, Bella tilted her head and simply studied him. "Why?"

Ford didn't pretend not to know what she was asking. He'd held her until she slept, then slipped out, leaving her pay on her dresser and double that amount, just for her, under her pillow. But that wasn't what she was asking him. He'd deliberately given her more than money in their hours together and he hoped it had left her restless, wanting something better than what she had here.

"Because you're pretty enough and good-hearted enough to make some man a damned fine wife. "

"But not you." It was less question than acceptance.

Her eyes held a touch of yearning that tugged at him but couldn't hold him. He almost wished it could.

"No." Ford let the regret come through. "Not me."

A rueful smile touched her lips as if his words confirmed a painful truth for her. "A girl doesn't get out of this business with a happy ever after. That's a fairy tale, cowboy."

"Some do," he said quietly. "You ever make up your mind to try, you look up Sheriff Hastings, Daniel Hastings down in Sherman. His wife Jenny will give you a hand, make sure you get a safe start."

She lifted her chin. "You sure about that? That I'd be welcome. People I've never met."

Ford was sure. When Slade and Jeb had come back to Texas for their starter herd, the three men had sat long into the night talking a little about life but a lot about people. About men like Preacher Barnes who'd treated his wife Hannah, Jeb's wife now, like a whore and townsfolk who'd regarded Katherine's daughter, an innocent little girl, with the same suspicion as the murdering Apache warrior who'd fathered her, and the sheriff who'd fallen in love with a young widow who'd lain with men as much to keep the loneliness at bay as to keep a roof over her head.

But all he said was, "Find a man, a good man, you can give your heart to and he'll trade his to keep it."

"Yeah? Where's your heart, cowboy?"

The smile she gave him was as sweet as any honey he'd ever tasted, but her question caught him off guard and he answered without thinking. "My wife took it with her to the grave."

Ford wished he'd lied, kept it light with some smartassed comment about not having a heart because now the sorrow that was never far away was reflected in the sheen in Bella's eyes. He touched his hand to her cheek. "Don't cry for me. I had the love of my life and now I have our daughter. It's enough."

He turned to walk away as she said softly. "It won't be enough forever, cowboy. Don't let it be. You're a man made to love a woman."

If he ever did, he thought, it would be a woman as strong and fierce as his sister, Katherine. But, for now, he didn't want another woman. He wanted Elizabeth. And he pushed aside an image of Maria Cordova holding a dead man's rifle to her shoulder in order to earn the right to keep it.

Evan Burch handed McKenna into the coach for Maria to take her. He gave Maria a wink as she lifted her arm for the baby and she suspected flirtation came naturally to him. She didn't encourage his attention but she didn't discourage him as strongly as she perhaps should be doing.

He was pleasant to talk with but she'd made sure he knew she was betrothed, a fact that still felt odd to her.

As good-looking as Evan was, he was not a temptation to her but she feared Ford Bellamy might be. She tried to focus her thoughts forward, to the life that waited for her, but she couldn't picture the man who would be her husband. No one had written to her of his looks or his manners or his intelligence, not her Papa nor her mother. Only that the family was wealthy and now owned much property which bordered their own on one side. That mattered to her Papa, she knew, but did it matter to her? Perhaps, it should. She did not want to live in poverty, certainly, but there was so much to life besides the things which money could buy.

Perhaps her betrothed would prove as handsome as Ford Bellamy. Perhaps he would look at Maria in the way Ford had looked at the lady who had stood with him in the street in front of the brothel. As if she were a treasure. Maria knew about brothels of course. Servants talked and she listened. What she didn't know much about was men or boys. Maria had no doubt that Ford had been a man with the lady from Celeste's. She looked at him as if he held her world. Would her husband know how to be a man? As Maria realized where her thoughts had led her, she blushed and turned her face toward the window in time to see Ford Bellamy swing his leg over the saddle. He glanced toward the coach and smiled at her.

No, she told herself sharply, his smile was for the little girl in her arms. His little girl. And his wife's, whose memory he would have with him forever. Maria was not a woman who would take second place. Not even to a memory.

She lifted her chin. She would make a life for herself

with the man her Papa had chosen for her, have babies of her own. Even so, she snugged McKenna a little closer to her breast for she was a sweet little one.

And the coach rolled out of town without Mr. and Mrs. Hanson aboard.

Ford found himself watching for glimpses of Maria and McKenna through the coach window. Not because he worried for McKenna's safety but because he'd begun to feel a hint of guilt. It hadn't taken him long at all to know that a coach was as uncomfortable a method of travel as a buckboard wagon, particularly when trying to protect a child against the worst of the jostling. Sure, his goal was Maria's safety as much as anyone's so there was benefit to her, but it wouldn't hurt to find some way to repay her willingness to burden herself with so young a child.

He figured they were about half way between stations, when a thought came to him. He guided his horse to the other side of the steadily lumbering coach, coming up beside Evan. "You mind if Miss Cordova rides your mare for a time and you tend McKenna?"

Evan gave him a curious look. "You reckon she'd want to?"

"I'm thinking if it were Elizabeth, she would. We'd switch up tomorrow morning between stations. She can ride my gelding and I'll keep McKenna in the coach. At least she'd get a chance at fresh air and a different view."

"Sure," Evan said agreeably, but Ford hadn't missed the glint of interest in his eyes when Ford mentioned switching up. That would give Evan time with Maria as well as give Maria an additional break from the coach. Ford thought about giving the other man a warning not to get too interested but it was none of his business, after all. And maybe the young woman would find herself as attracted to Evan as he was to her. Maybe she wouldn't care that he was a cowboy with nothing to his name but his horse, his gun, and what he carried in his saddle bag.

He wasn't surprised when Evan made sure to be at the coach door when they reached the first swing station, reaching up to take McKenna so that Maria could descend from the coach more easily.

When Maria returned from the necessary, she looked surprised to see Ford waiting for her at the door of the coach. "I thought you might like to ride for a while. Evan will ride in the coach with McKenna until the next stop."

Her quick smile answered as much as the, "Oh, I would!" she said on a breath. She glanced up to where Evan watched from the coach window, McKenna bouncing happily in his arms.

Ford had a moment's chagrin as he realized the lack of a sidesaddle but when Maria took the reins from his hand and stepped expertly into the stirrup he relaxed. This wasn't her first time astride. He doubted it was in Boston, but she'd done this before.

Another thought hit him and he glanced at her hat. It had a brim but he wished it were wider and offered better protection from the sun. Fortunately, the morning was cool with drifting clouds. They'd be lucky to escape a shower.

When Henry cracked his whip in the air above the mule team, Ford was careful to keep Maria between him and the coach. If trouble came, he'd get her back inside and Evan to his horse.

For a time, Ford entertained himself watching Maria's pleasure. He had to remind himself a time or two that his purpose in being on horseback rather than in the coach was to watch for danger. The lack of alarm in the occasional small animal and the birds that continued to wing low around them was somewhat reassuring, but he couldn't take the safety of their small party for granted.

Every now and again, he would catch Maria glancing his way. He supposed he was a puzzle, a widower with a small child headed to mostly unsettled territory. Sooner or later he expected her to ask a question or two and found himself surprised when he was the first to break the silence between them.

"How are the gambler and the preacher getting along?"

She grinned. "I think they've decided they have common ground enough not to fight about sin."

"What would that be?"

"They both believe a nip of whiskey is fine for curative purposes."

He raised a brow. "Curative?"

"Oh, my, yes. The gambler, Mr. Ellis, keeps a dry, sore throat that has nothing whatsoever to do with the cheroots he favors." Her voice had taken on an authoritative, lofty tone of mimicry. "He finds the occasional soothing swallow of whiskey keeps illness at bay."

Ford kept a straight face, enjoying himself with the exchange. "And Preacher Ridge?"

"It seems he spends a good amount of time walking back and forth in front of his faithful congregation and does so very energetically, which has caused an inflammation of his knee. A tiny bit of liquor eases his pain so that he can continue to serve the Lord."

"I can see how that would be beneficial."

"No doubt." She nodded vigorously, her eyes crinkling with laughter. "But they are fun and funny. I like them."

And Elizabeth would like *her*. The errant thought caught him off-guard and his pleasure in the moment faded.

They both fell silent and the creaking of saddle leather and the ring of mule hooves on hard ground seemed overly loud. Her voice, when it came, was soft and sympathetic. "You thought of her just now. Your wife."

His wife. McKenna's mother. The love of his life. He almost didn't answer. "I just had a thought that she'd like you, that's all. She took pleasure in people. She saw them for what they were but she didn't judge them for it. She was accepting, like you just were with those two in the coach."

Maria was watching him steadily. "I'm honored. And I'm sure I would have liked her as well."

Ford turned to scan the horizon, more to gather himself than for any sense of danger. Still, he knew he had to be watchful, not be distracted by Maria's sympathy or the remembered pain of his loss.

It was that last thought that struck him most. Remembered pain. He missed her still and always would but the devastating grief was distant now, remembered and hurtful, but not the gut-wrenching, ever-present pain he'd thought would never leave him. He supposed he could thank his decision to head West and make a new like for himself and his daughter.

Maria spoke again. "Will you tell me about her?"

He almost said no. But that—talking about his wife after her death—was something he'd never been able to do and not just because he hadn't wanted the depth of grief that came with the words. Elizabeth had lived all of her life in New Braunfels, they'd met there, married there, conceived their child there. She was known and loved by the town. There was nothing he could tell anyone about her, as a woman and a person, that wasn't already known. He *wanted* to talk about her, he found, wanted to keep the memories of the good that had come before the bad.

Ford kept his eyes on the horizon as thoughts of her flooded him. "I fell in love with Elizabeth the first time I ever saw her. I was seven. She was six. She wore her hair in braids and I'd pull them every chance I could. She was the prettiest girl in town even then and was still when I married her more than a dozen years later. And she was the sweetest and the kindest of anyone I knew."

But not the strongest. That was something he'd known but never admitted. And he felt guilty now, just thinking it. Elizabeth would never have come looking for him like his sister Katherine had done when he got himself in a tight spot. She'd stood fast, waiting for him, until he'd made it home but she would never have even considered riding out to find him with a rifle hung on her saddle. The thought made him feel disloyal to her memory. There weren't a lot of women as strong as Katherine, he reminded himself.

"That sounds like a fairytale," Maria murmured. "Loving someone from the day you first saw her."

"Not every fairytale has a happy ending," Ford said, his voice sounding rougher than he intended.

He turned to apologize for that but Maria's expression was calm, accepting, without the least sign of offense or backing down from the moment. "But at least you had it," she said. "You had that much and no one can take that from you. It's a gift you can give McKenna, that you loved her mother from the moment you saw her and that you forever *will* love her."

"McKenna's my reason for living, now, for going on." For everything.

"She's your reason for heading West?"

"In a way. My sister moved to Taos with her husband. And their best friends followed behind not long after. I want McKenna to know all of her family and I never want her to be afraid of seeing other places, of living her life however she wants." His glance swept the empty horizon ahead, then came back to her. "I'll take her back to New Braunfels someday because she'll always have family there, too."

"Take her back East, to the coast, as well! To see the cities and boatyards—the fishing vessels with their masts high alongside steamers that travel so swiftly. And the museums and lending libraries." She sounded almost breathless and then seemed to laugh at herself. "It was a gift to experience although I'd never want to stay forever. It's not where I'd choose to live the rest of my life, but I wouldn't have missed seeing it for the world."

Ford felt a sharp tug of curiosity about the sights Maria had seen. Maybe someday he *would* take McKenna to see more of the world. He started to say as much, but the cry of a wildcat raised the hair on the back of his neck. The horse beneath him snorted but held steady while Evan's horse, with Maria astride, stepped sideways and bumped into his. Ford pulled his rifle and waited as Henry's muttered curses carried back to them. The shrill squeal of dying prey that followed was a reassurance to Ford, but he noted that the sound drained the color from Maria's face.

She didn't say anything, nor did he, but he knew he'd rather a rabbit or prairie dog lost its life to a hungry cougar than one of them.

When the next swing station came into sight, Ford knew it was probably for the best that Evan would reclaim

his horse and Maria would take her place in the coach with
McKenna.

Chapter Eight

Slade rode his buckskin past the huge gate of the Taos plaza, where the windows and doors of every home and business opened onto the square. The adobe exteriors of those houses and those buildings created the wall enclosing the plaza. In the event of attack, the gates could be swung closed, providing an effective barricade against any threat.

That had happened just once since Slade had been in New Mexico and it had been a false alarm when the captain at Fort Union received a report that the Navajo nation was on the warpath, slaughtering white men and Spaniards alike. The actuality was no more than a small skirmish between a small band of the Navajo and a trio of Comancheros that had spilled over onto a rancher's property with some cattle killed.

Slade's destination lay a short distance from the plaza.

He dismounted at the rear of the Carson home and dropped the reins to the ground in front of a courtyard filled with late blooms. He smiled at the attractive woman who stood as he drew near. "Josefa," he said. "It's good to see you. How are the children?" As he asked the question, he noticed the bright eyes that peeked from behind her skirt and he chuckled.

"Welcome, Slade. They are well, as you will see once they realize it is you and come out of hiding. It is good to see you also. Kit will be pleased."

True to her words, the little girl clinging to her mother's skirt took a step forward then launched herself into Slade's arms.

"Teresina," Josefa chided her daughter softly. "Be a lady."

"Time for that soon enough." Her husband spoke from the open doorway behind her. "She's but five," he added as he stepped out, their son at his heels. Ford knew the boy was only a year, maybe two, older than the girl, but he stood straight and dignified, like his father. Kit wasn't a tall man, but he carried himself with an authority that the men around him respected.

He crossed the courtyard to his wife and kissed her on the cheek before extending his hand to Slade. Josefa took her protesting daughter from Slade, leaving him free to return the handshake. When Josefa insisted the boy go with her as well, Kit intervened in that quiet way of his. "Julian can stay."

Josefa gave a small nod, then carried her daughter into the house. Kit studied Slade's face a moment then gestured toward a bench. "Josefa will bring us something to drink soon," he predicted as they sat facing each other and stretched their legs before them. Julian took a seat beside his father and mimicked his actions although his heels barely touched the ground.

"Things seem well with you, my friend."

Kit nodded, his eyes searching Slade's. "But not so much with you." It wasn't a question.

Slade gave the Indian agent a sharp look, then realized Kit Carson was reading his face rather than expressing knowledge of why Slade was there. The man had a way of doing that. "The ranch may have a problem," Slade admitted. "We had visitors a few nights ago."

Kit's brows drew together. "Jicarilla?" Kit's charge included the Pueblos but his greater concerns were most often caused by either the Jicarilla Apache or their allies, the Utes, and sometimes both at once. By the time Slade and Katherine had claimed their land, the open warfare between the Jicarilla and the settlers had come to an end, but small skirmishes and deaths continued.

His role as Indian agent was how Slade had come to know him. Kit had visited the ranch shortly after he and Katherine arrived. They were still living in what would become the bunkhouse for the hands that had yet to be hired. Kit had cautioned them, on that first visit, that their treatment at the hands of the natives of the area would be largely determined by how they treated the natives in turn. Slade already knew that to be true. Although not regular army nor Texas Ranger, he'd worked for both until he and Katherine headed West. He doubted the natives of the New Mexico Territory were much different from the natives of Texas—rightfully resentful but weary from a war they'd come to realize they could not win. If treated with respect, most were willing to give respect in turn.

Katherine knew this even better than he. She also knew

their response if treated with disrespect.

His reply to Kit at that first meeting had sealed their friendship. Kit was convinced that the attacks on settlers, though few and far between, were acts of desperation as they saw their land overtaken and their food sources depleted. Slade tended to agree, although he knew he'd be less forgiving of a deliberate provocation. Fortunately, that hadn't been tested, although it now appeared someone might be determined to make him and Jeb think otherwise.

Kit asked few questions as Slade described the slaughtered bulls and the subsequent attack on the ranch, but his expression spoke volumes. The agent had done more than anyone to quell tensions between ranchers and natives, had soothed nerves and tempers with frequent visits and conversations, even bringing key leaders from both sides together. Kit's efforts were how Slade and Jeb had first met Jishnu. The agent wouldn't take kindly to anyone threatening the current, hard won peace.

"And you found just the one arrow."

Slade nodded. "I had the men scour each of the paddocks."

"But the youth lost two." Kit's eyes narrowed. "And you don't think he was lying about when and how?"

"He wasn't lying." Slade was sure of that. He was also sure that even if he thought the young brave was lying, he'd be hard-pressed to convince Kit of the same. Not because Kit was prejudiced in favor of the Apaches. He wasn't. But Kit knew, as well as Slade, that Jishnu kept a tight control on his small band. That control had kept peace for them thus far and the chief would yield up any malcontent who jeopardized the safety of the whole.

They fell silent as Josefa returned with two mugs and a

platter filled with meat and bread. Kit caught her hand as she turned to go and pressed it to his cheek. She gave him a searching look. "You must go?"

"Just for a day or two. I will set a guard at the door for you and the children."

"Surely that is not necessary," she protested. Her lovely eyes shadowed with concern at his words.

"Only to my peace of mind, my heart."

Her expression cleared at his assurance. "I will prepare a bag for your needs."

"Pack lightly, Josefa. I will be gone no longer than one night."

Slade watched the exchange. The two had been married far longer than he and Katherine but their affection burned as bright as if their vows had just been said.

When the woman re-entered the house, Slade waited for Kit to speak. "We will visit those ranchers neighboring your place and close to Jishnu's winter camp."

"One of those neighbors is recent."

Kit nodded. "So I heard. It could be a coincidence."

"It could," Slade agreed. "Hard to see how they'd benefit from open hostilities with the Jicarilla."

Kit's expression mirrored Slade's thoughts. "Maybe they're not the ones looking to benefit. Lots of unanswered questions to my mind. Lots of ugly possibilities."

Slade hoped there wasn't worse trouble brewing, a conflagration could be lit when the next arrow fell. Somehow, they had to get ahead of that.

Between tasks, Katherine watched the horizon for a sign of Slade. It was dusk when she saw two riders cross a distant hill. Even through the haze of distance, with little more than a shadow discernable, her heart knew one of the men was Slade. Her heart would always know.

As they came closer, Katherine placed three washbasins filled with clear well water and bars of soap and clean towels on the long wooden table near the door. She knew Jeb would be watching just as she had been and would head for the house as soon as he realized Slade was close.

She came back through the door after her final trip to the porch and automatically glanced at Hannah who sat at the table shelling peas. She was keeping a close eye on her after realizing Hannah's feet were showing signs of swelling.

Hannah smiled at her and said, "Stop worrying. It's normal."

"No, it isn't."

Hannah sighed. "Well, don't say that to Jeb. He barely lets me out of the house as it is. It may not be normal but I know it's common. I heard enough complaining in the women's Saturday social group back home."

And that was a world Katherine knew nothing about. The women of New Braunfels hadn't socialized with her after she was forcibly returned to the town. They'd seen her clutching a half-breed baby, heard of her cursing the soldiers who'd rescued her, and turned their backs on her. It mattered to no one save Katherine that she'd watched helplessly as those soldiers slaughtered an entire band of Comanche, women and children and babies. Shea had escaped death because she was in the arms of a white woman.

Nothing more than the memory of those grief-filled days lingered. Slade had erased the splintering pain of her past.

As she had predicted, Jeb rode his horse up to the house

moments before Slade and his companion dismounted. She recognized the Indian agent for the territory. Kit Carson didn't cut an impressive figure, but she'd learned in the time since they'd settled here that he was an impressive man. She liked and trusted him without reservation.

After making good use of the soap and water, he greeted her warmly. "Ma'am. You're looking lovely."

"Thank you for the kindness. It's good to see you again, Mr. Carson. Hannah and I will have dinner prepared before long."

She had the barest moment of time to notice when Jeb heard and reacted to his wife's name, to realize he was worried about her. More worried, it appeared, than Katherine's small concern with swelling feet. If something alarming had happened, she needed to know.

"Perhaps with some of those 'light as a cloud' biscuits of yours?" the agent asked hopefully.

She refocused her attention and gave him a smile. "The biscuits would be Hannah's but I'm sure she'd be happy to oblige."

Slade ushered the agent into the kitchen, touching Katherine's arm lightly as he passed her. At his gesture, the men settled at the kitchen table. It might have been more pleasant on the porch, but Slade always made sure that she and Hannah heard any conversation that affected them.

Slade's gaze tracked Katherine's movements across the kitchen as she did the bulk of the work. He noted each time she quelled Hannah with a quick glance, whenever the other woman lifted something lighter than a spoon to stir with.

Kit started the conversation. "So, now, you bought

four fancy beeves and two have been killed and left for carrion and a pretty mare down with an arrow from one of Jishnu's youngsters." He looked at Hannah, "And I'm rightfully sorry for that, ma'am," he said before refocusing on the threat still hanging over the ranch. "There's still one arrow missing. It could be out there somewhere spent or still in the hands of someone who means you no good."

"Or someone who means Jishnu and his people no good," Jeb countered.

Kit nodded. "That's on my mind as being just as likely. I figure some friendly neighbor-to-neighbor visits need to be paid, some friendly words need to be spoken."

Jeb raised a brow. "Warnings?"

"Advice is the word I'd use."

"Slade and I can't both go with you."

"No, I can see you wouldn't want to leave your womenfolk alone."

Slade waited a heartbeat for Katherine to chime in.

"I can outshoot most men with a rifle," she said, without heat. "Want to try me?"

Kit's eyes twinkled but his expression was solemn. "No, ma'am. I've got a reputation to maintain and I've no doubt you could best me and that's the gospel truth. But," and Slade watched as the twinkle disappeared, "having to kill a man isn't a position I'd like to put you in."

"It isn't the worst thing that can happen to a woman," Hannah said quietly.

The Indian agent shifted his glance to her and it warmed. Slade knew he had a real fondness for Hannah, a real appreciation of the strength with which she'd met life and started anew without whimper over what she'd been through. "No, ma'am," he agreed. "It isn't."

Jeb shook his head. "Katherine, you could shoot the wings off a fly, but I need you and that weapon of yours close by Hannah. Once my daughter is born, she can pick up her own gun if need be."

Hannah shook her head. "I'm having a boy, Jeb Welles, and being pregnant won't keep me from defending myself."

He sighed and shrugged. "Not arguing with you, Hannah, but we're not leaving you and Katherine alone here, either."

Slade nodded. "Wouldn't do for us to leave the vaqueros alone either, not right now. They're good men but they're not gunfighters."

"You trust 'em?" Kit asked.

"They've not given us reason to distrust," Slade said. But he knew there was a real difference in trusting and not having reason to distrust. He and Jeb had been more than fair to the men in their pay but greed could be a strong force in a weak man. Most of them he knew were strong enough to be honorable, but he was less than sure of two or three.

When Katherine piled a platter with Hannah's biscuits still warm from the wood-burning stove and placed it in front of the men, the talk turned to mundane things, weather and crops and the growing need for beef back East. The men served themselves from the heavy kettles in the hearth and settled contentedly to eat and visit.

Slade was considering a second helping when shouts of consternation too close to the house brought him to his feet. Jeb was already reaching for his gun as the men exited, automatically fanning out once they reached the yard.

A quick glance took in the vaqueros surrounding a lone Indian mounted on a sturdy sorrel and holding a nicely marked paint pony on a lead. The tension eased from

Slade's shoulders as he recognized the youth from Jishnu's band. The one whose lost arrows had been found and used by someone with bad intent. Slade's gaze swept the horizon where the lowering sun had tinged the clouds to varying shades of gold. There on the rise just beyond the barn, two mounted warriors stood watch. The only thing that moved around them was the breeze that stirred the manes and tails of their ponies.

Kit glanced at Jeb. "That the boy?"

At Jeb's nod, Kit stepped forward and spoke to the boy in his own language, then translated for Slade and Jeb. Slade recognized some of the Apache words although the exchange was rapidly spoken.

Kit looked at Jeb. "He wants to talk with your woman."

"Hannah's not coming out here."

"Yes, she is," Hannah said from the porch behind him.

Jeb turned in time to watch his wife descend the steps, careful of her balance. "Damnit, Hannah." Heaving a sigh, he stepped forward to take her hand.

Kit looked at the ground, but not before Slade caught sight of the grin he hid.

With Jeb at her side, Hannah walked up to the young brave who slid from his horse. The youth looked into her eyes and Slade knew he wouldn't find any animosity. Hannah wasn't that kind of woman. Had the mare been Katherine's, her sorrow would have turned to anger. Hannah's grief would only turn to more grief.

The young man began talking as much with his hands as with words and Kit translated in quiet tones. Not word for word, Slade knew, because some had no equivalent but it would be accurate enough for understanding.

"His name is Nantan. He's shamed his arrow was used to harm your horse. He's shamed he failed to retrieve his arrow. He wants to repay you with the gift of this painted pony. Says she's strong, but gentle, and will serve you well. She's not old and will live long for you."

Hannah nodded and kept her eyes on the brave as she said, "I'll accept this gift. She is beautiful and I'll treasure her."

Judging by the Apache youth's expression, Slade suspected her words didn't need translating but Kit did anyway. The youth held out the end of the rope and Hannah accepted it, nodding gravely as she did so.

The boy and the woman exchanged another long look then the brave grasped the mane of the sorrel and swung himself effortlessly onto the muscular back. He nodded at Jeb, then glanced at Slade and Kit, before putting his heels to his horse in the same instant he wheeled him about. Within moments, he'd reached the two who had accompanied him.

One of the vaqueros stepped forward. "Should we follow them to the boundaries?"

Slade shook his head. "No need."

Katherine stepped close and slipped her arm around his waist as Hannah laid her cheek upon the neck of the paint that had been gifted to her.

Slade wished the gesture would be the end of their problems but, since the young brave hadn't been guilty of anything more than losing an arrow, he knew that wasn't likely.

Chapter Nine

While Henry checked the rigging on his team, Ford watched through the window of the stage coach as Maria climbed on his grullo. Evan held one hand lightly on the reins even though he'd know, as sure as Ford knew, that the courtesy wasn't necessary. Ford's gelding was too well-trained to take so much as a step before his rider lifted the reins. He'd also warned Maria what not to do if she didn't want to be left in the dirt when the grullo reacted to a signal that called for immediate speed or a fast turn.

Ford shifted his attention to the baby in his arms. McKenna was his focus. Not some pretty Spanish girl whose parents could probably buy and sell half the New Mexico Territory if it suited them. But even as he told himself that, he was glad to catch her glancing toward the coach, toward the front where he and McKenna were seated.

In the end, that glance wouldn't matter. He knew that. Maria Cordova was young and pretty and doubtless the darling of her family, while he was a man who'd seen too much and lost too much and had a baby to raise. No, it wouldn't matter—but he was glad anyway.

For the first hour or so, he entertained McKenna by pointing to various things through the coach window then saying and spelling the name of each. He knew the spelling wasn't likely to stick but she'd be starting to talk soon. Every now and then he could recognize a word in her jabbering although he was doubtful she knew what any of the words meant. He'd started being more careful with his language around her. When she tired of that game, he whisper-sang nursery rhymes in a voice the good Lord surely hadn't meant for singing, but McKenna didn't seem to mind the occasional discordant note.

At the back of the coach, the salesman pulled out a pack of cards and held it up to the preacher. They'd both removed their jackets in deference to the heat, but the preacher kept his waistcoat neatly buttoned while the salesman had removed his tie and rolled his sleeves up to his elbows.

Ford had noticed the salesman taking nips from the bottle he kept tucked in a small bag he kept with him. They were small nips but they were regular and probably contributed to the dark pouches beneath his eyes. If the preacher had taken note of it, he hadn't commented on it, which Ford considered a good thing.

The preacher raised his brows, dark like his hair, but his green eyes held a gleam of interest. "Now, Mr. Ellis, you know a man of the cloth can't gamble."

Ellis winked, brushing a shock of straight, pale hair

away from his eyes. "No need to gamble, Reverend. Just a way to pass the time. Do you know how to play?"

"I'm sure I can recall a bit from my younger and wilder days."

Within moments, Ford was watching the salesman cheat his way through hand after hand. If money was involved, he might have taken a stand. As it was, he was just purely entertained. He was also enlightened as to why a salesman might be traveling as light as this one appeared to be. He realized the moment the preacher saw the sleight of hand and began to match his actions to suit, all with a quiet smile. Apparently, the man's younger and wilder days weren't so long ago that he'd lost his touch.

McKenna fell asleep in Ford's arms, the cards were put away, and Ford had too much time to think. To keep his thoughts focused in a good direction, he began imagining the house he intended to build, how large each room should be. He and McKenna wouldn't need much at first but if he planned well, he'd be able to add on as she grew. With Jeb and Hannah being so close to having their first child, McKenna would have someone near to her in age, someone to play tag with and learn to read and write and do sums with. At least he hoped they'd be living close enough for that. Slade had warned that the land claim could be tricky to negotiate. Ford had money from the ranch but money wasn't always the deciding factor. He'd tried to pray about it but prayer no longer came easy to him.

Even so, Ford read the bible aloud to McKenna every night, had since the day she was born. He'd begun because it was Elizabeth's and holding it helped him feel close to her even though every word had filled him with anger that first time and for days after. Over time, he'd begun to feel, and not just hear the words of hope and promise, that there was a life to come when he'd see his wife again and the anger had faded.

He'd shifted his thoughts from building the house to raising a barn when he heard Evan shout to Henry, "Whoa up the coach!" Ford tensed at the urgency in his voice.

It took a moment for Henry to bring the team to a halt. By the time he did, Maria was sliding down from the gelding. When she turned, she stumbled a bit. Her gaze went to Ford and she took a deep, steadying breath. He could see the fear in her eyes.

Ford made short work of getting out of the coach with McKenna. He didn't ask or wait for an explanation, but helped Maria up the steps then handed McKenna to her. "Your rifle is under the seat?"

Maria nodded, her expression tense but determined. Ford closed the door securely behind her and swung up into the saddle. He nudged the horse forward where Evan waited at the front of the coach.

Henry didn't appear the least impatient or concerned as he waited for Evan to start talking.

"Maria ... Miss Cordova needed a moment of privacy. I moved just a short distance away from the underbrush. When she came back, she was rushed and stumbling, and said she heard a woman scream."

Looking unimpressed, Henry spat expertly into the dust beside the wheel of the coach. "Huh, cougar, I expect."

Evan nodded. "That was my first thought but I moved off trail a bit to check things out and that's when I smelled smoke." He hesitated, looking grim. "And not just smoke. Something else."

"Well, hell." Henry sat silent a moment, staring off

into the distance. "Might be y'all need to take a look. Just in case."

Just in case there's anyone left to save. Ford could almost hear the end of the sentence. But he wasn't leaving Henry alone to protect the coach. Not with his daughter in it. And Maria. "Evan will stay here. Can either that preacher or that salesman handle a gun?" Ford knew the whip would have asked.

"Well, now that you mention it, preacher did say he'd changed his ways after the last man he drew down died on him. The sheriff chased him out of town, and he decided a different lifestyle might suit him better."

Ford considered the preacher's wiry build, the quiet, almost graceful way he moved, and nodded. He could see it. He stepped his horse back to the coach window and leaned in from his saddle. "Preacher, you still carry?"

"For protection only. Shall I climb out?"

"I'd be obliged."

The preacher closed the coach door behind him and said evenly, "On the box with Henry?"

After a moment's hesitation, Ford changed his plans. He suspected the preacher was more likely to shoot a man between the eyes than Evan was. He nodded. "If you don't mind."

Giving a nod, the preacher climbed to the box seat and pulled a rather wicked looking pistol from his vest.

Henry said, "We're going to move forward and expect you two to catch up."

Ford nodded and clapped his heels to his horse's sides. Heading back the way they'd come at a ground-eating canter. Evan caught up and took the lead, veering off the coach road at a point where a cluster of boulders forced the road to curve around them. That must have been where Maria sought privacy. Ford felt a quick wave of irritation that Evan had left the woman alone and unprotected for even a moment but thrust the feeling aside. Hell, he might easily have done the same. Everything looked peaceful enough here.

They'd crossed the first slope when Ford caught the drifting scent of woodfire. And the something else Evan had mentioned. The ugly, ugly smell of burning flesh. The closer they got, the more skittish their horses became. Ford understood. He didn't much want to get any closer either.

They topped a rise and the carnage came into sight, the charred wagon and the bodies—both human and horses. Two adults, two youngsters burned beyond recognition. Ford hoped like hell they were dead first. He heard Evan puking behind him.

When his retching eased, Evan moved his horse closer. His horrified gaze took in the scene below them where a handful of arrows littered the ground around the wagon. "I thought the army had the Indians quelled out here."

Ford sighed. "Only the ones who want to be. There are renegades here just like in Texas. Likely more of them."

Evan shifted uneasily in his saddle, glancing around at the scrub brush and scattered trees. "Where do you think they are?"

"Long gone or over the next hill." He had a sudden itch between his shoulder blades, a need to see his daughter and know she was safe. He turned his horse about. There was nothing he could do for these dead.

"Aren't we going to bury them?" Evan asked.

"It will be hours yet before that wagon cools down enough where we could get to them. Henry can send someone from the station." It would be too late by then, of course, but he didn't say so. The animals would get braver as the wagon cooled and they saw no movement from the humans. Sometimes Ford forgot how much Evan hadn't seen when they'd lived about the same number of years.

Evan nodded, looking relieved. Ford didn't blame him for that. It wouldn't have been a job he wanted, but he would've put his hands to it, had it been possible.

Maria rocked McKenna against her shoulder, knowing she soothed herself more than the little girl who hadn't so much as murmured in her sleep. From time to time, she bumped the heel of her boot lightly against the rifle stock, making sure it was still close at hand.

She tried to convince herself that she'd heard nothing—but she had. She knew she had. It was a woman's scream, one of pain and maybe horror. The sound had been shrill, piercingly so. And it had ended abruptly.

When Evan had left her alone to see if he could find the source, she'd felt chilled. Not even rubbing her hands up and down against her upper arms had helped. She'd felt that chill more when Evan returned. He didn't say anything, except they needed to get back to the coach, but his face had told a story. Maria had been terrified in the short time it had taken them to reach the coach. She didn't know what evil trailed them, or if it did, but her imaginings were vivid. The relief she felt at seeing Ford's face had been undeniable. The two men looked of a similar age, both muscular, though Evan had a bit more thickness than Ford, whose muscles were long and lean. But it was from Ford that she felt a sense of competence and maturity, the ability to make a decision and carry it through any hardship he might encounter. It was Ford she could imagine placing himself solidly between danger and his woman.

When the coach began to slow, she glanced back at the salesman who started in alarm at the change in the coach's movement. Maria leaned to look out the window. "It's them," she said in relief. "Ford and Evan." The fact that they held their horses to a slow canter rather than urging them to a hard gallop reassured her that they weren't being chased.

The salesman straightened his bulky shoulders, as if he'd never really been concerned, but his normally florid face was pale and a soft sheen of perspiration still lay upon his brow. "I'm sure they discovered that what you heard was nothing more than some wild animal," he said.

Maria just looked at him until he looked away.

After a brief conversation with the driver, Ford and Evan took their places on either side of the coach. The preacher didn't step down from the boot and the coach rolled forward. The salesman rubbed his neck and stared out the window.

Ford stared at the still-burning husk of the swing station. The acrid scent of charred wood and woodsmoke was better than the underlying odor that turned his stomach. He watched from across the clearing as Evan walked back from the barn which appeared to be unscathed.

"Four pair mules with arrows through the heart laying in the lot behind the barn. Several saddles hanging inside but no horses, dead or alive."

No surprise, Ford thought. The Apache—if that's what they were—had no use for mules. The horses would have value to them, but not donkeys or mules.

While Evan helped Henry water the mule team, Ford

began walking the clearing around the remnants of the swing station. After a moment, he realized the preacher had climbed down and was doing the same, crisscrossing Ford's path.

They slowed together in the center. "Three horses, at most."

"That's what I count," Ford agreed. "Almost like they tracked this up to look like more."

"Almost. Odd that one horse is wearing shoes."

Ford had noticed that as well, but he was surprised the preacher had. "Not so very. Likely stolen." He held out his hand and the other man shook it. "Just wanted to say thank you, Reverend. It was easier to ride back to check things out knowing you were shotgun with my baby girl inside."

"We'll keep her safe 'til you get where you're going." He cleared his throat. "Reckon you might as well just call me Ridge. I've about decided, preaching ain't my callin' after all."

Under other circumstances, Ford would've smiled but these were no circumstances for smiling. Some folks really were too old to change and some callings fit too well to change from. All he said was, "I'll appreciate any help comes my way."

Henry walked over to join them. He looked morose but then he usually did. "I don't like pushing this team another mile much less seven but that's what we got ahead of us. I can't push 'em hard but we need to be steady. And I can't take the time to dig through the ashes and bury the station keep and whoever's with him. I don't like that, but it's a fact."

"Sir," Ford said, "I doubt there's much you'll find to bury under there. I suggest we say a prayer and move out."

When the rest of their group had gathered, Ford took

McKenna from Maria. She was already getting leggy and she didn't like to be still when her eyes were open. And she was wide awake now. Maria would have a time when they were cooped back up in the wagon. Ford would manage until then. Besides, he liked the feel of McKenna safe against his chest.

When Henry looked toward Ridge to lead in prayer, the gunman turned preacher and back again shook his head. Shaking his head at the vagaries of his passengers, Henry started the Lord's Prayer in a voice rumbly with disuse and the others followed suit. Beside Ford, Maria's voice came clear and even, neither whisper low nor gratingly loud.

As Henry fell silent, Ford realized that the salesman hadn't joined them. A bumping noise caught his attention and Henry's as well.

"Hey, now," the whip called in protest. The salesman didn't stop or look back. He just kept tugging his case and a leather bag from the middle of the stack until he could tumble it from the boot to the ground.

Judging the distance to the ground, Ford was surprised the strap that secured the case from opening had held. He followed Henry's stumpy-gaited stalk back to the coach. "What in tarnation are you doing?"

"Leaving."

"Leaving? Where to?"

"Anywhere but ahead," Ellis said grimly.

"You're not going to make it if you turn back. We've come too far. You'll be dead before you get anywhere." Henry was genuinely bewildered. And visibly agitated.

"It's you folks that are going to die. Those savages are ahead of us and you just plan to trail right along in their tracks until they take a mind to turn. That's when they'll slaughter you and burn you alive. Well, I won't be with you."

"You can't carry your luggage much less enough water to survive. Not on foot."

The salesman slid a small pistol from the belt beneath the paunch of his belly. "I don't plan on it. You're going to unhook one of those mules for me."

"No, sir, I'm not going to do that."

The nose of the pistol angled toward Henry's heart, but the blast of gunfire came from behind the salesman. A splatter of blood erupted with the bullet exiting his chest. As Ellis toppled, Maria gasped and turned her face.

"I'm sorry, ma'am," Ridge said, stepping forward. "I'd never have wanted you to see that, but I've seen folks lose their senses before in situations like this. They tend to take innocent folk with them. I wouldn't be a man if I let his actions cause the death of you and that baby girl you've been protecting most of the day."

Henry heaved a sigh. "Going to be hard to explain losing a passenger."

"No, sir. He died a hero at the hands of these renegade Apache. He did his best to protect the women and children on board."

Henry's gaze met and held with Ridge's and, after a moment, the whip nodded. "He did at that. A hero. It'll comfort his family to know."

Ford turned away. It was the first time he'd felt completely uncertain of the decision he'd made to come West. If he lost McKenna, he'd lose his reason for living.

Chapter Ten

The decision for Jeb to stay behind hadn't been a difficult one. It had been the only one that made sense. Even so, Slade could sense Jeb's inner struggle as the three of them had talked through the evening hours. Slade knew he'd feel the same, needing to stay with his wife, but longing to ride with his partner. For now, they both knew that Hannah needed him most.

Slade and Kit made their plans before turning in for the night. They'd start with the Cordova spread on the east side of their ranch. Señor Cordova had proven a reasonable neighbor from the start and one Slade thought would be willing to sharpen his vigilance while still taking a wait and see approach.

Slade didn't like leaving Katherine behind but she was concerned for Hannah, too concerned to leave her.

"She seems healthy and the baby's kicks are strong," Katherine admitted as she pulled the brush through her hair, "but ... something's wrong. I can feel it."

Slade crossed from the window where he'd been standing, looking out across the moonlit horizon, to sit on the bed beside her. He took the brush from her hand, sliding it through the heavy strands with a far more gentle touch than her own. He felt Katherine shiver as his knuckles brushed the nape of her neck. He never tired of her reaction to him.

When he eased her back against the pillows, she sighed. "You should rest."

Ignoring the suggestion, Slade whispered her name just as he covered her mouth with his. Outside their uncovered window, the velvet sky held a glittering of stars and a three-quarter moon. A wolf howled in the distance as Katherine sighed and opened to him.

The Hacienda de Cordova was large but not pretentious. Two stories tall and built of solid adobe, it stood next to a scattering of trees that lined a small stream. Like Slade and Jeb, the man had wisely built with a water source as his priority rather than a majestic hilltop view. Unlike Slade and Jeb, he had built much closer to that water source. Perhaps it was that he'd never experienced the ravaging floods of a wet winter or perhaps the stream had cut its way closer over the years.

Señor Cordova met them on the long verandah as they dismounted. Slade had no doubt he'd been told of their approach soon after they had crossed the boundary of his property. They encountered a number of his vaqueros who had tipped their hats and continued on with their business.

Two men on horseback, however well-armed, would not be perceived as a threat to them. Likely, too, Kit's face was well-known. Part of his work involved knowing and understanding the concerns of the landowners who might have occasion, for good or ill, to interact with the Indians in the territory.

Slade didn't expect the man to recognize him although he and Jeb had made themselves known to the neighbors on both sides and to the south of their place shortly after securing their claim through the governor's office. He was mistaken.

"Señor Slade, Señor Carson, your visit is a pleasure." Cordova was tall and rangy like the cattle he ran, his face weathered by the seasons, his thick hair white from the sun.

He welcomed them into a wide, sparsely furnished room that seemed to serve as both entrance and hallway. The dim interior was a pleasant respite from the dust and heat of their ride. Straight back from the entrance, another set of wide double doors opened onto a courtyard where servants garbed in cool, loose white clothing carried trays and pitchers of refreshments. Cordova spoke politely to the women who placed their burdens on the wood-planked table that centered the space. They smiled pleasantly at the guests then disappeared into a doorway to one side.

"Sit, please," Cordova said as he ushered Kit and Slade further into the courtyard.

The area was open to the sky where white clouds mixed with the blue, visible between the bare planks that crisscrossed the entire rectangle of space. Heavily leafed and flowered vines twined the planks, providing significant shade, a relief from the glare of the sun.

"Eat, drink," Cordova urged. "Then we will talk of

why you are here."

Kit reached for a slice of bread and spread it with what appeared to be jam from an earthenware bowl. "You don't think we're here to be sociable." It wasn't a question.

Slade lifted the pitcher and poured water into the cup before him. The water was sweet and cool.

Cordova seemed to consider Kit's question then shrugged and smiled faintly. "In the fall, after the cattle are sold and the remainder settled for the winter, we will have a gathering, a festival as we always do to celebrate God's favor. Mr. Slade and Mr. Welles and their wives did not join us last year and this year I hope they will. But, now, no, I do not think you are here for a friendly visit."

"Well, it's friendly enough," Kit noted. "What we're here to tell you may prove a problem—or may prove to be nothing."

"But you think it is a problem."

"I do," Kit said bluntly.

"I am listening."

Kit didn't embellish. There was no need. Even told and retold, the events sounded ominous to Slade's ear.

When Kit fell silent Cordova sat with his elbows propped on the table, hands in front of his face, fingers locked, the tips of his forefingers touching. His gaze was distant and filled with what appeared to be genuine worry.

He turned to look straight at Slade. "Do you think this is an attempt to drive you from your property? To make you fearful for your wives?"

"I don't. And if it were, it was a pitiful effort."

"I agree." Cordova sighed. "I think someone would cause trouble for Jishnu."

Something inside of Slade eased at his words. There was no undertone of animosity for the Apache chief.

More, there was a hint of frustration at the probability.

Kit nodded and leaned back in his chair. "Crossed my mind as well. But to what purpose?"

"I have heard the Comancheros are unhappy with him. He refuses to allow them to trade on the lands where his people dwell."

Slade stiffened. "They've tried? Near us?" There was little he despised more than the men who traded on both sides, bringing guns and whiskey to the Indians under the pretext of providing them with food staples.

"Tried and failed. Jishnu spoke with me about it."

Kit shifted in his seat. "Any reason neither you nor the chief thought to bring it to my attention?"

His tone remained mild where Slade would have been cursing.

Cordova looked embarrassed even as he lifted one brow in a quelling look. "I do not bring every small thing to do with Jishnu to the Indian agent. Not even such a good one as you have proved to be. Jishnu thought it was settled. I let it go."

"But now it may not be."

"Or it may still be and this other is unrelated." Cordova kept his equanimity.

"You don't believe that."

"No," Cordova admitted. "I don't."

"And something's got you worried."

"Not worried," Cordova insisted. "My daughter travels home from the East coast by coach. I would not want her subjected to any unpleasantness." He took a deep breath. "She is heavily guarded to ensure her protection. I made sure of that. Two vaqueros were sent to accompany her home as soon as she departed the steamer at the Texas coast."

The Comancheros considered the coach lines easy pickings but with two armed guards added to the coach's shotgun rider they would find the coach no easy prey. Slade, however, gave a thought to Katherine's brother who might also be traveling West to Taos. Ford was far from the reckless young man he'd once been. He would have been cautious in ensuring his daughter was adequately protected … still the nudge of concern was there. Katherine would be devastated if anything were to befall her brother or her niece.

They took their leave soon after. Kit looked Cordova in the eye. "Keep your guard up. If you hear anything from any direction, I need to know of it as fast as a horse can ride."

The Spaniard nodded. "It will be so. Again, you are welcome to stay. Mi esposa would welcome you."

"We'd best get on," Kit said. "We've two other landowners to warn."

"Señor Arellano, no doubt, is one?"

Slade nodded. "With Jishnu encamped directly above me, the least I can do is talk with the landowners on each side of me."

"Time I met Arellano, anyway," Kit commented.

"He is an honorable and reasonable man," Cordova assured them. "I have agreed to a betrothal between his heir and my daughter." He watched as they mounted their horses and lifted a hand in farewell. "Go with God."

When they were out of earshot, Kit grunted. "Arellano might be an honorable and reasonable man but I sent his heir packing out of Taos not long ago."

"Raisin' a little hell?"

"More than a little. Arellano needs to settle him down before someone puts a bullet through his gut."

Slade added Kit's assessment to what Katherine had told him of Arellano's visit to their place with his nephew and sighed. The last thing he and Jeb needed were problems with neighboring landowners over some young fool of a man.

They swung south as they left Cordova's and found a decent place to camp near a stream. The water was shallow and clear, and they entertained themselves in the last light of day by angling for fish with hooks painstakingly carved from bone that Kit produced from his saddlebag. When that proved unsuccessful, Slade sharpened tree limbs and they managed to spear enough for a meal.

As the fish cooked, Kit's good humor faded. "There's war coming."

His words fell into the quiet evening. Slade knew the possibility existed, had heard talk from some who were gleeful and others who were fearful. Because the prospect of war was on Kit's mind, he suspected Kit had seen or heard some recent communication. The agent was frequently in and out of the nearby army post.

"Somehow the idea of us warring on each other seems far-fetched to me," he said at last. Even as he spoke, he knew he and Jeb had been isolated from much of the tension that brimmed between the two factions. Neither believed one man should own another but they also didn't believe one half of their country should be forced to concede their beliefs to the other half.

"You've been pretty much focused on your cattle ranch." Kit didn't make the statement sound like an accusation.

"It's all we've had time to think about." But Slade knew Kit was right. Mostly, he and Jeb were able to ignore the whispers and rumors and outright calls for war in the day-to-day work of ensuring their cattle ranch prospered, and because they rarely left the ranch. Beyond the borders of their land, and even the New Mexico Territory, animosities simmered and would eventually boil over if left unchecked.

He stirred the fire with a stick and sighed. "Maybe cooler heads will turn it all around."

"Don't seem to be cooler heads on either side."

Slade looked him in the eye. "Then I'll hope to God any fighting stays outside the borders of this territory."

Kit shook his head. "If war comes, it'll come here as well. You can count on it."

They were up with the first glimmer of sunrise and reached the next spread before the sun had risen very high into the sky. Two young men were headed from a small adobe house to the barn and looked up warily at their approach. It took a moment for Slade to realize that one of them was a female dressed in men's clothing. Because of the loose clothing and the hat that covered much of her face, he might not have done so had the other not stepped in front of her protectively.

They were Americans rather than Spaniards, a young couple not long married, Kit told Slade as they rode closer and stopped. The man relaxed as he recognized and greeted Kit.

"Good morning, sir. It's good to see you again." He turned his gaze toward Slade while Kit made the introductions between the men.

Benjamin Warren shook the hand Slade held out to him then said, "And this is my wife, Johanna. We just finished breaking our fast so coffee's still warm and we've biscuits and ham left aplenty."

While Kit politely declined the offer and explained their early morning arrival, Slade studied the couple. Johanna looked a good bit younger than Katherine and Hannah. It could be she got lonely from time to time for womenfolk. He'd remind himself later that he or Jeb might bring them to visit. But that couldn't happen until Hannah's baby had arrived safely and this current threat, whatever it proved to be, was resolved.

Benjamin, her husband, was older, maybe more than a little older, but age wasn't always easy to tell when a man spent his days in the sun. His expression as he listened to Kit was calm and his gaze was steady. At one point, when his wife shifted and their arms brushed, he gave her a reassuring glance.

When Kit finished, the man didn't immediately jump in with a response and when he spoke, his words were measured. "I haven't met this Indian chief but I'm inclined to trust your judgement, Mr. Carson. But not too far, if you don't mind my saying. Even so, if anything troublesome should happen, we'll ride into Taos with word. I won't leave my wife here unprotected." He glanced toward Slade and added, "Two bulls and a good mare is a lot to lose."

"The mare is the hardest. My partner's wife set great store in her."

"I've got but two bulls here, so losing even one would be serious loss and we have no more than a few horses that are suited to ride yet." Benjamin looked worried.

"If you need help, our place is closer," Slade offered. "Either my partner or I could ride with you, and our wives and vaqueros are real handy with guns."

Benjamin nodded. "Obliged."

But Slade noticed he neither accepted nor refused the offer and that was fine, but a man should always know his options. If trouble came, he couldn't see himself leaving Katherine behind. Nor could he see her agreeing to being left.

"We'll let you get on with your day," Kit said.

As they mounted and turned their horses toward the northwest, Slade found himself looking forward to speaking with Arellano—and perhaps meeting the man's nephew. One or both needed to be put in their place.

No one threatened his wife or Jeb's.

Katherine's heart jumped as she touched a match to the kerosene lantern and turned to see Jeb seated, with his elbows propped on the table and his head resting in his hands. It was barely dawn and still dark out.

"Jeb?" He raised bleary eyes to her as she asked, "Are you alright? Is Hannah?"

"Yeah. She's resting," he said tiredly. "Finally."

Katherine brought the lantern closer and frowned at the exhaustion on Jeb's face. "What's going on?"

"Nightmares. They started a few nights past and they're getting worse. She wakes up crying like her heart's broken, thinking she's lost the baby."

"What?" Katherine struggled to make sense of what he was saying. "Why? She's past the danger point. We talked about this. She's been fine."

"I think it just caught up with her that she's six months pregnant and she was six months along when those bastards made her lose her first baby."

Katherine pulled another chair from the table and sat down. "Damn."

"Yeah."

"Jeb?"

He sighed and just looked at her.

"Go to bed. Lorenzo and I have this. We'll manage. Go."

To her surprise and added worry, he did. Jeb was as strong as Slade. He must not have slept for several nights.

Damn. This should be a happy time for them not a scary one.

Chapter Eleven

Ford stepped out of the station into the moonlight. McKenna slept peacefully on her pallet next to Evan. Ford wished he could sleep. They'd left San Antonio five days ago. They should be past the half-way point of their journey but they weren't. It wasn't the driver's fault. Things happened. Things that couldn't be helped. But he hoped the worst was behind them. The moon wasn't full but it was bright enough for him to see the shadows of the trees laying across the clearing that separated the long, low building from the cluster of cottonwoods that surrounded it.

He nearly jumped when one of the shadows moved toward him. Maria.

"What are you doing out here?"

"Same as you, I suppose. I couldn't sleep and tired of

my clothing twisting about me as I tried to be comfortable."

That brought an image he'd rather not have had in his mind. He cleared his throat. "Not real safe out here with what's been going on."

"But now you're here," she said simply, as if that made everything right. "Can we walk, please, just for a while? It's peaceful and pretty in the moonlight."

"Just for a little while." Ford was reluctant for more reasons than one, but she sounded so plaintive he didn't have the heart to tell her no. "And we stay close to the cabin." But not so close they could be heard.

He fell into step with her. The wind soughed through the small stand of trees around them. After a moment, he sensed her move closer to him and wasn't surprised when she slipped her hand into the crook of his elbow. Just as he wasn't surprised how good it felt to him even though he wished otherwise.

"When we were talking ... before ... it sounded as if you will miss the East coast."

Her hesitation lasted barely a moment. "I think that is not the correct word. Every moment held excitement, some new adventure, and I took joy in that. Even so, I longed to ride free as I was taught, not constrained to a quiet trot down a winding lane or across someone's field. It grew tedious to remember not to laugh out loud or shout for joy because someone was always at hand. When I did forget, no one condemned, but I would wonder if they felt embarrassed for me. In New Mexico, it may be that each day will feel too much the same as the one before it but they will hold the freedom that I have missed." She grew quiet then added, "And I go home to be married, mistress of my own household, so there will be much to learn and to do."

Ford felt both relief and regret. He didn't want to be drawn to her, didn't want the risk of another loss in his life. If that meant missing the joy along with the grief, he was fine with that kind of exchange. He had McKenna to cherish and he had women like Bella to enjoy. Women whose real names he'd never know, never whisper in the first light of morning, or call out as he came to the porch for a noonday meal. He understood the relief. He didn't want to explore the swift feeling of emptiness.

"Then I suppose I should wish you joy in your marriage." A whole lot of questions fought for space in his mind but he shoved them back. Her life was not his concern.

"I don't expect to find joy, but I hope there will be contentment," there was a long pause, "and respect."

His steps slowed at the edge of the tree line farthest from the swing station. "Marriage should be more than that."

"Yours was." It wasn't a question.

He felt the familiar lump in his throat, the ache. He swallowed hard. "It was everything I ever wanted."

"I'm sorry for your loss," she said gently but took his breath when she added, "but I hope never to hurt like that."

"It was worth it," he said suddenly, fiercely. "You deserve more than contentment." Every woman did.

Her hand slipped from his elbow, but before he could wish it back, she turned to face him and placed both hands on his shoulders. Looking down into her eyes, glittering with the rays of the moon, he felt his heart thud in his chest.

"I can live with less. But—I do not know this man I am to wed—and I do not want him to be the only man I have ever kissed."

She lifted her face to his but did not close her eyes. He meant to do no more than brush his lips against hers then step back, but at the first touch he leaned in and deepened the kiss as his arms slid around her, pulling her close and lifting her to fit the length of him. Her breasts were full and firm and he hardened in response. Immediately he thought of Elizabeth but when he would have stepped away, she curved her arms upward, pressing her palms against his back, pulling him to her.

He growled deep in his throat and kissed her again. Only when he realized that her legs were trembling did he take his lips from hers. But he didn't release her. He turned her so that her back was to his chest. He wrapped his arms around her, under her ribcage. He would have given every coin in his possession to turn his hands palm up and cup the weight of her breasts as they rested against his arms.

Feeling Maria warm against him, his words came back to him. The time he'd been given with Elizabeth had been too brief but it had meant everything. And what they'd shared *was* worth every aching moment since.

After less time than he wanted with her, he walked Maria back to the door of the station and watched as she walked inside. She didn't look back.

Maria didn't sleep. Even without a mirror, she knew there were dark circles under her eyes. She pulled her hair tight to begin coiling and pinning the heavy length and wished she could ride beside Ford when they left the station. She had the same thought again when she stepped out without eating the food that had been prepared for them. It hadn't looked appealing.

What she wished wasn't practical, of course. The men

were wary and vigilant. Henry and Ridge were already up on the box as she walked toward the coach. Ford and Evan would ride on either side of the coach. Maria would keep McKenna safe inside.

As she reached to pull herself up into the coach, she felt a hand on her back to steady her. Securely inside, she turned and met Ford's gaze and flushed at what she read there. He handed McKenna up to her. The little girl cooed as she put her arms around Maria's neck and Ford's eyes darkened. He opened his mouth as if to speak, then turned away.

The morning passed slowly, too slowly. McKenna proved fretful and tired and slept more than normal which gave Maria little to do in the tedious hours between team changes. At each of the two morning swing stations, she climbed down with Ford's assistance and walked the stiffness from her legs while he held his daughter. The first time she could feel him watching her as she paced back and forth. When she turned, their eyes met and held for a moment. At the second station, Evan chose to walk with her.

Maria would rather have been alone but she made herself smile at him. His eyes looked haunted by the horrible deaths of whoever had been in the charred remains of the wagon and at the swing as well as the sudden, violent death of the salesman, Mr. Ellis. She supposed hers held that same look.

"I don't reckon this trip is what you expected it to be," he said.

"I think it is not what any of us expected."

"Ford, maybe did," he admitted. "He tried to warn me."

"Yet he brought his daughter." She didn't mean it as an

accusation and hoped it didn't sound as one.

Evan shrugged his shoulders and glanced ahead of them where Ford walked with McKenna held upright against one shoulder. Maria smiled at the way the little girl looked around her with lively interest. "He'd never leave her. She's his life now that Elizabeth is gone."

"Perhaps he will wed again someday. A little girl should not grow up alone." She felt a tiny stab at the thought of Ford finding a woman to wed, sharing the intimacy that she had dreamed of in the night, having a baby together.

"Well, they'll be settling close to family so she'll at least have cousins."

She was glad when Evan turned the talk to more inconsequential things and even more glad when they were called to return to the coach.

The midday stop was actually in the midst of what appeared to be a small settlement, not quite a town yet, but perhaps one day. The swing station, however, was still no more than a barn with a log shanty for the stock tenders. Henry sent the passengers walking along the short dirt road to the other end of the settlement where a boarding house of sorts offered a hot meal. Maria found the food better than she'd expected with some kind of tender greens stewed in salt meat and biscuits served with honey. At the end of the meal, the proprietress was kind enough to wrap a biscuit with honey in a cloth for Maria to take for McKenna to enjoy later.

Ford lingered, speaking with the boarding house owner. Maria had no good reason not to fall in step with the others. She forced herself not to cast a backward glance. Ford was a man well able to take care of himself and his daughter. He wouldn't let them get too far ahead and she could see in her mind his long strides closing any distance between them.

She felt someone move closer to her side and cast a quick glance. Mr. Ridge gave her a nod and a faint smile. "Mind?"

"Of course not." It was the truth. From what little she knew, she surmised he was a gunslinger but how could she begrudge the man a profession that was helping to keep her safe?

"You're not afraid of much, are you?" The words could have been praise. The tone seemed something different.

She looked up at him, tilting her head against the sun. "Should I be?"

"Might be wiser if you were."

"Of you?" Perplexity colored her voice. She could hear it and had no doubt he could as well. "Of a man who sits with his gun alongside the coach driver, himself exposed to danger the better to protect us."

"Maybe I'm a man who just likes to kill."

For a moment she didn't speak, remembering the violence of that moment, the sickness that hit her hard and fast. When she did answer, she stopped in the middle of the dirt road, forcing him to do the same or leave her standing. He stood looking down at her, expression guarded, but not guarded enough. "No, Mr. Ridge. I saw your eyes afterward. Whatever you are, you are not a man who likes bringing death to others. You're not afraid of it but you take no pleasure in it."

She turned and began walking toward the station and the coach that awaited. She was almost surprised when he kept pace with her. She was even more surprised when he spoke again.

"I wore a sheriff's badge for fifteen years."

Maria stayed silent, simply waiting, watching the dust that kicked up around her skirts.

"Our town was small but not quiet. Not nearly. Too close to the border. I kept it clean as long as I could then I started to see that I'd become a calling card for some."

"Young men with guns looking for a chance to prove their manhood," she murmured.

He gave her a quick, startled glance and nodded. "I finally had enough. Moved on. Found another little town."

"And they found you." She imagined it wouldn't have been hard. Bad news traveled faster than good.

"And they got younger and younger. I took to shooting them in the hand to keep from killing them. The last one had a gun in each hand."

"No way to stop him without killing him."

"He was sixteen."

Maria kept walking but put a hand on his arm. "He made a man's choice. He died a man's death."

"Sheriff didn't see it that way. Asked me politely to move on."

She gave a small chuckle. "But … a preacher?"

He shared the laugh with her. "I reckon that didn't work out any better."

"So, now you're going to Taos?"

"Not to stay. Going to see an old friend, then keep heading West."

"Will that be enough to keep the young guns from finding you?"

"Probably wouldn't have been but that sheriff that asked me to leave? He did me one last favor. There's a tombstone in that town with my name carved on it."

"Oh." Sadness hit her hard. "But what of your family? Your friends?"

"Got none."

"I disagree."

He was silent for a long while. "I reckon you'd better call me Tom."

"Is that what your friends call you?"

"Yes, ma'am, once upon a time. The few that I had."

They had reached the coach and she took her hand from his arm. "Thank you, Tom. I'll be proud to call you by your given name."

He helped her up into the coach. A few moments later, the others reached them. Ford gave her a searching glance as he crossed to her with McKenna. As careful as she was to keep her expression neutral, her heart skipped a beat at the heat in his eyes. Nor did she miss the sharp glance he gave Tom Ridge.

With an effort, Ford pushed aside the image of Maria standing in the road, staring up at the gunman, her hand on his arm, and focused instead on their surroundings as the coach lumbered steadily over the well-worn trail. This team of mules, like the previous, impressed him. They'd only ever had the two plow mules. When the first one began to show signs of age about the time Ford was entering his teens, he'd been retired to a corner pasture and replaced by the second. Neither were named, both were simply called *mule*, but both were treated like family.

The mule teams that pulled coaches were trained far beyond what Ford had experienced. They were calm and steady and cooperative with Henry and with each other.

Because he was paying attention, he became aware almost as soon as Henry when one of the leads began to limp slightly.

Henry pulled the team to a gradual stop and climbed down from the box. Ridge followed suit as Ford dismounted, dropping his reins to the ground.

"Right front," Ford offered, knowing the whip maybe couldn't tell which leg though he likely knew which of the pair from the bobbing of the mule's head as he moved.

Evan rode around from the far side to join them.

Henry grunted and picked up the outside, front leg. He lowered it carefully, gazed up at the sky, then looked at Ford. "Shoe's gone."

Ford knew they'd taken longer than usual at the last stop by walking down the road for a meal and back again. Henry had suggested it, likely suspecting a hot meal would put his passengers in a better frame of mind. The journey so far had been more than difficult. That delay hadn't been a concern at the time but it would be now.

"We're about halfway between, now, aren't we?" Ford asked.

"Yeah. Take just as long for one of us to ride back to get a spare mule as to ride forward to the next station."

Ford rubbed the back of his neck. A man on horseback could travel twice as fast as the mules could pull the coach but he wouldn't be able to watch his back at the same time. And Ford didn't like the idea of the wagon sitting here in the open for the time it would take to return with the mule's replacement but didn't have much to offer in its stead. He looked across at Evan. "What do you think?"

Evan dismounted. "I'd rather get this guy going if we can. He'll have to walk to safety either way. I need leather to cover the bottom of his hoof with something to pad it and leather strips to go up his leg to tie it."

Without saying a word, Ridge climbed down from the box and walked around to the boot where he began untying the salesman's bag. The others watched in silence as he dumped the man's clothes on the ground and began cutting his leather bag into circles to place below the hoof and bands to secure it.

Evan took a few minutes more than that to fasten a hoof covering with several layers of leather to pad and protect. He was careful in tying the leather strips so that they were secure above the fetlock but didn't cut into the mule's leg. To be doubly sure, he placed one layer of leather between the ties and the strips.

Henry's scowl eased but his look of concern didn't fade. They'd lost time they couldn't afford to lose and dark was likely to catch them some distance from their final station. But all he said was, "Let's move out."

Chapter Twelve

Slade silently admitted to being impressed as he and Kit rode up to the front entrance of Arellano's adobe home. Not because the two stories rose tall and extremely large and would have taken untold hours and dollars to build. And not because the long front verandah was almost completely shaded by an incredible fall of vividly colored flowers. What impressed him was the fact that every vaquero they passed ceased their work and followed behind, silent and non-threatening. Rakes and pitchforks were set aside. Horses being lunged or brushed were left secured. Wagons carrying forage and supplies were left with their teams ground-tied.

He heard Kit murmur, "What the hell," as he looked around them and Slade wondered the same. Without making a show of the action, Slade pulled his rifle from his saddle and cradled it across his arm.

By the time they had reached the double front door of stained hardwood, they were accompanied by two dozen or so vaqueros. When they stopped the horses, those men fanned out around them, faces calm but purposeful.

The double doors swung open and two men stepped out. The older one smiled. "Mr. Carson, you are welcome here, as is anyone who rides with you." He lifted a hand and the men who had left their jobs dispersed as silently as they had gathered. "Please, put your guns away. Come in to my home."

Now that they were no longer surrounded, Kit dismounted and Slade did the same, sliding his rifle back into place.

"Unusual welcome." Kit didn't sound impressed.

Arellano shrugged. "A bit of unpleasantness. A bit of precaution. But come, we will eat and drink and then we will talk."

They followed him into the house and along a corridor where doors stood open onto a lush courtyard. Two servants, both older men, were placing platters of food and bottles of wine down the length of one table. One man walked with a limp and Arellano placed a hand on his arm to stay him as he passed by. They spoke in Spanish, but Slade understood enough to know Arellano was suggesting he rest for the remainder of the day, that he'd been too much on his feet. The servant shook his head vigorously and Slade could see the gleam of pride in his eyes.

That exchange had Slade adjusting his opinion of Arellano, at least slightly. A man who had a care for those in his pay had earned a degree of respect. Whether or not he retained that respect, would have to be seen.

Following Kit's lead, Slade filled his plate but

disregarded the wine. Wine had never been to his liking, though he didn't mind a sip of whiskey on a cold night. To his knowledge, Kit didn't touch alcohol at all, at least Slade had never seen him do so.

The food preparation proved above average. Light, crusty bread spread with a preserve that Slade suspected was figs and honey. Fish that flaked when touched with a fork. Vegetables stirred into oils and herbs, yet retained a crunch when eaten.

Slade didn't notice Arellano make any gesture but a servant appeared at Slade's elbow with a glass filled with clear water. Slade murmured his thanks and drank. The water was as sweet as the food was tasty. He said as much to Arellano who beamed.

"My cook will be gratified by the praise."

Slade simply nodded. He planned to let Kit take the lead in conversation. He wanted an opportunity to observe Arellano's responses and expressions.

Kit's first question surprised both of them. "Where's your nephew?"

Arellano looked uncomfortable for the first time since their arrival which piqued Slade's interest. "Javier?" He shrugged. "He broke his fast late. I suspect he is riding with some of the vaqueros. There is always much to be done on a place this size. No single aspect can be neglected."

"I reckon he has much to learn," Kit said bluntly.

"I cannot argue that truth. However, Javier is a willing student."

"I'd hoped to meet him." Slade sat back in his chair.

He had kept his comment noncommittal but Arellano gave him a keen look. "I should perhaps apologize for my nephew's hasty reaction to Mrs. Welles' challenge."

"Challenge?" Slade laid his fork aside and stared the

man down. "Did you take it as a challenge when Hannah reassured you that my partner and I had not left our wives without protection?"

Arellano forced a chuckle. "No. Of course I did not. But I am older and my blood is much cooler than that of a young man. But it is odd, do you not think, for a fragile female to wield so powerful a weapon?"

Slade snorted. "If you'd ever seen Hannah Welles wield that weapon, you wouldn't be thinking of her as fragile."

The laughter from the Spaniard came more easily, but Slade couldn't help but wonder if Javier were truly away or if his uncle had ordered him to remain from sight.

"How old is your nephew?" Kit asked unexpectedly.

Again, something flickered in Arellano's gaze. "Twenty and three years of age."

Three years older than when Slade had been forced to kill or be killed. Old enough not to be making stupid mistakes on another man's land, around another man's wife.

"You believe he is … old enough to be taking on a property this size?"

Although Kit's tone was quiet, his intent was clear and Arellano flushed. "I was much younger when my father died and I became head of my family. I doubled the size of our property and have ensured four sisters suitably wed and a brother educated so that he can take his place in our world."

"I've no doubt you're an exceptional man, Señor, and I mean no offense to your nephew. Your uncle built an empire here. It would be a shame if your own nephew failed to hold it."

"He will not fail." Arellano seemed somewhat appeased by the comments but his words were firm. "And, truly, I have little choice. My father is old and failing. Our holdings in Spain are much larger and I am his heir. It is my duty to return. Javier must hold these lands in my place. He will care well for them and eventually I plan that they will become his own."

Kit nodded. "If he encounters a problem he can't handle, have him send word. I'll do what I can." He looked Arellano straight in the eye. "But not if it's a difficulty he creates because he's young and brash. You'd be wise to leave someone to keep him in check."

"My nephew has no need of a caretaker. He will not create trouble, nor will he back away from it. Besides, he will soon be too busy raising a family to wish to look for trouble or create it where none exists."

Kit sighed and Slade knew the Indian agent had a thought he wouldn't share, most likely because it was certain to fall on deaf ears. A man could be blind when it came to his own kin.

Like Slade, Kit seemed to recognize the time had come to turn the conversation. "We came with a purpose, Señor."

"I suspected that to be the case. One moment."

Arellano clapped his hands softly and a trio of servants entered the courtyard quietly and began clearing the table. As they left, a young woman entered with a tray and cups of coffee, the hot liquid sending steam into the air. She placed the tray on the table and exited as silently as the others.

Slade lifted his cup appreciatively. The brew was dark and savory and he declined the offer of a sweetener or cream.

"You may speak now," Arellano said. "We will not be disturbed."

Again, Slade let Kit carry the conversation while he

kept his gaze on the Spaniard.

"I've got my eye on something happening around Jishnu's band. Someone is stirring trouble and pointing the dirty stick in their direction."

Arellano leaned forward as if interested, but his gaze remained mild.

"One of his youth lost a couple of arrows while rabbit hunting and at least one of them found its way into one of Slade's animals."

The Spaniard nodded thoughtfully. "The natives have been known to take a beef when food is low."

"Food is plentiful and will be until the first snow," Kit reminded, adding, "and the animal was Mrs. Welles' mare in a barn paddock."

And too damned close to the house for Slade's comfort.

"You, of course, cannot be certain that the arrows were indeed lost."

Slade had noticed that Kit didn't challenge Arellano's initial not so faint suggestion that the Jicarilla had lied about the arrows being lost. It seemed, however, that the Spaniard was determined to push the issue.

Kit didn't take the bait, didn't so much as blink when he said, "I'm certain."

Slade had to give Arellano credit. His expression remained unperturbed as he shrugged. "It is to be hoped they do not betray your trust in them."

"Any man would be unwise to do that."

Kit's expression was too open and mild for anyone to have perceived his words as a threat. Nevertheless, their host stiffened as he agreed softly, "Unwise indeed."

"Just as any man would be unwise to stir trouble where none exists." Before Arellano could respond, he continued, "Your hospitality is appreciated and I've done what I came to do. I'd be obliged if you'd pass the word to your nephew and to your vaqueros to be watchful. Whoever is trying to cause Jishnu problems is likely to try again."

Kit reached for his hat and stood, and Slade did the same.

Arellano got to his feet gracefully as well. "You are always welcome in my home, Señor Carson, and you as well, Señor Slade. The hour grows late. You are welcome to stay the night within the safety of my walls."

"We'll be on our way. I promised Josefa."

And, that, Slade thought, was the thing that mattered most to Kit. His promise to Josefa.

Slade couldn't imagine living as Kit lived, mostly gone, leaving a wife and a number of children to wait for his return, wondering if they were safe and in good health. As an Indian agent, Kit's territory extended far beyond the town of Taos.

Slade's own thoughts turned to Katherine as they mounted their horses, rested and watered by Arellano's servants. He was ready to be home. Slade's gut told him there would be more menace in the days ahead and his place was by her side.

He hadn't disregarded Kit's warning that the brewing war would reach them, that they would be impacted, but he wouldn't take up arms unless it was to protect his home and his family, which included Jeb and Hannah and their child and soon would include Ford and his young daughter as well. And he'd protect them from any threat, regardless of philosophical agreements or differences.

Chapter Thirteen

Maria stared out the window of the coach as darkness fell. The horizon held a deep purple tint that glittered with stars even before the last faint light faded. Ford's little one slept, worn out from bouncing up and down on the seat and lulled by the swaying of the coach. Maria supposed the men were growing anxious to see the lights of the station. The midafternoon stop had proved uneventful and she was glad for the chance to step down and rest, but equally glad to be on their way again. The journey had begun to weary her just as her thoughts of Ford and her own future wearied her.

The air held a noticeable coolness that hadn't been there when they'd left San Antonio. She couldn't be sure if it was the result of the change of seasons or the difference in altitude or a combination of both. Earlier, she had pulled a warm wrap from her bag to place around the little girl in her arms.

Their stop for the night was in a town larger than the last, but still, nothing like she'd grown accustomed to in the East. Even so, she was glad to see it and not inclined to complain as the coach rumbled to a stop in front of a small house with a weathered front but cheery lights from every window.

Ford and Evan dismounted to stand in the street with Ridge while Henry went to the door and spoke to the owners. The couple, older and unsmiling, stepped out on the porch to look at their small group. Ford met Maria at the door of the coach to take his daughter who stirred sleepily. Maria clambered down unassisted.

"Dinner's hot and ready for us once the team is settled. The Clanahans have one large room for female passengers and one off the barn for the men. Both rooms have several beds and the bedclothes are clean."

Maria noted Ford's faint frown at the arrangements, but he said nothing. She knew Evan would help him with McKenna just as he had at the previous boarding house. She knew he would have access to ladies of the evening just as he had the night before. And none of that was her business. McKenna was his daughter. Maria was not part of their life. Still she touched Ford on the arm. She couldn't help herself. He glanced at her.

"Perhaps you would rather McKenna stayed with me in the night."

He looked hesitant and, suddenly uncertain, she started to retract her offer with a lighthearted remark. Then his face cleared. "I'd be obliged … if you're sure you won't mind."

"No, of course not. She's a pleasure to me." It was true, she realized. She'd grown more than fond of the little girl. His daughter had the biggest smile and a cheerful, inquisitive nature. She loved rhymes and songs, even Spanish songs whose words she likely could not understand. At least she seemed not to, but they made her smile and clap her hands. And, so often, those hands reached up and patted Maria's cheek with affection. Maria would miss her, she realized. And she would miss McKenna's father.

She wished abruptly that she hadn't offered, but he was shifting McKenna to her arms and when she felt the warmth of the small child against her chest, she was glad that she had.

"I'll help Henry with the coach and team and bring your bag in if you don't mind taking her in for a moment. I'll make sure she eats her dinner then bathe her before I get settled out back with the others."

"I don't mind," Maria said. "and I will appreciate your bringing my bag but I think we'll sit on the front porch until you return. It's nice out and I'd rather not be closed in any more than I need to be."

Maria couldn't interpret the look that crossed Ford's face but all he did was nod and say, "I'll be quick."

As she climbed the steps and eased herself and the child into a rocking chair, Maria didn't mind how long it took the men to do what needed to be done. She'd been honest about not wanting to be closed into the boarding house room, although it was likely to be a large one as it accommodated several beds. She missed being outside of the coach. She missed riding side-by-side with Ford, or even Evan.

* * *

When Ford walked back to the porch, McKenna was awake. She sat facing Maria with her feet in the rocking chair on either side of Maria's hips. They were a woman's hips, he couldn't help but notice, not narrow flanked like some. Maria sang some kind of song to his daughter, her voice soft but musical. It was a happy sound and McKenna made gurgling noises that weren't musical at all. But they were happy ones. Ford's heart lifted. This journey had started to rasp on his nerves, keeping him doubting his decision to leave the only home McKenna had ever known. Seeing her feel so safe and so content with a woman who had been a stranger just a few days before reassured him that McKenna would adjust, she would be happy. And he could be, too.

When he said his daughter's name from the base of the steps, Maria jerked her eyes to his and looked embarrassed, then stricken. McKenna just turned and cooed, holding out her arms to him.

Ford walked up the steps, took McKenna and tossed her lightly in the air, never quite releasing her from his grip but the action thrilled her as if she were flying and she squealed with delight. As he caught her close to his shirt front, he turned his attention back to Maria and frowned. She looked even more upset.

"Maria, what is it?"

"I should have asked," she said quickly. "I didn't think. Perhaps you would rather I not sing to her in Spanish. It's just a silly child's song."

Ford didn't say anything for a moment, then he just shook his head. "No reason for her not to know more than one language." Midway through the sentence, he switched smoothly to Spanish and watched as her face cleared.

"Maybe a silly song to you but it made my baby girl smile and I'm grateful for that."

He held out his hand and offered it to her. Her hand felt warm in his, small and warm, but strong. Her fingers were long and slender. At the door of the dining hall, Maria slid her fingers from his.

The rest of their small group were all seated when they entered. At one end of the table, Mrs. Clanahan presided over a large tureen of soup and silently filled bowls as they were passed to her and then passed around to each other.

Ford accepted his gratefully and focused on feeding McKenna rather than himself, blowing carefully on each spoonful of broth and mashing the vegetables on the side of his bread plate before adding some of the broth to give her a different texture. After a few minutes, he felt a hand on his shoulder and glanced up to see Mrs. Clanahan. The woman held out her arms for McKenna. Ford hesitated because the woman still didn't smile but there was something in her eyes, a warmth, that eased him.

He turned, letting McKenna see the outstretched arms, letting her decide. The little girl gazed solemnly up into the face that held more than a few wrinkles, then held out her arms. And Mrs. Clanahan smiled. Ford watched as she carried his daughter to the opposite side of the table and sat, so that McKenna could see her father. To his surprise, she scooped a small amount of tiny field peas from the soup, placed them on a saucer to cool, then slid the saucer closer to McKenna. After a moment, McKenna mashed one pea into the saucer then picked up another. Mrs. Clanahan guided McKenna's fingers to her mouth. McKenna swallowed that first pea then immediately picked up another and placed it in her mouth herself. And then another. His daughter was eating by herself. The realization caught him off-guard.

From her seat beside him, Maria said softly, "It's hard, isn't it?"

Ford blew out the breath he hadn't realized he was holding. "It's getting easier." And he knew that was true. A little easier each day. For the life of him, he couldn't say if that was a good thing or a bad thing. McKenna was growing up. He wasn't sure he was ready.

At the end of the meal, Mrs. Clanahan handed a drowsy McKenna back to her father and gave him a grateful smile. "She's a sweet thing."

"Thank you, ma'am. She's got a bit of temper sometimes."

The woman smiled. "She'll be stronger for that. Women need to be strong." Ford wondered what lay behind the faraway look in her eyes as she spoke but he didn't ask. "Will you or your ladies be needing anything else?"

"Could I trouble you for warm water and a cloth to bathe her?"

"No trouble at all. I've got water keeping warm on the stove. I'll be right back with what you need."

It was only as the woman bustled away and he turned around did he absorb the woman's words. Your ladies. The odd look on Maria's face embarrassed him. He should have noticed and corrected the assumption.

"I'm sorry … I'll let her know that you—that we're not married."

Maria shrugged. "It doesn't matter, really. We'll never see her again."

Something in her expression made Ford suspect it did matter to her. But he didn't say anything about it when

Mrs. Clanahan returned. He'd likely make things worse no matter what he said.

Maria reached for McKenna as the woman handed him the pitcher filled with water. Judging by the warmth of the container, he suspected the water was just the right temperature. Mrs. Clanahan smiled as she turned to Maria and pulled a cloth and a small bar of soap from her apron pocket and handed both to Maria. "That's what I use on my face."

Maria raised the soap to her nose and sniffed with a look of pleasure. "Castile soap! Mama's sister sends a large package of it from Spain twice a year."

"It's dear to come by but, please, use it for yourself as well."

"That's generous. Thank you."

Ford walked with Maria to the room where she and McKenna would stay. An oil lamp burned low on the chest of drawers. Maria poured some of the water into a bowl that stood beside the lamp as Ford placed McKenna on the bed and removed her food-stained dress.

With Maria standing close, holding the bowl of water, the act of bathing his daughter felt oddly intimate. These were the moments he had never been able to share with Elizabeth. The moments he grieved most for *her*, more than for himself. Because of what she was missing.

When he had McKenna bundled into fresh clothing, he nuzzled her before releasing her into Maria's arms in the night-darkened doorway.

"You can find where we're bedded down if she needs me?" But the thought of her leaving the safety of the boarding house, stumbling in the dark to find the barn made him uneasy.

Looking like a Madonna as she cradled the sleepy child against her chest, Maria nodded. "I can but, truly, I think she will sleep the night through without waking. It's been a long day for her." She spoke the words softly. That whisper and the shadowy room behind her created an intimacy that tugged at Ford's senses and he took a step backward.

Maria's smile seemed to fade as she moved into the room and closed the door. Ford waited until he heard the lock twist before he turned to go.

Evan waited in the hall just outside the long bunk room. "Thought maybe we could go find a drink."

The suggestion caught Ford off guard. It had been a long day for all of them. He paused, trying to word his refusal such that Evan would realize what a damned fool notion he'd had without Ford having to phrase it that way. "Probably not a good idea for either of us. Henry's pushing for an early start to try to make up time and I'm already dog tired."

For a moment, Evan seemed to hesitate then he turned away. "I won't be long."

Ford started to call after him, to go with him. He didn't want to but he had a sense of responsibility for Evan he wished he didn't have. But, damn, he was tired and he didn't want a drink. He wanted sleep.

Settling into his bunk he reminded himself that Evan was a man grown with a couple of years on Ford. If he couldn't take care of himself in this sleepy little town, hell, he probably couldn't manage on his own anywhere.

As Ford's head touched the hard mattress, Henry rolled over in his bunk and snorted before drawing another snoring breath, then another. Ford smiled in the dark and thought he might not get any rest after all.

* * *

Ford awakened abruptly and felt disoriented for a moment. He'd fallen asleep to the rhythmic sound of Henry snoring. That hadn't changed, but something had.

As Ford gave his eyes a moment to adjust to the dark, Ridge spoke softly from a bunk halfway down the room. "Reckon we better go find your friend? Thought he'd be back by now. Seems a little green to leave on his own too long."

Ford had all kind of thoughts on the comment. None of them good. A foreboding dug into his gut.

Ridge pushed up to a sitting position on his cot as Ford swung his legs over the side of his own and slid his feet into his boots. Like Henry and Ridge, he'd lain down fully clothed. There wasn't much light coming through the narrow window at the end of the room, but he could hear Ridge buckling his gun belt in place. Funny, how natural the man had seemed as a preacher but how easily he'd slid back into his former role.

Ford closed the door on Henry's snores and followed Ridge from the room. A quick check proved Evan's horse was still stabled with the others. If Evan had fallen asleep beside one of the ladies in the house at the other end of town, rousing him could be awkward. Ford knew allowing Evan to tag along carried some risks. He tamped down his irritation, knowing he'd done far worse. A hell of a lot worse, truth be told.

The few oil lights that had burned along building fronts had been extinguished, but the moon and a heavy scattering of stars lit their way. A coyote yipped in the distance and a dog barked closer by. Ridge stopped in front of a building with a single sign with the words Drinks and Women. The painted letters were dark against the weathered gray wood, as if they'd been recently repainted. The oil light in front of the door was extinguished, the windows darkened.

Ridge gave a soft grunt. He'd clearly been hoping to find the place still open. Ford stepped past him onto the narrow porch, intending to pound on the door until someone opened but a low, harsh sound nearby had him pausing with his hand lifted. Ridge heard it as well. He turned and scanned the dirt road to either side. There were no sidewalks, just ramshackle buildings and road.

Ford stepped off the porch, listening. The sound came again, a rasp of labored breathing, and he followed it around the low porch to the corner of the building. He saw the shape which appeared to have toppled from the porch end. His mind rejected the sight before he recognized it for what it was. He dropped to his knees in the dirt, sickened at the amount of blood that soaked Evan's shirt and seeped into the dirt around him, dark against dark.

"Evan. Jesus."

Evan's eyes were open, staring at the stars above him. They flickered faintly as he tried to focus on Ford. "Tell . . . tell my pa. Sorry. So sorry."

"Damnit, Evan." Ford fought nausea and tears. "Damnit."

"Didn't know she was married." Evan closed his eyes. "Swear to God."

Saying a word as ugly as any in the English language, Ridge turned and walked out into the middle of the street. He looked around at the darkened buildings then lifted his gun and fired a shot, then another. Ridge stood motionless in the brief silence that followed while Ford cradled Evan's head and heard his friend take his last two breaths before he stilled. Tears burned his eyes and anger burned his gut.

One or two doors opened a distance away, then closed and stayed closed. Ridge turned and fired yet again, this time striking a post on the porch of the saloon. Ford closed Evan's eyes and then rose to stand as a lantern was lit in a room above. A shutter opened a crack and Ridge's next bullet hit the siding above the window. The shutters were flung wide and a man leaned out, spewing curses. Ford couldn't see much of his face, whether he was old or young, bearded or clean-shaven. But none of that mattered. What mattered was that Evan, a friend he'd known all of his life, lay dead. Murdered.

"You kill this boy?" Ridge's voice sliced through the profanities.

"Boy? He looked man enough when he was poking my wife."

"He was unarmed."

"Unarmed and bare assed." The laugh was more coarse and obscene than the curses had been. "Thought he could just walk out and walk away after he had my wife naked and spread under him."

Ridge's voice was low and calm. "Regardless of his sins—or hers—only a coward shoots an unarmed man. What's your name?"

"Who wants to know?"

"The man who's going to see you pay for killing this kid."

"Ain't no sheriff here." Ford heard the first bit of uncertainty in the man's voice.

"Don't need one," Ridge said laconically. "Reckon I don't need your name, either, if you don't care to give it. I won't be carving your grave marker. Get your gun and come down."

"Go to hell."

"I can come up."

Another string of curses was followed by the slamming of a door above. Ridge slid his gun back in its holster and waited. Ford stood beside Evan's body and cradled his shotgun in his arm. He wasn't fast with a pistol like Ridge but he was accurate. He didn't miss when he sighted down the bore of his shotgun. Grief and anger boiled in him and he didn't plan to give Ridge first shot.

As footsteps pounded down the staircase inside, hard and heavy and angry sounding, Ridge looked Ford's way through the darkness as if he could see to the heart of him. "Don't do it, son. It ain't something you'd want to live with."

Ford stayed silent. He had to live with plenty, already, more than most. He could live with this, too, if he had to.

When he didn't answer, Ridge sighed and said, "I won't miss."

Some of the rigidity seeped from Ford's shoulder as grief pushed at him once more. No matter what he did, no matter what Ridge did, Evan's death couldn't be undone. The dog that had barked earlier, barked again. Once. The silence that settled after that one yip was heavy, broken only by the clump of boots on the staircase inside the saloon.

The door to the porch swung open and the hair raised on the back of Ford's neck as starlight glinted on metal. He didn't bother shouting a warning to Ridge who waited in the street. He lifted his shotgun and fired and heard the pop of gunfire, saw the flash of gunpowder from Ridge's gun in almost the same instant as the blast from his own gun.

The man who'd thought to catch the gunfighter off-guard grunted in disbelief. He swayed as his body acknowledged the bullets that ripped through his chest and dropped him in his tracks.

"Not a shred of honor in the man."

Ford thought the words a fit epitaph.

Ridge looked at Ford. "Obliged."

"You didn't need me, after all."

"Obliged all the same."

They'd never know which bullet killed the man, but it didn't matter in the end. They'd both done what needed done.

A light seemed to dance in the doorway behind the dead man and a feminine form moved through the opening. She lifted the small lantern she carried and cast a glance sideways at the dead man. Still silent, she walked down the steps then peered toward the road as Ridge came forward.

The woman, not a girl but a woman grown, looked wraith-slender and ethereal in the light of the lantern. Her dark hair hung long and loose. The wrap she clutched tight revealed more than it concealed.

Ridge came forward then stopped in front of her. "Ma'am." That was all he said. Just that one word.

What the hell, Ford thought, but he waited in silence to see what would come next.

"Guess he won't be giving me any more black eyes."

"No, ma'am. I reckon he won't."

"Still, he owned this place, him and his brother, and I don't and I'm out of a job and a husband. A black eye every now and then and handing out whiskey to fools was better than whoring. I've never done that and never would no matter what he said to me."

For a moment Ridge didn't move or speak then his voice came low and soft. "Come morning, our coach will leave after we bury Mr. Burch. Should you care to be on it, there will be no black eyes or expectations of whoring."

She gave him a long look and nodded, then stepped back over her husband's body and closed the door behind her, leaving him where he lay.

Whatever Ford had expected when Evan asked to go with him, it wasn't that he'd be placing the man six feet deep in a place so small it wasn't even a town, just a cluster of homes and a few businesses without signs to identify them. But it had a graveyard with a white picket fence. Evan's was the fourth hole dug there. The Clanahans seemed to hold sway with folk and declared that being shot without a gun to defend himself made Evan Burch the innocent in the event. He would be buried first and not share that space of time with the saloon owner who'd killed him.

Maria stood close to Ford, her eyes bright with unshed tears as Evan was lowered into the ground. If anyone thought it ironic that the gunman who'd avenged his death was the same as the man who spoke words over his burial, the thought went unsaid. He'd refused for the gambler but offered for Evan. Ford suspected the difference for Ridge lay in whose bullet had ended the life.

When Ridge fell silent, Ford handed McKenna into Maria's arms and fought the lump in his throat as he and Ridge shoveled dirt over the hastily constructed pine box.

Henry stood scowling and Ford had no doubt his concern was for the ever-increasing delay to the mail delivery that was of greater importance to him than passenger fare. Still he'd made no secret of the fact that without the passengers he'd been lucky enough to have on this trip, he'd likely be lying dead somewhere along the way, killed either by robbers or Comancheros or Indians. He owed them, he told Ford, owed Ford and Ridge and Evan, and he was a man who paid his debt.

No one spoke as they walked away from Evan's grave.

Outside the white picket fence, the dark-haired woman waited. Ridge stopped briefly to pick up her bag then offered his arm, as if he were the gentleman preacher he'd tried to be for a little while, and walked her to the coach.

Ford didn't miss the fading bruise along the left side of her face, where it darkened the cheekbone below her eye. Underneath that bruise was a beautiful woman. It'd be interesting to see what Ridge did with her now that he had her, but Ford doubted he'd be around long enough to know.

Chapter Fourteen

Jeb rocked his chair back on two legs and propped against the wall behind him. This porch had been one of his favorite places from the day they'd laid the final board. He watched the sun sink in the multi-colored horizon with a feeling of contentment, still amazed at how quickly and completely the New Mexico Territory had felt like home to him. It wasn't the longest he'd lived anywhere, but it was the first place that seemed right to him, truly right, and not just because Hannah was here with him.

Or, maybe that was it, after all, Hannah and Katherine and Slade. Even so, the land had a beauty that was at once more rugged and filled with more grandeur than the Texas plains that had been his home for most of his life. And more danger, too, he knew. Were he younger and single, without a baby on the way, he might've wondered if it was danger that held the allure for him. He knew better now. He wanted the beauty, but he also wanted peace for his child and his wife. He wanted to grow old and prosper so that his sons and daughter could prosper after him.

Hell, he snorted to himself, he sounded like an old man.

"What kind of sound is that?" Hannah's spring water cool voice behind him made him jump and almost topple his chair and him with it.

"The sound of a man's foolishness." She came close enough for him to slip an arm around her waist. Lowering his chair so that all four legs were securely on the porch, he pulled her onto his lap.

She laughed and protested, "Jeb, I'm heavy."

"Are you calling me weak?" Jeb nuzzled the back of her neck, brushing silky tendrils aside until he could press his lips against tender skin, sliding lower into the curve of her shoulders. He felt her shiver and the surge of lust that hit him was hot and hard.

She moaned softly but leaned forward so that she could twist to look at him. "No, I'm calling me fat."

Jeb chuckled. "That's not fat, that's my daughter you're talking about."

"I'm having your son."

"Reckon we better place a wager on that."

Hannah just laughed at him and leaned back against him, looking toward the horizon as he had been doing. "Are you watching for Slade?"

"Not so much but I expect he'll be home by morning."

"Yes. He said he would and he does what he says. You both do."

"I love you, Hannah Welles."

"I love you, too."

He turned his head and kissed her neck again, feeling her quiver through every muscle and sinew of him. "Let's go to bed," he whispered.

And his whisper held a determination to love her long enough and thoroughly enough that she slept dreamlessly, keeping the nightmares at bay.

Slade and Kit parted ways at the edge of Slade's property.

"You're welcome to bed with us for what's left of the night," Slade offered.

But Kit declined with the same reply he'd given Arellano. "I promised Josefa."

And Slade understood. He turned his buckskin toward home and his thoughts went to Katherine as they always did.

Slade's first glimpse of home was not the peaceful, darkened windows he expected. Oil lamps lit every room of the main house as well as the bunk house. His pulse quickened and he put his heels to his tired horse.

Mateo separated himself from the small group of men near the bunkhouse and took the reins.

"Katherine?"

"Is well," Mateo assured hastily. "Carlos did not return at dark. We have been searching where he would have been but the moon, she is not helping tonight."

Slade strode toward the house. There was no need to give instructions. Mateo would care for the buckskin just as Slade would do.

Jeb looked up as Slade walked through the kitchen door. The relief on his face was unmistakable. A quick glance gave Slade a pretty good understanding of his concern. Katherine leaned against a wall, dressed in men's clothing, a rifle slung over her shoulder and her hair tucked under one of Slade's hats.

Hannah stood by the stove with a disgruntled look on her face tending to what he hoped like hell was a pot of coffee.

Slade gave Katherine a squeeze and took a seat beside Jeb who had several crudely-drawn maps in front of him. Across the table, Lorenzo nodded at him gravely.

"What's crossed out has been searched," Jeb said quietly.

Slade scanned the drawings, most of the areas marked were in Carlos' quadrant of the property. "Carlos' men … no one heard or saw anything?"

"No, he heard a calf bawling and turned back just before dark. Told them to go on, he'd catch up. He didn't."

"We have to go back out," Katherine said fiercely. "We have to find him."

Jeb shook his head. "I agree but every man here needs sleep. We'll go at the first light."

Slade rubbed his jaw. Like Katherine, he felt a sense of urgency but, if Carlos was not in the area he managed, he could be anywhere. There wasn't enough moon or star light to help in a search. And dawn was but a few hours away.

He rose and took Katherine's hand and tugged her out onto the porch. She pulled her hand from his and immediately began pacing. "I hate doing nothing. Hate thinking of him lying hurt and alone." Or worse. The unspoken words hung in the air.

She turned and came back to him, met his gaze and stepped closer. With a sigh, she laid her forehead against his chest. "I know," she said quietly. "I already know. They're exhausted. We all are."

The door behind them opened and Lorenzo stepped out onto the porch.

Jeb, just behind him, stopped at the door and said, "I'm taking Hannah to bed."

Slade nodded. "We'll be in soon."

As Lorenzo reached the steps leading to the yard, Katherine said his name.

He turned. "Yes, Señora Kate?"

"Get some rest," she said gently. "Tell everyone to rest as best they can. Tomorrow will be long. We will need to be strong. For Carlos."

He nodded. "Sleep well, Señora."

Slade didn't see much hope in the gaze that slid from Katherine's. Truth be told, Slade didn't feel much hope himself.

The hands gathered in front of the porch before daylight, straightening when Slade and Jeb and Katherine and Hannah stepped out onto the porch. Every man on the ranch stood in front of them.

Slade just shook his head and Jeb sighed and said, "Mateo, Santiago, Antonio ... separate your men into two teams. One team rides with each of you to search for Carlos in your quadrant. Pick a lead for the other team to watch your herds. Lorenzo, you take half of Carlos' men to watch the herds in the north quadrant. Alejandro, you'll have charge of the other half of Carlos' men to guard the house and the barn. And my wife."

Alejandro nodded gravely, clearly pleased at the trust placed in him. "She and your son will be safe."

Jeb caught Hannah's faint smile. The men humored her determination to bear him a son.

Jeb looked at Slade who stepped forward. "Katherine will ride with you, Mateo. I'll ride with Santiago. Jeb with Antonio. When Carlos is found safe, fire four separate shots, one breath apart and everyone is to return to their positions with the cattle. If there is danger and help is needed, fire three rapid shots. Each of the search teams will follow the sound of the shots. Those with the herds will remain with the herds, prepared to use your weapons."

Jeb hadn't liked placing Katherine with one of the leads any more than Slade had, but neither of them doubted she'd strike out on her own if left behind, and she refused to ride with one of them and leave one of the three vaqueros without an owner at his side.

Jeb also didn't like kissing Hannah on the cheek and leaving her behind, knowing she wanted to go with them. The risk to her and their child was too great. Jeb had no idea what they were going to find, but he doubted it would be anything good and suspected it might well be dangerous.

At the moment of full light, they dispersed in different directions.

Katherine felt Mateo's frequent glances her way. As pleased as he was to be trusted with her at his side, she knew he felt the weight of that trust as well. He didn't know her past, didn't know she could shoot as well as any man. And that she would shoot to kill if necessary.

She didn't need his protection any more nor less than he needed hers.

The men behind them were quiet until they reached the east quadrant where they fanned out at Mateo's orders. Each man was to stay within sight and hearing of the man on his left. Katherine and Mateo rode slightly ahead of them. And she knew that would worry Mateo as much as anything. If danger lay ahead, the two of them would be the first to encounter it.

The crisp air of early morning quickly gave way to the steady blaze of the sun. Katherine eased her arms from the sleeves of her jacket which was actually one of Slade's winter shirts. She could feel Mateo watching her, worrying for her, and she shot him a smile. "The sun feels good," she called softly, just enough that her voice would carry.

As much as she tried to place a good distance between them, the more ground to cover, Mateo seemed determined to keep it as little as possible. After a while, she gave up and soon they rode side by side.

Before the sun had reached its zenith, they reached a shallow but swift moving stream. Mateo lifted a hand in signal as he dismounted to let his horse drink. Katherine followed suit, watching as the men on either side of them caught up and did the same.

Ignoring the line of sweat that rolled between her shoulder blades, she scooped water to drink and dampen her face.

Mateo stepped close as she straightened. "We could rest here a bit, Señora Kate."

"Not for me. Not while Carlos waits to be found."

He said nothing but she saw the flash of sorrow in his eyes.

"You think he's dead," she said softly.

"I hope he is not."

"I, as well, Mateo. We cannot give up hope until hope gives up on us."

He nodded and gave the motion for the men to remount. Looking around, Katherine saw that most of them had already done so and were waiting patiently for the signal to ride. They would not give up as well.

At the next stream, they stopped to eat and rest the horses. Katherine heard low murmurs of conversation from the men around her, but there was no laughter nor even humor in sound of their voices. She supposed, they waited, as she did, for the rifle fire that would tell them Carlos had been found. The only sound was the lowing of cattle in the distance and the rustle of wind in the trees.

Each time the terrain became hilly, she worried that they would somehow not see Carlos lying hurt, even unconscious, in some crevice or behind some boulder. Her eyes grew dry from staring around her.

The single gunshot when it came made her heart leap in her chest. She held her breath but there was only the one.

Mateo looked at her. "Señora?"

She shook her head and took a deep breath. "It could have been a shot fired at a snake or a cougar. We ride."

"We are close to the boundary of the ranch."

"I know." Even to her, her voice sounded flat and strained. They were to go no farther than their property line. She and Jeb and Slade had agreed on that.

And they were right upon that boundary when a call came up the line to them. Immediately, she wheeled her horse to the left and urged him to a canter, already seeing the gathering of men near a small stand of trees. One of them stepped out, waving his hands in the air for them to stop. Katherine slowed her horse but didn't rein him in completely and the man was bold enough, or desperate enough, to grab her horse's reins.

Mateo's sharp rebuke jerked the man's gaze to him but

Katherine saw the look upon his face as surely as Mateo who gave a low groan of dismay.

While the man who'd stopped her held her horse, she dismounted and gravely thanked him. As she moved forward on unsteady feet, he pled, "Señora, do not."

Mateo reached her side and they walked together where the men parted, revealing Carlos' body. He was impaled upon a tree by so many arrows she couldn't count them all.

Fury swept through her, swept aside—at least for the moment—the grief that would haunt her later. This man was loyal to them, trusted from their first day upon their land. She looked at the men who watched her.

"How did he die?"

Those close enough to hear looked at her in bewilderment. "Señora?"

"There is no blood here. How did he die? Take him down and tell me."

They made haste to do as she asked and Mateo touched her arm. "The gunshots?"

"Fire four, one breath apart."

Mateo looked hesitant, clearly wanting to bring Jeb or Slade to them with three rapid shots.

"There is no danger here, no need to signal for help. Whoever did this has no courage in them. We will take Carlos home."

Mateo lifted his rifle and fired four shots with a heartbeat between them. Then he nodded at the men nearest the tree. Katherine watched with clenched teeth as the arrows were broken from the trunk of the tree and Carlos' body was lowered. One of the men turned and vomited into the dirt. If Katherine had tried to speak in those moments, she would have done the same.

Another man approached her and Mateo.

"Rafael," Mateo said softly, "what do you see?"

"A knife wound through the heart, from behind, without courage." His nod to Katherine gave credit to her assessment of the murderer. "The back of his shirt was soaked with blood that is now dry. You are right, Señora, the arrows did not kill Carlos and he did not die in this place."

"We will place him on my horse and I will ride behind Mateo."

The man straightened. "No, please, Señora. The men ... we have talked. We will place him on one of our horses and we will take turns leading the horse that returns with Carlos."

She took a deep breath and then nodded. "Thank you."

"It is our honor to do so."

Slade reached them before they were halfway home. He took one look at Katherine's face and reined his horse in beside hers and together they escorted Carlos home.

Chapter Fifteen

Maria watched the horizon, empty save for the slowly-purpling clouds. This was the landscape she had missed in her years in the East. Boston had beautifully colored fall weather with multi-colored leaves against bright blue skies, but winter came in varying shades of whites and grays. The tall, dark facades of homes and businesses blocked all but the briefest glimpses of the harbor from her aunt's home. Nor was it a place for a casual stroll by a young lady.

Winters in New Mexico were ferocious and strikingly beautiful. They could also be deadly with northern winds that drove bitter gusts of blinding snow across the mountains.

"Your little girl's pretty."

Maria looked up in surprise. The woman hadn't spoken

a word all morning, not since murmuring a subdued "Pleased," when introductions were made. Her name was Tess Kelley.

"She's not mine," Maria corrected her.

Tess tilted her head. "But you wish she were, I think."

Maria didn't know what to say to that. She wasn't sure that was true, but she wasn't sure it wasn't, either. She didn't respond to the comment, simply gestured toward the window beside her where Ford rode a few yards away. "That's her father, there. On the grullo."

"Good looking man. And a kind looking one."

"He's a good father." That was as much as Maria wanted to comment about a man who'd rarely left her thoughts. Not since the morning she realized he'd been with a lady of the evening. Even more so since the night she'd insisted he kiss her.

Tess seemed lost in her own thoughts for a moment, then said, "I was going to have a baby. Been a few years back. He didn't want it. Slung me down the stairs when he found out and I lost it. There weren't any after that."

Although she was often quiet, Maria was rarely speechless and she honestly didn't know what to say to that other than an apology that it had happened. Something stopped her. Perhaps it was the thought that the woman wasn't sorry not to have born a child to a man so violent. What kind of life would a son or a daughter have had?

Tess's next comment confirmed that suspicion. "Just as well. He'd likely have found a way to kill it." She turned her face away. "I couldn't have borne that."

Maria pressed her cheek lightly to the top of McKenna's head as she wondered what her husband-to-be would be like. What he *was* like. She wanted a good man, a good father. A capable, strong person. Someone like Ford Bellamy.

And a little girl just like McKenna. She couldn't imagine kissing that dimpled cheek good-bye and never again seeing those huge eyes looking at her with such trust.

Her thoughts depressed her and, like Tess, she turned her face toward the window, trying not to watch Ford as he and his grullo covered the dusty miles effortlessly beside the coach.

Ford winced and muttered a curse as the first streaks of lightning split through the clouds. They were headed straight into what looked to be a hellacious storm. There was a time when he'd never given a thought to lightning, even after he'd seen a man split nearly in half by the force of a bolt. But that was before McKenna was born, before the death of her mother. Ford was all his daughter had to keep her safe.

He wasn't afraid to die, but he was scared as hell of leaving his daughter to go through life without his protection. Even so, he wouldn't climb into the safety of the coach, such as it was. Ridge sat atop the box once more and Ford knew he kept careful watch from that vantage, ready to give warning at the least hint of danger. Ford did the same from beside the coach, but he was all too aware that Evan no longer guarded the other side. His sorrow for the loss of a friend remained but he couldn't afford to dwell on it. Regrets would come later, he knew. Now wasn't the time or the place.

Henry stopped the coach long enough for them to unroll the leather covers for the windows.

Maria held his daughter up to the opening as Ford

stepped out of the saddle and dropped the grullo's reins to the ground. When he climbed on the wheel to reach the straps holding the window cover, McKenna squealed at the sight of him so close to her. When he leaned in to kiss her cheek, she reached for him and said, "Papa," very clearly and Ford's heart jumped.

He glanced at Maria who was smiling at him. "We've been practicing," she said softly, her pretty eyes large and luminous in the fading light.

Ford grinned. "Papa. That's a nice thing to hear." He had to fight an urge to kiss her as he reluctantly lowered the leather cover between them.

Ford's smile faded as he climbed down. His little girl wouldn't be learning to say mama. There was no one for her to say that to. And Maria, not McKenna's mother, had taught her to say papa. That stung, but not as much as it once would have. He didn't know yet how he felt about that.

When the heavens burst open under the weight of the rain, the downfall drenched all three men in a matter of moments. Despite his long, oiled leather coat, rain slid under Ford's shirt collar and soaked his pants legs from the thigh down. There was no point in complaining. Their last stop of the day was someplace ahead. They had only to get there. At least McKenna and the two women were sheltered from the driving rain and the mule team moved steadily forward under Henry's expert handling.

The station wasn't what Ford had hoped. No town. No boarding house with home cooking and comfortable beds. The stock tenders were quick and efficient at getting the mules unhitched and into the barn for the night but the station keep, a man of middle years with slumped shoulders, sighed and coughed his way through sleeping arrangements. He waved his hand toward a large pot simmering atop a cook stove. "I've been poorly a day or two, but my wife made fresh soup just today. And bread. She's a right good hand with both."

Ford handed Tess's, then Maria's, bags up into the loft but kept his daughter with him until the women had changed their gowns and climbed back down the narrow ladder. Behind a curtained alcove, he spread his long coat on the floor, dry side up and let McKenna play with the cloth doll Aunt Dee had made for her. McKenna babbled at the doll as she ran her fingers lovingly over the embroidered eyes and nose. Every now and again, he heard the word "Papa" and each time the sound of it tugged at his heart.

When he emerged in dry clothes, McKenna in his arms, Maria stood near the hearth staring into the fire that burned low but steady, dispelling the damp chill of the evening. Walking toward her felt natural. It felt right. And he didn't have a clue what to do about it.

The storm proved to have been a front for colder weather behind. Morning dawned bright and clear with a light frost on the ground. By the first station stop to change mules, Ford's throat felt as if he'd swallowed barbed wire. He thought of the station keep with his slumped shoulders and his cough and sighed. By midday, he ached. Everywhere.

Dismounting, he tied the grullo and Evan's horse at the boot of the coach. Grateful to find his legs steadier than he'd expected, he walked around to the side and opened the door. When McKenna held her arms out to him eagerly, he lifted his gaze to the woman holding her and drew an unhappy breath. "Maria, I don't think I should hold her."

Maria's gaze moved over his face and she nodded. He wondered what she saw ... if he looked like hell, which was how he felt. She turned her back to him and, with McKenna in one arm and a hand on the edge of the opening, she stepped carefully out of the coach. Ford kept both hands on her waist, guiding her movements and ready to catch both the woman and his child if Maria took a misstep.

Maria's waist felt delicate, small above the curve of her hips, and Ford struggled with the unexpected image of those curves beneath a woman's undergarments. It occurred to him that perhaps he wasn't as bad off as he felt.

When the others went inside to eat, he walked around to the side of the building to sit in the sun, his back propped against the rough exterior, and dozed. At one point, Maria stepped out with a cup of steamy liquid that he drank without question before closing his eyes again.

When he heard the scuffle of boots on the porch, he got to his feet. Henry met him at the corner. His keen eyes drew together in a frown. "Get in the box with me, boy. Ridge can ride your horse or Mr. Burch's."

Ford shook his head. If he was sick because the last station keep had been sick that meant he could pass it on to the whip. "I just needed a rest. I'll ride."

Henry scowled and grunted but he didn't argue.

Soon after the midday break, the landscape shifted to a rocky incline. At Henry's apologetic suggestion, Maria and Tess climbed out with McKenna to walk. "Your weight ain't nothing to these mules," he assured them, "but it's going to get fair uncomfortable inside for the next while. I'm hoping to reach the next stop before dark. The settlement hasn't been there long, but the accommodations are good and we can all get some rest."

Something in his tone and his glance made Maria wonder if he was growing concerned by Ford's illness as well.

"It will be good to stretch our legs," Tess said.

Henry gave her nod. "Just be sure to walk close to the coach. And beside it just ahead of the wheels," Henry cautioned. "Any further back and you'll be swallowing dust."

It *would* be a nice change to be outside of the confines of the coach. Maria agreed with Tess on that. She hadn't minded the previous few occasions Henry had asked his passengers to walk for a while, but now she had McKenna to carry. On those other times, Ford had taken his daughter up on his horse. Maria knew he didn't want his daughter too close for now and she wasn't sure he was even strong enough to balance her safely for any length of time.

"When the little one gets heavy, I can carry her awhile," Tess said as if reading her mind. At Maria's hesitation, Tess looked hurt. "I won't taint her."

Maria met her gaze. "Of course, you wouldn't and I appreciate the offer."

"But?"

Sorting through her thoughts, Maria blew a strand of hair from across her lips. "It's that she doesn't belong to me and it feels odd to make decisions for her." But that's what she'd done more and more, as Ford became comfortable with her, as their situation grew increasingly difficult, first with the attack on the coach, then danger of the burning wagon and station keep, Evan's death, and now Ford's illness.

Tess looked from her to Ford, his pallor evident though his spine was straight and his eyes continually scanning the landscape for threats. "If that man don't get some rest and healing time, might be you'll be making a lot more decisions. I've seen folks die from a fever left untended."

Maria's heart leaped to her throat as Tess gave voice to her greatest fear.

"Of course, you could find some family to tend her if that happened. Henry could always send word to Ford's kin where to find her."

Maria looked at her appalled. "No! I'd never give her over to the care of someone she doesn't know, someone who doesn't know her and love her. Who might not keep her safe." She didn't even voice what she felt at the possibility of Ford getting much worse and, perhaps, not getting better.

Tess lifted a brow and a smile played along her lips. "Didn't think you would, honey. And I expect you'll have more on your heart than you'll know what to do with when you and that baby's father both get where you're going."

Maria bit her lip, then sighed. That was a comment best ignored, mostly because Maria feared it was true. Instead she said, "I'll be glad for you to carry her when my arms tire." She knew that wouldn't take long. McKenna was a solid little girl. "You're a good woman, Tess. The men have been kind but it's nice to have another female for company."

"Men can be tiresome for sure."

But when Maria glanced at Tess, she saw the woman's gaze was on Tom Ridge who had shifted in his seat to look back at them. Clearly, Tess didn't find the gunslinger tiresome.

The road they traveled lay between what looked to be

two small mountain peaks. Watching the coach bounce along the road, Maria suspected Henry's caution that things would be uncomfortable inside was mild to what the reality would have been. The whip allowed the lead mules to pick their way around the worst of the terrain and the pace was so slow that neither Maria nor Tess had difficulty keeping up. They were young and strong and handed McKenna back and forth between them. The little girl seemed as glad to be out of the coach as the women who entertained her with songs and rhymes or simply by pointing out colors and objects and giving them names.

There wasn't a lot of variety to the land around them except for a few birds and lizards and the often-pretty colors of the tumbled rocks that littered the path, but McKenna didn't seem to mind as long as they talked to her and listened to her nonsensical chatter in return.

Maria turned her gaze toward Ford as often as Tess glanced up at Ridge but she told herself it was for different reasons. Ford's health was her concern. And she told herself that the heat in his eyes when their gazes happened to meet was due to the fever.

The land leveled somewhat after their second stop and Henry hoped to make up time by keeping the fresh team at a ground-eating trot as long as they could comfortably sustain it. Maria and Tess and McKenna returned to the interior of the coach but when Ford assisted Maria stepping up with McKenna, Maria's heart sank. The calloused hand that brushed against hers was too hot by far.

Maria watched as the neat cluster of buildings nestled at the base of a mountain came into view. A settlement Henry had called it but it looked larger than many towns. There was no sign hung for either a bank nor telegraph office but the boarding house, run by two maiden sisters, looked solidly built and neat as a pin on the outside.

The two women with gray braids wrapped neatly around their heads stepped out on the wide porch to greet the passengers as Henry stopped the coach in the street. While the men unloaded bags from the boot, Tess and Maria climbed the steps where the women introduced themselves as sisters. Twins, if Maria judged by their looks. Both taller than most and slender to the point of being thin. Anne wore spectacles. Josephine didn't but her eyes were the same hazel as her sister's.

Anne smiled warmly. "Let's get you settled."

"I just love the little ones." Josephine beamed at McKenna. "We have a couple of trundle beds that will work nicely."

Maria took a deep breath. "Do you have private accommodations? McKenna's father isn't feeling well. I'd like a place to tend him that won't disturb anyone else."

She heard boots on the steps behind them as Anne nodded. "We do but it costs a bit more." Her eyes strayed to Ford as he stopped beside Maria who thought her gaze held a hint of wariness. "Do you know what ails him?"

"He got drenched in a storm," Maria spoke firmly, "then took a chill. The extra cost isn't a concern. He just needs good food and time to rest."

Anne nodded, looking a little less anxious but not entirely reassured. "We've both."

Ridge moved to stand beside Tess. "My wife and I would like a private room as well."

Faint color stained Tess's cheeks as she slid her hand into the one that Ridge held out to her. Maria felt a sudden and unexpected twinge of envy. She had no inclination to judge either of them. Their life belonged to them and they could make of it whatever they wanted. The thought appealed but she knew that kind of freedom would never be a possibility for her.

Chapter Sixteen

When they dismounted between the ranch house and the barn, Slade reached for Katherine and pulled her close to him for a moment.

She leaned against him ever so briefly then gave him her smile, sad and weary but intended to reassure. "I'll take care of Carlos. You have other things that will need to be done."

Slade nodded. Life had made his woman strong but that didn't stop his worry for her. Even so, she was right, he had things yet to do. He called Mateo to him.

"I'll need you to help Katherine prepare Carlos."

"I would rather hunt for the guilty, Señor Slade."

Placing a hand on the man's shoulder, Slade sighed. "I would, too, but I think we're up against a snake and won't see the head until he's ready to strike again." He hesitated.

"I'd like for you to choose someone to manage your herd for now. I'll want you close to the ranch house."

Mateo's plain features tightened. "You fear harm to the Señoras."

"I think it's a distinct probability that someone will try."

The vaquero straightened his shoulders, looking unexpectedly dignified beneath the sweat and the dust from their search for Carlos. "They will not succeed. My promise." Slade knew he was mindful of the honor and trust given him.

Slade nodded, grateful for the loyalty of his men, but no less concerned. He unsaddled his own horse inside a small corral, waving away the youngster who ran to help him but giving him a weary smile for his willingness to work. The other groups trickled in as he scraped the sweat from the buckskin and gave him water to drink.

Jeb rode straight toward him, face grim. He dismounted and threw his hat on the ground, looking as sick and disgusted as Slade felt. "What the hell, Slade?"

"I wish I knew." He hesitated. "We've both made enemies." And he'd never discount those enemies. He'd brought many a man to justice and sometimes justice meant death.

"Well, damn, we both have enemies, probably more than a few," Jeb agreed. "And they have kin, and kin have a long memory, but a man who's pissed—or his brother or his pa—he's going to come gunning for us, me or you, whether face to face or to our back. I don't see this. I don't see someone like that going after one of our hands."

Jeb had touched exactly on Slade's worry. What had been done to Carlos reeked of cowardice and ugliness, not straightforward revenge. But neither could he come up with any other reason for what had been done.

"I don't see that either," Slade said finally.

Jeb scooped up his hat and dusted it against his pants leg. "Maybe someone wants to make the men nervous enough to quit and move on."

Slade rubbed the back of his neck. "Maybe." But why?

"Reckon we better send someone after Kit," Jeb said.

Slade stared at him blankly for a moment. "Aw, shit," he said. Neither of them attributed the arrows to Indians, knowing Carlos had taken a knife to the back. But the man had come to them at Kit's suggestion. He was kin to Josefa. Slade didn't think it was a close kinship but even so, family was family.

"I'll take care of it," Jeb said. "I need to go in to Hannah, now, but I'll find Juan on my way up to the house and ask him to ride to Taos for Kit and a priest."

"Send a man with him," Slade said tiredly. "I'd rather no one travels alone for now. Tell them to be watchful and trust no one."

Jeb handed his horse off to the youngster who still hovered not too far away, anxiously hoping to be needed. If Katherine were with child and as close to term as Hannah, Slade would have done the same, much as he preferred to care for his own mount. The buckskin had been his partner for many years. Slade hoped he would be for many more.

Morning brought no answers, just Kit and Father Benicio. Slade was not surprised that Josefa hadn't come with them. Kit wouldn't have permitted her to ride into possible danger and Josefa, though a strong woman, was also an obedient one. Katherine would never have let Slade leave her behind.

While Katherine had washed and tended Carlos' body, men had built a box for him and dug his grave. Slade had walked out in the moonlight with Jeb to choose the site.

This would be their first grave but it wouldn't be their last. This was their land and they would stay. They'd planted their roots deep here. Men would come and work, alone or with their wives. Accidents would happen. Illness would happen. Death would happen. Wherever Carlos was laid to rest would be the site of future graves. At some point, he and Katherine would lie there together as well. He wanted a long life with her and he'd fight to have that but, eventually, death would come. Death always came.

They'd chosen a hillside next to a peaceful thicket of trees. In the weeks to come, Slade planned to have men build a stone wall around the hillside. Carlos would have a protected place to rest.

Every man not needed to keep the cattle safe stood in a semicircle around the open hole. Their hats were in their hands, their heads bowed.

Father Benicio spoke quietly but with a strength to his voice. He talked of Carlos' love for his family. He'd never married but was a good son and brother and uncle. He talked of Carlos' love for his God. He was a good Catholic. He talked of the need for forgiveness. For Carlos' family and friends to forgive those who had taken his life and defiled his body.

But while the priest talked of forgiveness, Slade vowed vengeance in his heart. Carlos had been a good man and his future had been ripped from him. Slade didn't take well to that, wouldn't forgive it, and damned sure planned to avenge it.

He said as much to Kit as they sat on the long porch afterward. Slade and Jeb sat on the broad steps while Kit leaned against the wall of the house, legs stretched out in front of him. A short distance away, Father Benicio walked and talked with a few of the men who had been closest to Carlos and felt the loss of him and the manner of his death the most.

Kit nodded at his words but didn't speak for a moment. When he did, his tone was as soft-spoken as ever. "I'll help you when that time comes. My gut tells me that Carlos was in the wrong place at the wrong time. That his death had nothing to do with Carlos."

"Then what?" Jeb sounded as frustrated as Slade felt.

"I'm no preacher nor priest," Kit admitted, "but it seems the church has got a pretty good handle on the seven deadliest sins. Seems to me y'all have been too busy with this place to turn a man to wrath unless he comes from your past. Also seems to me, if that were the problem, it'd be you or Jeb with a knife in the back or a bullet through the heart."

Slade nodded. Kit had touched on his own thoughts.

"A man might lust after Katherine and Hannah but he'd have to be mighty brave, or dumb as dirt, to take one of them on and he'd know he had to kill both of you to get to either of them. A greedy man wants more than he owns. An envious man wants what another owns. A slothful man is too lazy to work for what he wants. A prideful man is back to vengeance if his pride had been wounded, but a prideful man would face you down."

Jeb half-smiled. "I gather you don't think gluttony has a place in this."

Kit shook his head. "I think someone wants what you have."

A thought slid through Slade's mind. "Or maybe something I want?"

Both Kit and Jeb shifted to look at him. Jeb nodded.

"Ford's land claim."

"Ford?"

"Katherine's brother. He lost his wife about a year ago. Childbirth. He's planning to settle next to us with his little girl. He may already be on his way. I picked out some land that's just to the south of us but adjoins ours at the tip. We crossed over it when we stopped by the Warrens' place."

Kit was silent for a moment and Slade suspected he was mulling over possibilities in his mind. "Warren or anyone file an opposing claim?" he asked after a bit.

"Not that I know. Could be something I need to check into."

"Why don't you let me do that checking? I've got business in Santa Fe. I could meet with Rencher and ask some questions about what new property owners I can expect. It's a conversation we've had before. Rencher was how I knew you were here first time I came out." Kit sighed. "I expect I'd better make a swing through Fort Union. Give them a heads up that someone out this way is casting suspicion on the Indians and there could be more trouble to come."

"Do you think this is aimed at Jishnu's band?"

"Not in particular. I looked at those arrows your men retrieved from Carlos' body. They're a mix of Ute, Pueblo, and Apache and one or two I don't even recognize."

Slade sighed. "If someone's trying to drag the Indians into this, they're not drawing a very clear picture of who's to blame."

And, he acknowledged to himself, that might be the intent.

Chapter Seventeen

Ford's teeth were chattering by the time Maria guided him to the room Josephine had shown her. "McKenna," he murmured.

"Safe with Tess. Just until I get you in a bed."

Ford's lean muscles were almost a heavier weight than Maria could manage, even with him still on his feet and moving forward. They barely reached the bed before his strength gave way. Maria heard him sigh as he sank onto the mattress. Her own sigh held equal relief.

She pulled his boots off as Josephine bustled in with a basin of hot water. She placed it on the table near the bed and pulled a rag and a small bar of soap from her apron. "The dining hall is to your left as you go back into the front room."

Maria opened her mouth to protest and the older

woman silenced her with a stern look. "You'll eat my good cooking while it's hot, young lady. I've bathed more than one man in my days. I'll manage just fine without help." Her gaze softened. "No need to fret yourself. I've only ever lost one patient and that was his own fault. He ran off before the law caught up with him and his bullet wound. They found him two days later toes up in the snow. I could've saved the damn fool."

Nothing worth saying came to mind, so Maria nodded silently and left Ford to what she hoped were the gentle ministrations of their landlady.

The others were seated when she entered the room and found an empty seat. To her surprise, Tom Ridge was holding a sleepy McKenna who still had crumbs on her lips. Tess sat at his side. Whatever Henry thought of the abrupt deviation from normal stage coach sleeping arrangements, he kept it to himself, never so much as raising a brow as he nodded in silent greeting and kept eating.

In addition to Henry's coach passengers, there were three additional boarders at dinner. Over what was left of the meal, she learned all three men had tickets for Henry's coach north to Albuquerque. One of the three commented that he'd been a shotgun rider a time or two and Henry looked almost cheerful at the news.

When Anne came to clear the table, she stopped near Maria's chair. "There's no apothecary anywhere near, but the general store next door has some herbs. One or two might be helpful to cool the fever in your young man."

"Thank you. I'll go as soon as it opens in the morning. If I can find a bit of honey, I can make an elixir for him to drink." She'd already accepted that Ford wouldn't be able to continue the journey in his present condition. Nor could she leave him with no one to care for McKenna. Or him.

"Let me get things put away and we'll go over. I've a key."

"The owner won't mind?"

"Not a bit."

When Maria cast an uncertain look toward McKenna, Tess waved and nodded. By the time Anne had the table cleared, Maria had eaten all she could. She rose to follow the other woman and had a moment's surprise as Tom Ridge handed McKenna to Tess and fell into step with the women. They exited the boarding house by a side door that led straight into what appeared to be a mercantile as much as a general store.

Ridge caught on first. "You own this as well as the boarding house."

Anne nodded and Maria caught the faint sorrow that crossed her face but then she turned away to study the dried herbs that hung from the ceiling along one wall. Their words carried to her from across the room, but she let them drift past without comment.

"My man took care of the store. He died about a year ago, quick like. Didn't have no illness and I didn't have no warning. He was there and then he was gone."

"Must be a lot to manage, just you and your sister."

Anne nodded. "Fact of the matter is, we'd like to move back to Texas. This New Mexico Territory was Jacob's dream, not mine, and Josephine wasn't about to be left behind when I followed along after him. It's just me and her now and we're tired of trying to keep up with everything."

Their landlady fell silent and Ridge crossed to Maria who'd gathered a few things into her arm. "Finding what you need?"

"I think so but I can't be sure."

"How bad do you think he is?" Ridge asked.

"I wish I knew," Maria admitted. "He's strong, stronger, I suspect, than anyone I've ever met but the cough and the fever are wearing on him."

Anne stood near the counter, her expression patient as Maria made her choices and came to her. "Do you have honey?"

"Not here but we've some at the boarding house. I took what I wanted over there as we got low here. It'll be summer before we get a good supply back here."

Maria felt a pinch of worry. The dried herbs were what she needed but the honey would help Ford get them down.

"You're welcome to what you need. We'll make do with molasses for the sweetening when the honey runs out."

"Thank you," Maria said gratefully. She'd manage with whatever she had as long as Ford would drink the mixture. She found molasses nasty, at best, although she knew some liked it. With luck, she wouldn't have to find out if Ford was one of those who did.

As Maria paid for her purchases, Ridge peered into corners and shelves, looking at the merchandise. "Do you sell liquor? Sometimes a whiskey mix can make medicine a bit easier to swallow."

"Did for a while. Jacob found it more trouble than the money is worth. He always said he wasn't a peacekeeper and, if you deal in liquor, you'd best be one." Anne snorted. "I'm no peacekeeper. Josephine can be when she takes a notion but I'm not and never will be."

Maria gave Ridge a curious look as he wandered about the space peering into corners, but she said nothing. The man's business was his own. Still, she had a feeling he hadn't asked about the sale of whiskey on Ford's behalf. At least not entirely.

* * *

The night proved excruciatingly long. By morning, Maria accepted that Ford would not be able to continue on with the coach which meant she could not either. He'd slept fitfully but not well, swallowing the honey mixtures Maria had brewed with Anne's assistance, one with elderflower which Anne said came from England, the other with echinacea. The first time she tried to place a cool rag against his head, he'd flung it aside. She scolded him and replaced it and he left it alone, allowing her to replace it at intervals after that. From time to time, she napped in the rocking chair Ridge had carried in under Josephine's direction. And all the while, McKenna had slept peacefully on her pallet on the floor.

Around midnight, Tess knocked softly, stepping in when Maria opened the door to her. "Do you need anything? I can sit awhile so you can rest."

Maria shook her head at the offer, knowing she wouldn't rest for wondering if Ford was alright. "He's cooler now than he was but he won't be able to travel by tomorrow."

"Tom and I wondered about that. Even if he's better, he'll be mighty weak."

"And I won't leave him."

Tess smiled. "Didn't suppose you would."

For a moment, Maria wanted to tell the other woman how happy she was that Tess and Tom Ridge were together but she wasn't sure how real that was, how long it would last. She knew only that this woman looked altogether different from the one who'd stood outside the circle of mourners who'd laid Evan Burch to rest. The bruise was still faintly visible upon her face but her lips were no longer pressed flat and she had a softer look to her.

When Tess had gone, Maria locked the door behind her. She stood staring at the solid surface for a long moment, then she went and laid down on the bed beside Ford and wrapped her arms around him and slept for what was left of the night.

When McKenna roused at daylight, Maria changed her and slipped from the room to find one of the sisters. Both were close at hand, Josephine in the kitchen stirring a pot of what looked to be a dark gravy and Anne in the dining hall, placing plates and forks upon the table.

Anne looked up and smiled as Maria entered with McKenna. "There's that sweet baby girl. And how's the patient?"

"He's better, I think, but not strong. We'll need our room for another day or two at least."

The woman nodded. "Your pastor's wife spoke with me a bit ago. Said her husband wouldn't dream of leaving one of his flock behind and they'll be staying on until you can all continue on."

Maria blinked, speechless, but Anne didn't seem to notice anything amiss and beamed as she added, "I didn't realize you were traveling together... more than as passengers on the same coach, I mean. That's a real nice thing, looking to start a church somewhere there's none yet."

Moments later, still bemused, Maria stepped back to check on Ford then carried McKenna out into the grey half-light of dawn where she sat with her at the farthest end of the porch in one of the several rocking chairs. A still-sleepy McKenna dozed and Maria let the rocker slow to a stop.

Henry didn't notice her as he came up the steps as Tom

Ridge was walking out. The two men stopped, eyeing one another.

"You sure about staying on here?" Henry asked. "Can't rightly see you turning pastor again."

"Well, looks to me this place is growing. It'll need a sheriff sooner rather than later. Might as well be me."

Henry gave him a studying look. "You know, I thought you looked familiar that first day in front of the station."

Ridge said nothing. Just stood there waiting.

"If a man asked me to guess," he said thoughtfully, "I'd say Tom Ridge wasn't all there was to your name. I'd say you're T.R. McCleod."

Maria's heart thudded in her chest.

"I hope no one asks. I left that man in a grave a while back. I'd like for him to stay there."

Tom waited patiently and Maria found herself holding her breath. Tom Ridge wanted a new life, one that didn't include young gunfighters wanting to test their skill against his. She'd like for him to have that. Him and Tess.

"No reason anyone would ask. No reason for me to say. Not with T.R. in his grave," Henry said after a thoughtful moment. He looked Tom straight in the eye. "Anybody ever mourn the man?"

"I doubt that. He was an orphan and no one took very kindly to him being around, so he mostly made his own way as soon as he could. Always thought he'd come to a bad end."

"Some do," Henry said, "and some start over. Too bad Mr. McCleod never got that chance."

"He made his choices," Tom said.

Henry nodded. "We all do. I'll be sorry to see you leave the coach but glad for you to get the chance Mr. McCleod never had."

Ridge nodded his gratitude.

When Henry turned to go, his glance fell on Maria and he nodded at her. "Reckon you're wanting the rest of your bags unloaded." It wasn't a question.

"I'd be obliged. Mine and Ford's. We'll need passage on the next coach through."

Henry nodded. "I'll send word your fare's paid."

"That would be kind of you." She hesitated. "If the coach is met in Taos, someone looking for me, you'll tell them I'm safe?"

The whip peered at her and she wondered if he saw the things she didn't want seen. "Reckon I can tell them you were safe with the sheriff and his wife until the next stage came through."

"Thank you," she said simply, wanting to say more but not knowing what. She had no way of knowing if he was a good whip or just adequate or not as good as most. She did know he'd done his best to keep them safe and he cared that passengers had died along the way.

When he walked away, she turned her gaze on Tom Ridge. "Miss Anne was quite impressed with your dedication to your flock, Pastor Ridge," she said solemnly. "Thank you for not leaving us behind."

His lips barely twitched at her words but amusement, and perhaps relief from his exchange with the whip, brightened his eyes. "That would be very unworthy of me. I'll bring your bags to your room when they're off the coach."

"That would be most helpful." For some reason, her heart felt lighter as she rose from the chair to carry McKenna back inside to her father. She passed Miss Anne in the hall with a smile and wondered how the sisters would reconcile the transition of Tom Ridge from pastor to sheriff. It wasn't her problem, she reminded herself, but it was interesting to contemplate.

Ford awakened slowly, tentatively. The pounding in his head was gone. The uncontrollable shivering of muscles wracked by fever was gone as well. He stretched slightly. All he felt was an incredible weakness and the warm curves of the woman curled against him. He had no idea how long he'd been sick or where he was, but he knew it was Maria beneath his arm.

He felt his lack of strength when he instinctively lifted his head to look for McKenna who lay curled on a pallet on the floor. A glance toward the door assured him that it was locked and it was safe for him to sleep again. And he tried, but his hand cupped the curve of Maria's breast and her breathing was soft and even, both facts drawing his attention to her when he tried to think of other things.

He told himself he should shift positions, move his arm from its protective curve, move his palm before his fingers curved more possessively. But he lay there, enjoying the feel of her and knowing he shouldn't.

It seemed both forever and the barest moment before she stirred. He could almost feel her eyes fluttering open, her consciousness telling her of the arm around her, the hand that touched her more intimately than anyone had a right to do. And the arousal that pressed against her lower body where it curved into him.

He wasn't sure what he'd expected her to do but it was for sure not what she did as she shifted to face him.

"Good morning," she whispered.

"Good morning. I'm alive, I guess."

She smiled. "Thankfully."

He felt suddenly embarrassed that she'd awakened to his hand on her breast and his manhood pushing into her backside. "I need to apologize for... for touching you. I didn't mean to—I mean, I wouldn't have." He sighed, frustrated as much by his lack of grace as by the ache that hadn't left his body, an ache that told him he wanted her spread beneath him, not looking at him as if she'd taken his embarrassment for her own. "I guess I was sleeping hard after being sick for so long ..."

"Please. I understand," Maria said quietly. "I am betrothed to another. You are still in love with your wife." She rolled away and got to her feet. "It is nothing. Truly."

But it was something to Ford. He just didn't know what. And the damned thing was he wasn't at all sure he *was* still in love with Elizabeth. Love her. Yes. Forever and a day. His love for Elizabeth would never die. But *in* love? He wasn't as sure. His wife was gone, an increasingly ethereal memory. A man couldn't be in love with a memory, could he? And the thought of another man with his loin pressed against the curve of Maria's hip, his hand cupping the weight of her breast was something Ford didn't want in his mind.

Chapter Eighteen

It was full dark out when Slade poured himself another cup of coffee and sat back down beside Katherine on the bench that lined one side of the long table. Jeb and Hannah were opposite them in chairs that one of the men who had come to them as a vaquero had painstakingly put together with hand-carved pieces of wood. When Hannah had noticed the craftsmanship in what Emilio considered a hobby, she had immediately pulled him from working cattle and given him a list of furnishings she wanted for the house. A cradle first, then chairs for the kitchen--still a work in progress--then rocking chairs and porch swings and tables of various sizes for various rooms and chests of drawers. Slade figured Emilio had at least another year or two of work on her original items. Jeb had just shaken his head over the loss of a good hand with the horses.

Likely, after this house could hold no more, she or Katherine would put him to work in the one Ford would build, which thought made him wonder what kind of mess Ford was riding into here. And when he would arrive. Stage coach travel wasn't without risk and he knew Katherine fretted from time to time, standing on the porch and watching the horizon.

Slade's gaze skimmed his wife's face then took in the faint purple shadows beneath Hannah's eyes. She and Katherine were worn down. Hell, they were all exhausted but he sure wished Hannah, at least, would go to bed. He knew she wouldn't, not before everyone else did. She'd proven tougher than he'd ever thought she would at his first glimpse of her. Jeb had chosen well.

After a sip of the coffee he'd poured, he placed the cup on the table, keeping one hand cupped loosely around it. Katherine laid her head on his shoulder and he put his arm around her. He heard her soft sigh and knew they should all go to bed. He'd found it impossible to sleep after returning with Carlos' body and knew it would be just as hard for him to rest that night. But still they sat in the silence, pondering what had happened and what might lay ahead.

"What now?" Hannah looked from Slade to Jeb. "We can't just do nothing."

Jeb sighed. "For now, nothing is about all we *can* do."

Slade agreed. "Nothing … at least as far as it looks to anyone watching. The vaqueros are sworn not to talk about Carlos. Not anything that happened or anything they saw. Not even the priest knows how he was murdered."

Hannah frowned. "I don't understand."

"We're in the middle of something we don't understand. The only one who *does* understand is the guilty person.

Sooner or later something will be said, something will get by, and it'll help us. But Carlos' death isn't the end of it. There's a purpose to everything that's happened."

Katherine straightened and nodded in comprehension. "So, we wait to see who talks about it? But how will we even know? This isn't New Braunfels. We rarely have visitors."

Slade never had to wonder if New Braunfels was someplace Katherine missed. The town she'd lived in since birth hadn't exactly been kind to the girl the Indians had stolen that long-ago day, and some had been even less kind about the baby girl who'd come back in her arms.

"People can't settle for waiting, especially guilty people," Jeb said. "He'll come, wondering what we know, watching to see what we do."

"You can't think just one person did what was done to Carlos." It wasn't a question.

Hannah grew even more pale at Katherine's question, at the reminder of the atrocities upon the dead man's body. Slade suspected her imagination had filled in any gaps left by their determination to protect her from the sight of him.

Jeb reached out to clasp her slender fingers as he answered Katherine. "It wouldn't take more than one man, but I think we're dealing with a coward, and cowards rarely work alone. If anything, they want someone nearby they can blame, someone they can throw to the wolves."

Slade wished Hannah hadn't heard quite so much— not while she was pregnant—but they didn't keep secrets from one another. There was too much at stake. At least she hadn't seen Carlos' body, either pinned to the tree or laid out to be tended after he'd been brought home draped across a horse's back.

Jeb stood. "Not much left of the night but we need

what rest we can get." He tugged Hannah to her feet. "If any of us can."

Just after daybreak, Slade was gentling a two-year-old gelding in a small corral, when a youth of eleven or twelve rode his pony hard into the barnyard, stirring dust and scattering the laying hens. The gelding spooked at the unexpected chaos and Slade hit the ground hard with a curse. When he stood, he dusted off his pants, and his pride, and gave the youngster a measured look. He saw excitement but not fear and gave a sigh. He swept his hat off the ground and brushed it against his thigh before returning it to his head.

"Señor Slade, two riders come this way!"

"You're with Antonio, aren't you?"

"Si, Señor. Antonio sent me to tell you."

"Just two?"

The boy nodded vigorously. "Antonio thinks they will not be a danger but that you should know."

Slade nodded. "Antonio is right and you did well. See Señora Katherine before you return to Antonio. Tell her what you told me and that you would appreciate something to eat or drink and a moment to rest."

The boy's eyes lit at his words and he scrambled to tie his pony to a post. There was almost certainly something a youngster would enjoy, resting on the stove. A youngster or a grown man. Slade allowed himself to smile as he watched the youth walk hurriedly to the back porch then turned his attention to remounting the gelding, but only long enough to be sure the animal knew that every dismount had a remount.

Slade made a slow circle around the corral, casting a wary eye as he caught sight of the boy walking back for his pony. Perhaps knowing himself fortunate for not having earned a scolding at getting the Señor dumped on the ground, he kept his movements quiet as he untied his pony and swung into the saddle. But, as Slade suspected he would, once he was away from the corral, he set his heels hard to the pony's side. The gelding beneath Slade snorted but held steady and Slade chuckled and shook his head. He couldn't remember being that young, but he doubted he'd been much different.

After another few rounds with the two-year-old remaining quiet, Slade unsaddled and groomed him before turning him out. He'd planned to work the horse longer but, as much as he trusted Antonio's judgement, he wouldn't be caught distracted as their visitors approached. If they *were* visitors and not just traveling through.

As it turned out, he recognized Benjamin Warren and his wife when they rode into the yard. The woman was once more dressed in men's clothing. Slade recalled Hannah's rape at the hands of renegade soldiers and wondered if Johanna Warren's choice of clothing was as much for protection as for practicality.

Benjamin swung down from his horse. "Mr. Slade."

"Just Slade."

The other man nodded. "You'll remember my wife, Johanna."

"I do and I'm pleased to have you here."

Benjamin's gray eyes darkened to slate. "Not much to be pleased about. I reckon we need to talk with you, after all."

Slade sighed. "Let's walk up to the house then for

something cool to drink. I'd like you to meet my wife. Whatever needs saying, I'll want her to hear and my partner's wife as well. Jeb's out with one of our lead vaqueros and his herd, else I'd send for him."

Katherine was waiting when they reached the porch and held the door wide.

"No need for us to come inside, ma'am." Benjamin looked uncomfortable at the idea of it.

"And no need for you not to, although I'll admit it's more pleasant on the porch." Katherine smiled at them. "I burned a pan of bread earlier and the smoke hasn't entirely cleared out. Please have a seat and Hannah and I will be right out with some tea."

Some of the stiffness eased from Johanna's shoulders at Katherine's admission and easy smile. She gave a tiny nod to her husband who nodded at Katherine in turn. "We'd be obliged for the rest and for something to drink, if it's no trouble."

"None, I promise you."

Slade took a seat on the steps and gestured to the Warrens to take a chair. Benjamin hesitated but there were clearly enough places to sit. He'd have to realize that Slade hadn't taken the steps out of necessity but preference.

Katherine returned with a tray of drinks and Hannah carried a smaller tray piled with biscuits.

Slade looked up with quick interest. "I thought those were burned."

Hannah grinned. "Those were Katherine's. These are mine."

Slade made introductions and the Warrens accepted Katherine's concoction of squeezed fruit juices mixed with water and a bit of honey. He didn't ask any questions, just waited until Benjamin was ready to talk. After a third biscuit, which Hannah didn't have to press the man too hard to accept, he dusted his hands and looked at Slade.

"I've got a dead bull," he said bluntly. "That's not something I can afford to lose."

Slade exhaled a long breath. "No, sir, I know it's not. Do you know what killed him?"

"I do." Benjamin's jaw jumped. "It was meant to look like it was a blade, made to look like it was, but I was close enough to hear the gun shot and the animal bellow when he was gutted."

Slade leaned forward. "Did you see anyone?"

"No, just the sound of horses leaving the area. It took me a bit to find the carcass. I looked for tracks after I realized he'd taken a bullet through his eye. Once I found the tracks of the horses, I followed as long as I could. They led this way, across the tip of your land, then turned a sharp west toward the river. I lost them in the water and the rocks on either side."

"How many riders?"

"A half dozen or so, at least."

Slade thought it a good thing the man hadn't caught up with them, but he didn't say so.

"Shoes?"

Benjamin looked at him blankly. Slade stifled a sigh. "Were the horses you followed shod?"

His answer, a shrug, was pretty much what Slade had expected. The man was a rancher through and through. He'd never tracked a man, probably couldn't even picture in his mind now, how those tracks had even looked against the hard dirt.

His wife seemed to catch on faster, giving Slade a sharp look. "You suspecting Indians?" She looked less frightened at the thought than she did angry. He'd thought her timid but wondered now if it was her pale coloring that gave him that impression. Hair, eyebrows, eyelashes and freckles were all the same fawn brown and her eyes were barely darker. But those eyes held a sharp look that spoke of grit and resilience.

"No, ma'am, but what I am suspecting is that someone would like us to believe Jishnu's band has gone renegade."

"And why would they do that?" The question came fast but her expression remained neutral.

"What better way to keep us looking in the wrong direction?" Slade asked.

Her husband's brows drew together. "Or is removing the natives the goal?"

"I asked the same question of Kit," Slade admitted. "He doesn't think so but it's still in my mind as a possibility."

"Have you lost any more animals?"

"Lost a man." The thought of Carlos was still a punch to the throat. "Killed from behind." He wouldn't say more in front of Mrs. Warren nor did he care to bring the images she'd seen to Katherine's mind again.

Benjamin studied the boards of the porch beneath his feet, then lifted his gaze back to Slade. "I'd like to leave my wife here with you until this is settled."

Johanna had begun shaking her head halfway through his statement and uttered a fierce "No" before he'd finished.

He swung his head to look at her. "I can't risk losing you. I need to know you're safe."

"And I need to know *you're* safe. I need to see you come in from the hills at the end of the day."

Katherine touched Slade's arm and he swore he could read her mind.

"Ma'am," Slade said, "you're welcome to stay here and your husband would know you're safe, which is no small thing. But I can tell you both there's not a chance in hell that Katherine would let me leave her someplace for her safety." He turned from her to Benjamin. "I can spare a few good men, good shots. You set one to watching the house by day when you're gone and the other to watching it by night when you both need to be resting. And a third to go with you when you're tending your cattle to watch your back."

Benjamin shook his head reluctantly. "I can't be beholden to you for the work of three men, especially not knowing what or when the end will be."

"You won't be beholden. Every damn one of us will need each other at some point. I'll expect you to come when I send word. It's my turn to help first, is all."

There was a lengthy silence before Benjamin stood and held out his hand. "I'll return favor for favor. You've my word on that."

Jeb came in for the midday meal and greeted their visitors. Over Hannah's stewed chicken and Katherine's corn bread, Benjamin repeated what had brought them to the ranch.

Jeb nodded at Slade's plan to send three of their better marksmen. They had more than a few. None of them were gunslingers but any of them could bring down a buck deer in full flight.

The two of them talked through options while Benjamin listened, his expression as unrevealing as his wife's. By the time they had selected the men they thought would fit best, Katherine was serving a skillet pie stuffed with apples. Slade took a moment to notice that Johanna had finally settled. No longer clenching her hands together in silence, she actually spoke now and again to Katherine or Hannah.

Later, as they watched the couple ride out with three of their hands, Katherine leaned against Slade. She wanted to ask "Now what?" as Hannah had last night. But she knew Slade and she knew the answer. When the time was right, Slade would go hunting and she wasn't in a hurry for that, not when she couldn't go with him. Any other time, he'd demand she stay behind and she'd simply saddle up and follow him. She'd done it before and had no qualms about doing it again. He was hers as much as she was his and where he went, she would go.

But now there was a baby on the way. She'd yet to tell him, waited a day or two to tell him, waited to be sure, but she knew it was time and it would change things for both of them. She would never risk their child unless it were to save the father.

Slade surprised her when she told him of her pregnancy as they lay together in the dark of their room.

"I know." Just those words, but she heard the satisfaction in them, the contentment.

"How?" She'd barely figured it out herself. When it hadn't happened month after month, she'd begun to believe it wouldn't, that she was one of those women who couldn't conceive a child. The thought had made her sad but it hadn't been devastating. All she'd ever asked in life, all she truly needed, she had in Slade. But the realization that a life grew within her had filled her with an unexpected joy.

Slade chuckled as he nuzzled her neck. "Woman, I've had my hands on you every night for the past two years. How could I *not* know?"

It was true. Even when exhaustion from their day overtook everything and they simply fell into bed to sleep, Slade's hands were someplace on her body, his fingers splayed over her belly or running lightly over her ribs, his palms cupping her breasts or her womanhood in those last few moments before sleep claimed them.

She wanted to ask him what signs he'd seen or felt— how he'd known and she hadn't—but then those hands and his mouth distracted her and afterward she slid dreamlessly into the sleep she desperately needed.

Chapter Nineteen

Maria toed the weathered board beneath her soft boot to keep the rocker moving. Ford rested and Maria, with McKenna in her arms, had chosen the porch to escape the bustle of the front rooms of the boarding house.

She still felt bewildered with the speed at which decisions had been made and events had moved. The sisters, whom she found very sweet and dear, planned to leave on the noon stage the next day, the first leg of a journey back to their Galveston home. They had bags packed to take with them and boxes packed to be sent by Tom and Tess later.

Tom, it seemed, had decided that the settlement was large enough to suit his needs, at least for now, and that right here was far enough west, at least for now. One day, the place would need a name and a sheriff. That seemed likely to happen sooner rather than later. The settlement had doubled in size just in the few years the sisters had been there, at least according to their estimation. Until that time came to be, Tom thought the boarding house and general store—both of which he now owned—would be enough to keep him busy. Him and Tess.

Maria wasn't surprised when the door eased open and Tess slipped out to the porch.

She looked as bewildered as Maria felt. "He wants to marry me," she said and sank into a chair next to Maria.

Maria studied her face. The bruises she'd borne were barely there and more often than not she wore a smile, but she wasn't smiling now. Tess looked almost panicked as she stared at her hands folded in her lap.

"What do *you* want?" Maria asked.

"We've only known each other a few days."

It wasn't an answer but, perhaps, Tess had no answer. It wasn't always easy for a person to know what they wanted. But at least they had those few days of acquaintance—and intimacy—Maria had no doubt. Some women wed with neither, just as she would. "Sometimes that's more than enough to know," she said quietly.

Tess lifted her eyes. "He makes me feel safe."

That was no small thing but was it enough for marriage if you could actually choose? But could Tess choose? How would she live, otherwise? There weren't many opportunities for a woman to make it alone. Maria wished she were in a position to offer Tess options.

"Safety is important," she agreed. "Being happy is also." She thought of Ford, felt the weight of his child against her breast. How was *she* going to feel when they parted? But this was Tess's moment, her decision. Maria had nothing to decide. Her future was fated and no part of Ford's life. Or his daughter's.

Tess lifted her eyes at last. "I'm happy with him. I never thought I could be."

For the first time in this odd conversation, Maria found she could smile. "Then I'd say that's a fine start to a new life for both of you."

Slowly, Tess let out a long breath and, even more slowly, she smiled back at Maria. "It is, isn't it?" An almost mischievous look crossed her face. "Tom says I can be whatever I want to be. I can cook and clean in our home or I can run this boarding house or I can run the general store. He says even if I don't marry him, I can have one or the other to manage." The bewildered look was back but the happiness was there as well. No doubt Tom was a type of man Tess hadn't encountered before.

Maria tilted her head as she took in Tess's look. "I'm guessing you told him he should find a housekeeper. I think I see a businesswoman before me."

Tess smiled and sat a little straighter in her chair. "I think I will be a good one. I really do."

One more night, Maria thought, as Ford closed the door to the room they shared. Because of the mistruth she'd encouraged the sisters to believe when he was so ill, she and Ford were husband and wife. Staying together one more night seemed the better course, although Ford no longer needed her to place cool cloths on his face and hands or to lift his head and encourage him to drink her concoctions. He no longer needed her to tend his daughter. He seemed stronger by the minute, as if the illness had never been.

Just the night before, he'd fallen asleep exhausted while she bathed and held McKenna until she, too, was ready to sleep. Then she'd slipped under the covers beside Ford, listening to his quiet breathing, grateful he was no longer wracked by fever. It had been a healing sleep.

Before, being so close in the room with him felt innocent, natural. Now they were too aware of each other or at least she was too aware of him.

He'd walked McKenna up and down the hall outside their room to give Maria a few minutes of privacy to wash and ready for bed. Now she kept her back to him as he was using the cloth she'd carefully wrung and the clean water she'd left for him.

The silence felt too awkward to let it continue. "I guess your sister will be worrying about you by now since you weren't on the coach with Henry."

When he didn't answer, she glanced over her shoulder at him. He gave her an odd look. "I didn't send word when I was leaving. I suppose I should have. I've been on my own so long, I just didn't think about it."

"Well, at least your brother-in-law won't be out looking for you and McKenna."

"Huh," Ford grunted. "It wouldn't be the first time Slade's had to come looking for me."

Intrigued, she turned and propped a hip against the wall.

Ford grinned at her quick interest. "A few years back, I thought I was grown enough to be out on my own. I found out real quick that being strong and tough is no match for good judgement. Turned out I didn't have a lot of that. I got in trouble because I was young and stupid, landed in jail. I managed to get myself out before I got hung for being young and stupid. It was Slade who cleared my name with the law."

"I'd say you turned out just fine," Maria said softly. "McKenna sure thinks so." There was no doubt the baby adored her father and it was equally clear to Maria that his little girl was everything to him. "I'll miss both of you."

Ford said nothing, just studied her face. Maria couldn't read his expression and wished she hadn't spoken.

After the sisters boarded the coach at noon the following day, Tom crossed into the general store and returned to the front parlor where Tess waited with Ford and Maria. He carried a family bible. He cleared his throat. "I saw this that first evening when we were looking for herbs."

"I was looking for herbs," Maria corrected dryly. "I realize now you were looking for something entirely different."

"And I found it," he said with a smile. He was a handsome man when he smiled. He looked from Maria to Ford and added, "Thank you both for standing with us on our wedding day."

His gaze went to Tess who wore a dress the blue of a summer sky that made her eyes and her hair even darker, her skin more creamy. He held out his hand to her and she gave him hers to hold. "Tess," he said simply, "I promise to love you and take care of you from this day through forever. I'll be honest and faithful and provide for you and any children that come to us."

Tess tried to speak but had to draw a deep breath before she said, "And I promise to love you, Tom, and stand by you all the days of my life. I'll be honest and faithful and give my life to caring for you and any," her breath caught on a little hiccup, "any children that come to us." She smiled at him through the tears in her eyes.

They wrote their names carefully in the front of the bible. Below that, Maria and Ford signed their names as witnesses.

Tom cleared his throat. "I'll pay the fees to have this recorded, Tess, so the marriage will stand. Should something happen to me, all that we have here will come to you."

"You'd best make sure nothing happens to you, Tom Ridge," Tess said forcefully.

And he took her in his arms and kissed her so long and thoroughly that Maria had to look away. All she could think about in that moment was the memory of waking from sleep with Ford's hand cupping her breasts and his arousal pressing against her bottom. She knew she blushed at the memory and could only be grateful that no one could read her thoughts. But, dear God, how could she bear another man, a man she didn't know, to touch her now?

Ford had stood almost numbly as he watched the exchange of vows. He thought of the vows he'd made to Elizabeth in front of their families and their friends. 'Til death do us part ... and it had parted them and nothing he did could stop it. He felt again the grief that had wracked him on that last visit to her grave, the words he'd spoken into the silence of the woodland glade where she rested through eternity, where he'd thought to rest beside her one day. *"I'll love you forever, Elizabeth. God knows I will and I think you know it, too. I'll never love another woman the way I love you."*

He still carried the grief and always would but it no longer burned through every other emotion. He looked at Maria and knew that he wanted her in the same way and just as strongly as he'd ever wanted Elizabeth. It shook him that she was promised to another man and he knew he needed to keep his distance.

Maria had moved her things to another room as soon as Anne and Josephine had climbed into the coach. It was for the best. With his fever broken and his appetite returning, he didn't need her to nurse him. And with the sisters gone, there was no need to keep up a pretense that they were a couple. Tom and Tess already knew better. God only knew what they thought but, whatever it was, they'd never say anything to anyone. Ford was sure of that. They thought far too highly of Maria to sully her name.

But, when she walked by and his daughter reached out her arms, Maria took her with a smile and Ford knew that distance between them was the last thing he wanted.

The next morning, he heard the blast of the coach horn as it neared the boarding house. Their bags were ready on the porch; his horse saddled and at the hitching post out front. They would have one last meal with Tom and Tess and the incoming passengers, and then he and Maria would become just two more passengers continuing on their way north to Taos. Soon they would part company and likely never see each other again.

With no appetite, Ford gave his daughter into Maria's keeping yet again and went in search of Tom while the passengers feasted on steaks and vegetables from neighboring farms. Tom had already found a young woman from a nearby family to cook for them. Tess was learning what it meant to be Tom Ridge's bride and it looked good on her, to Ford's mind. She smiled at him as he stuck his head into the kitchen and asked for Tom.

"He's just behind the house talking with the coach driver who's supposed to be in here eating." Her tone was just a bit tart. "Tom says the coach is only given a little bit of time for each stop."

Ford grinned. "I'll let him know he won't want to miss this meal."

She arched a brow at him. "But you're going to miss it?"

"Well, I thought maybe you'd wrap up a bit of something I could eat later."

She was still scolding him as he ducked out the back with a grin to find her husband.

The whip was already walking toward the house and gave Ford a nod as they passed. Tom leaned against a tree looking contentedly around him. Ford knew he had plans to reopen the store soon, but he and Tess were still rearranging and deciding what else they needed to stock.

He smiled as Ford approached. "I guess you're ready to be on your way. You've got family waiting."

"It's time, I reckon," Ford agreed. "I'm glad I met you, Tom Ridge." He held out his hand and Tom shook it firmly.

"Same. Me and Tess will miss you and Maria."

"With luck, our paths will cross again someday."

"With luck."

Ford sighed. "I've left Evan's horse in your stable. For you and Tess. A wedding present. Evan would like that, I think."

Tom nodded. "That's a fine gift and we'll accept with gratitude. Finding a horse was something I knew I'd have to take care of sooner or later. I'll be proud to take care of him for Evan."

"A man needs a good one and you won't find one better."

They started to shake hands again, but then Tom's arm came around his shoulder with a slap of affection on his back. Ford knew he'd made a friend he wouldn't forget.

On his way back through the house, Tess pulled him close for a hug and thrust a bundle at him. "Just some bread and butter with a nice steak tucked between," she told him.

He gave her a kiss on the cheek. "I'm obliged. You and Tom take care of yourselves. If you ever need help, send for me up Taos way."

"We'll be fine."

And he believed they would be.

Maria waited with McKenna in front of the coach. She gave Ford a smile as he approached. "Our bags are loaded and strapped down."

"I'll just get my horse tied to the back."

"I've got McKenna," she said softly. "You'll be happier riding. Just don't get over tired."

Ford hesitated. He shouldn't lean on Maria more than he already had, but the sunlight and fresh air called to him. "Are you sure?"

She nodded. "Very sure." Then she laughed softly. "When you do tire, you'd best sit in the front with me."

Because of the twinkle in her eyes, he leaned to look into the coach at the middle seat he and Evan would have shared. A thin woman of uncertain age looked back at him with more than a hint of suspicion in her eyes. On the seat beside her sat a bird cage with two small yellow birds inside. He thought they were canaries, simply because of their bright color, but couldn't really have said for sure. He didn't know much about song birds, just predators like eagles and hawks and owls.

He turned to look at Maria. "Thank you. I'll ride for now."

And it was for the best, he told himself. It wouldn't do to spend too much time pressed leg to leg with Maria, but not for the life of him was he sitting next to two birds in a cage.

Chapter Twenty

After clearing away the midday meal, Katherine walked out to the porch. She could see the paddock where the men were saddling to go back to their herds, Jeb and Slade somewhere among them. Hannah had agreed to lie down for a while because only then would Jeb agree to go back out with the men. Both Katherine and Jeb were breathing a little easier, Hannah's appetite had returned and the nightmares seemed to have ceased.

As Slade and Jeb rode out with their men, Katherine gave a sigh and lifted her gaze from the barnyard to the north where distant hills edged their property. She found herself watching that horizon most days as the sun rose and as it faded and at moments in between. She wasn't sure when Ford would come, when he would bring the baby girl she longed to meet. She didn't like worrying but she couldn't help a bit of it, couldn't help the nagging sense that he should have been here by now. She wished he'd been more precise in his timetable of when he would leave Texas and when he thought to arrive in Taos.

But her brother wasn't a specific kind of person. At least he hadn't been. It was Ford's recklessness and wanderlust that had brought Slade to her door that fateful day, that had linked her destiny to Slade's as she struck out across the Texas plains to find her brother and bring him home. Had marriage changed Ford? Or the birth of a daughter? Or the loss of a wife?

Elizabeth had been Katherine's truest friend and Katherine's heart still ached at her passing. She'd been the one friend to stand by Katherine when she'd been returned to New Braunfels after being taken by the Comanches, as if the time with them had been of her choosing. Even Evan Burch, who'd long had a crush on her, had looked at her with just that bit of distrust after the soldiers had brought her home and dumped her, kicking and cursing, into her family's hands. Into Aunt Dee's hands. She thanked God every single day of her life for Deidre McKenna, her mother's sister, the woman who had raised her and Ford after their father's passing. Aunt Dee had understood that the longing Katherine had felt for home during her captivity couldn't diminish her horror at the slaughter of innocent women and children, which had led to her return. But Dee was family, as was Ford. The only person not family who had understood and accepted all that Katherine felt had been Elizabeth.

Elizabeth had loved Ford truly and forever, as Ford had loved her. And now she was gone, leaving Ford's heart shattered and Katherine with no chance to say goodbye. She had left them only with her daughter to love and

Katherine longed to see McKenna as much as she longed to see McKenna's father.

But, as much and as often as she'd watched the horizon, Ford had yet to appear. With a sigh, she started to return to the house when a movement caught her eye. Not in the north, toward Taos and the coachline, but to the east. She tensed, but the rider was solitary and posed no threat, else he'd never have made it past the guards that Slade and Jeb had set. Even from a distance, she thought she recognized Javier Arellano and acknowledged a moment's gratitude that Hannah was resting peacefully in her room. The fiery redhead didn't need the stress or the excitement, not when she'd just begun to regain the peace she'd had early in her pregnancy.

Katherine decided against returning to the house and watched as he drew near. It was no surprise to her when Bartolome and Lorenzo left their work with the *remuda* and other livestock and came to stand with her upon the porch.

On an impulse, she asked Lorenzo to ready her horse. By the time the young Spaniard had reached the house, she was walking toward the paddock. Her divided skirt swung against the dust with each long stride. Lorenzo had saddled her horse—and his. She sighed. The man had no idea the life she'd led before coming West with Slade or her ability with a gun. No idea what she was capable of doing if need demanded.

Javier reached the corral as she took the reins from Lorenzo. A quick glance assured her that her gun hung in its customary place.

Lorenzo gave her an anxious look. "I will go with you, Señora. Shall I send Bartolome for Señor Slade?"

"There is no need to bring Slade from his work. I'm sure this is just a neighborly visit." From a man who didn't feel neighborly toward them at all, she suspected. "Is my gun loaded?"

"Of course, Señora, as always."

"Then there's also no need for you to accompany me. I will stay within sight of the house and the range of your rifle. Please wait for me on the porch, for Hannah's well-being. She rests now. I know I can trust you to ensure she is not disturbed."

Although he didn't look happy, Lorenzo nodded and stepped back as she swung into the saddle. She immediately angled her horse's path so it would intercept the Spaniard's. He was dressed far less grand than on his last visit, with no fine silver or gold thread running through his clothing. His shirt and britches were dark brown and unembellished although they looked to be of a costly fabric.

He reined in his horse and gave her a smile. "Señora Slade, good day to you."

She nodded with just the faintest uplift at the corner of her mouth. "And to you, as well, Señor Arellano."

"Please ... Javier."

"As you wish." But she did not offer him the use of her given name.

"May I ride with you a bit?"

"Certainly, although I've not the time to go far. I just needed the afternoon sun and fresh air on my face."

He turned his horse so that they rode side by side. "It will not be so enjoyable soon. My uncle tells me the bitter winds will begin and last for months."

She nodded. Only this morning Emilio had spoken of bad weather coming across the hills. For now, the sun warmed the air and the sky was blue. But she trusted Emilio's warning. Last year, near this time, it had been much warmer, yet he'd warned of the approach of a winter storm with startling accuracy.

But Javier Arellano hadn't ridden this far to talk of the weather. "What brings you to us today?" Katherine tilted her reins the slightest bit so that her mare began a slow, almost imperceptible arc, keeping their path in the valley that cradled the house. Javier's mount kept pace with hers.

"My uncle believes I have offended you and Señora Welles."

"Your uncle is a wise man."

"Indeed, I have found him to be. Therefore, I felt I must come to apologize—to you and to Señora Welles."

"I'll accept your apology for both of us. If it's sincere."

A jackrabbit bolted across their path, a flash of silver and brown in the bright light of the afternoon. Her mare stayed steady. Javier's fancy stallion snorted and whirled. The young Spaniard brought him back around expertly, but Katherine could see the anger in his eyes. She wasn't sure if it was the horse's behavior or her words that had angered him, but he covered it well with a pleasant expression.

"It is very much sincere." He hesitated as if choosing his words. "I realize things are different here in this country. Women here are different. I was rude by the customs of this country."

Katherine stopped her horse and he did the same. "You were rude by the customs of any country."

He watched her a moment and she wondered if he would argue the point, then he sighed. "It is so."

She nudged her mare forward, uncaring if he resumed their walk or turned his horse toward home now that he had said what he came to say. His stallion fell into step with the mare once again. For several minutes, the only sounds were the horses' hooves on the hard ground beneath them and the faraway cry of a hawk.

"I am to wed a young lady who was raised in this country so it is important that I give respect to those differences," he said.

"You'll wed an American?" For some reason, that surprised her.

"She is of fine Spanish blood, but Maria Cordova was born in this New Mexico Territory."

Katherine mulled that over. So, the young Arellano heir would wed the daughter of his neighbor—and theirs. Interesting but not unusual.

"I will be glad to meet your young lady."

"As will I."

She shot him another look but held her tongue. Arranged marriages did still happen in many cultures.

"And I'll be glad for her to meet you and Señora Welles. A gently raised young woman, a young wife needs friends, those she can turn to for advice on things to do with women."

Katherine felt a laugh bubble deep in her throat but swallowed it back. She and Hannah were probably the last women a 'gently raised' young lady should turn to for advice. She'd be much better turning to her mother though a husband might not think so.

Instead of making that point, she shrugged and said, "I can teach her how to make decent cornbread and how to hit whatever she aims a gun toward." She could almost read his thoughts and waited for him to tell her that no wife of his would ever need to hold a firearm.

"Those things, too, are good skills."

Without giving him warning, Katherine wheeled her mare about to face Javier. He looked startled, just as she wanted him to feel. "Señora?"

She had his attention and she'd let this go as far as she

intended. "This conversation is a far cry from your last visit. Too far for me to swallow."

He had the grace or the wisdom to look embarrassed. "My apologies once more, Señora," he said stiffly. "It is true my uncle warned me that I had offended you on my last visit. He was displeased with me and that stung my pride. Upon reflection, I was displeased with myself. If I am to have him see me as a man, I must behave as a man. If I wish Señors Slade and Welles to respect me, I must show myself to be worthy of respect."

"And is that what you wish? Their respect?"

"And yours, if we could begin again. If you are willing for me to have that opportunity."

"I'm not unwilling but, for now, I have to get back. I've work to do."

"As do I, Señora Slade. As our neighbor, you and your household will receive an invitation to my wedding. It is my hope that all will attend."

Katherine watched for a moment as he rode up the hill toward home. When he reached the crest, he turned to wave at her as if he'd known she waited and watched. As perhaps he had.

Her only thought as she turned toward the ranch house was that he'd said *my* wedding, not *our* wedding. As if he alone mattered. And Katherine could believe that was how he felt despite his pretty words.

Lorenzo met her at the barn, searching her face as she drew near. She knew he'd been watching their every move, trying to discern from her actions, her behavior, if he needed to come to her aid. Worrying that he would have missed a sign of trouble. Whatever he saw now must have reassured him because he simply nodded and held the mare to be unsaddled. He'd learned by now that, on rare occasion, she might ask for her horse to be saddled but she always removed the saddle and groomed her mount afterward.

Hannah was awake and kneading dough for bread when Katherine walked in from brushing her mare.

"How was your ride?" There was a hint of longing in Hannah's voice. Katherine knew she missed being on horseback, but not enough to risk the baby once she grew ungainly with her pregnancy.

"Hmmm," Katherine brushed her hair out of her face, "fine except Javier Arellano decided to join me."

Hannah's hands ceased their work and she frowned at Katherine. "I thought it was one of our men I saw with you. What did that jackal want?"

Katherine lifted a brow and grinned. "Jackal? That's quite an insult for a man who sends you his apologies for his rudeness."

"But fitting," Hannah muttered, giving the dough a punch. "I don't like him."

"Nor do I."

"Good. We need to be wary. I don't trust his eyes."

Katherine stepped back to the porch and pulled a dipper of water from the barrel before returning to Hannah and their exchange. The water felt cool against her dry throat.

"I don't trust any part of him," Katherine agreed. "He's a coward and cowards are dangerous. They'd rather not give an opponent a fighting chance, not when it's far too easy to strike from behind."

"So why did he come and why didn't you just send him right back where he came from?"

"Because the best place to keep an enemy is where you

can see him and the best place to learn about your enemy is from your enemy."

Hannah placed her dough in a pan and covered it with a damp towel. "And did you?" she asked. "Learn anything, I mean."

"A little. His uncle scolded him for his behavior. His words told me he came to make amends. His eyes told me he's mad as blazes at the need." She smiled. "We're invited to his wedding to a 'gently raised young lady' that he hopes will come to us for advice."

Hannah gave a gurgle of laughter, much like the one Katherine had chosen to swallow when talking with Javier. "He better hope like hell she doesn't come to me if he wants to keep his manhood intact."

Katherine's lips twitched at the comment. Hannah could be as bloodthirsty as a Texas low-country mosquito.

"I'm going to get the sheets off the line. Emilio is convinced we'll see a northern storm before daylight. Javier said his uncle thinks the same."

"I'll help so we can fold them into the basket as we take them down," Hannah offered. "My bread needs to breathe and rise a few hours before I touch it again."

She followed Katherine to the porch where Katherine picked up the basket at the corner. They worked quickly and quietly as they most often did but when Hannah reached for the basket filled with clean bedclothes, Katherine intervened. "You don't need to be lifting anything that heavy."

"Probably best you don't either. Now."

Katherine gave her a quick look of surprise. "You know?"

"For a week now."

Katherine rolled her eyes, but smiled. "You and Slade."

Hannah chuckled. "I'm not surprised he realized as well. He watches you all the time."

"As if Jeb ever takes his eyes off you," Katherine shot back, then laughed. "I'm happy our babies will have each other to play with and learn together."

"Me, too," Hannah said softly. "I never want my child to be lonely."

As Katherine knew how alone Hannah had been through her brief, too-young marriage to a preacher who never saw the good in her.

Lying in the dark with Slade's arms wrapped around her, her back to him and her body curved into his embrace, Katherine heard the first strong winds sweep down from the northern hills and strike the house. Emilio had been right, once again.

Chapter Twenty-one

Ford felt the shift in the weather after the first swing station stop. It had seemed natural for him and Maria to gravitate to one another, to walk and talk together in the small amount of time allowed for them to stretch their legs. At first, she'd been reticent, lingering in her seat with McKenna until the other passengers had left the coach. He thought, perhaps, she was trying to gauge their standing after his illness and waking up with him wrapped around her. He'd been careful to act as if he'd put the incident from his mind when, in fact, he thought of little else with every glimpse of her.

At the second stop, he made sure to be at the coach door when it was opened. Seeing him waiting there, the spinster with the canaries held back while he helped Maria and McKenna safely to the ground. McKenna lurched toward him with a squeal and he caught her, struck by the solid weight of her. She was growing up too fast.

Nearly unbalanced by the little girl's movement, Maria grabbed Ford's arm to steady herself. It surprised him when she laughed at herself and the sound pulled a burst of laughter from him. In that quick moment, the awkwardness between them melted away.

The whip helped the spinster to the ground and she swept past them with an offended glance as if the light-hearted sound was somehow an insult. Maria lifted her brows at the sniff she gave them, but Ford winked and her smile returned. Holding his daughter in one arm, he offered the other to Maria, glad when she placed her hand inside the crook of his elbow. He instinctively pressed his arm to his side, pulling her closer, and she didn't pull away.

"Do those canaries sing?"

"I haven't heard so much a peep or a chirp from either one." She gave him a sidelong glance. "I'm not sure she gives them much to sing about."

"The ladies in the back tried talking to them, but she quickly covered their cage with a cloth so they couldn't see, which I thought was rude."

Ford thought for a moment, wondering if he should just keep his thoughts to himself but Maria was watching his face. "What?"

"I suspect the older woman was even more offended by those two than she is by us and she probably thinks we're man and wife."

For a moment, she didn't say anything at all. "Perhaps we should clarify what we are to one another."

"Perhaps we shouldn't."

The words had popped out before he thought and, if she questioned why he felt that way, he'd be damned if he could give a reason she'd understand because he didn't understand. The truth was, she'd begun to feel like his wife and McKenna's mother but he couldn't say that to her, not when she was going home to marry another man.

Fortunately for him and maybe her as well, her mind was on a different track. "Why would she be offended if that's what she thinks?"

"Some spinsters don't cotton to men at all and don't care for those who do."

"Well, but the two young ladies behind her have been nothing but kind. And they don't wear rings so she has no reason to think they are married."

Ford chuckled and shook his head. "Maria."

Her eyes narrowed at him, then widened in understanding. "Are you saying, they are *that* kind of women?"

She turned to look at the women who were dressed as plain as any housewife, not like Celeste's women. No man would mistake them for anything but what they were. They leaned against the side of the swing station. One stood sideways with her weight on one foot, one shoulder against the building and one hand on her hip so that the cloth of her gown was tight against her stomach. The other leaned against the wall, hands behind her back, thrusting her bosom forward. Two of the stock tenders stood close by, gazing from one to the other. They stood far closer than was necessary for conversation, if Ford was any judge of distance.

"Oh." That was all she said, just that one word. Then, "Well, that's a reason to make a husband keep his distance, I suppose, but a bird?"

Ford's shout of laughter drew her gaze to his face and

her own laughter broke through. "What a nonsensical conversation this is," she admitted.

"Maybe the best kind," he suggested and they kept walking until the whip gave a short blast on his horn to gather them to the coach once more.

At the door to the coach, he advised, "At the next stop, we need to pull a cloak for you and a blanket for McKenna from the baggage." Maria studied his face gravely, then nodded. "I won't forget." But she didn't question him. Ford tried not to take pride in that thought. Could be she was a woman who didn't question much, but he recalled her insistence on being given Lem's firearm and he doubted that was the case.

Maria watched Ford through the window, his daughter warm against her chest. She couldn't have said what she was feeling in that moment unless it were to admit to a sense of loss. That was ridiculous, she knew. He wasn't hers and she wasn't his. There was nothing to lose when she'd never had ... what? She couldn't put a name to it. To do so would make it impossible to relinquish at the end of their journey. They would go their separate ways and live their lives. But she would think of him. She knew that now. She would think of him in the years to come. And wonder.

Restless, she twisted in her seat and caught a glimpse of the hills in front of them. The sky was a leaden gray and far from a reassuring sight. She leaned back and looked at the ladies in the back of the coach. "If you've warm cloaks in your bags, you'll want to find them and get them out on the next stop. Ford says there's cold weather ahead."

"That your man?" the redhead on the back seat asked. "He's mighty fine looking."

Maria smiled. "I agree, he is handsome." They could take it as they would, but she wasn't giving either of them an open field with him. "And he's rarely wrong. If he says it will be cold, then it will be cold, indeed."

"Maybe he could keep all three of us warm," said the more slender of the two. Dark brown curls tumbled from a loose knot at the top of her head and her eyes hinted slyly of knowledge a respectable woman wouldn't have.

"Perhaps he could … but I choose not," Maria softened her words with a smile. She truly believed they meant no harm.

"Don't blame you, sister girl." The redhead gave her a wink. "I wouldn't be sharing that man either."

"Jezebels," the spinster hissed as she pulled her bird cage closer.

Before either of the girls could spit back an answer, Maria said softly. "If you need a warmer covering for your sweet birds, I think I have a cloak to drape over the cage. As for our fellow passengers, they've said nothing untoward. Nor have I."

The older woman cast her eyes toward the floor. When she lifted them, they were more anxious than angry. "You'll give my babies a warm covering?"

"Of course," Maria said softly. "At our next stop. We'll all need our warmest clothing before the afternoon miles." And as she spoke, she found herself wishing that Ford had a warmer jacket. He could not afford to grow ill again. She didn't doubt that he was weak yet, though he hid it well.

A swirl of dust through the window caused Maria to turn and shield McKenna with her body. She heard Ford's shout and the whip's answering curse; the coach slowed then stopped. It was Ford who loosened the strap of her window while the whip loosened the strap on the other side of the coach.

Ford's expression was set as he touched McKenna's curls through the window. The back of his hand brushed against Maria's cheek and she caught her breath. Had he touched her intentionally? Was it a caress, a careless gesture, or simply an unintentional contact? Her gaze searched his but read nothing.

"Are you alright?" he asked.

She took a deep breath and smiled to reassure him. "We're fine. Thank you."

He nodded and lowered the leather covering between them. Maria quickly secured her side with the strap while the redhead shifted to the middle seat to do the same on the other.

Before she returned to her seat, she looked at the spinster who was visibly shaken by the thought of bad weather. "I'm Jessie." She pointed to the back where the brunette watched with lively interest. "That's Candida. We'll take care of you."

The spinster nodded but didn't speak. A moment later Maria heard her take a quivering breath and felt bad for her, but she could offer no real reassurance of their safety. These ladies may or may not know what a New Mexico Territory winter storm looked like, but she knew. Although it was still early in the season, it wasn't too early. If it struck with force, her focus would have to be protecting McKenna while her father did what he could to help keep the coach moving forward toward safety.

She could hear the whip urging the team on and felt the coach begin the incline. When the first hard gusts rocked the equipage, she bit her lip. The team would be struggling against that force. The spinster whimpered low in her throat. Thankfully, McKenna slept on. The wind along the crest of the hills was the worst, but lessened as they descended into the valley beyond.

McKenna roused at the sound of the whip's horn, signaling the next stop of their approach. Maria sighed in relief, as the coach rolled down the narrow road of a small town rather than into the dirt yard of a small way station.

"Well, I'm glad that's over," the redhead—Jessie—said fervently. "I thought it would be a lot worse."

Maria looked at her in surprise and hesitated before saying, "I fear we may not have seen the worst, yet." And though she didn't want to alarm the others, she felt compelled to add, "In truth, I am certain we have not."

"Well, damnation."

The spinster didn't so much as bat an eye at Jessie's profanity.

Maria kept still with McKenna until the other women had been handed out of the coach. Ford stepped up to take his daughter and then help Maria to the ground. One look at his face made Maria's heart sink. Ford thought as she did—that they were in for much worse weather than the little they'd experienced. She took notice of the additional baggage on the low, weathered porch of the boarding house.

Their whip stood at the door of the dining hall as they entered. "Eat fast, folks, we need to get to our next stop before it worsens."

Their meal was ready and serving bowls and platters were passed in haste. Maria focused on McKenna who sat in Ford's arms across from her. The little girl was playing with her food more than she was eating it and Maria worried she'd be hungry later. It was too late to regret feeding her the bits of bread and butter she'd brought onto the coach with them. She'd just have to make sure she tucked something away to take with them on the next leg of their journey.

She paid attention to the three gentlemen at the table, suspecting they would be joining the coach from here. They all bore a resemblance to one another but were decades apart in age. All medium height, medium build, with no distinguishing features. And not one of them said a word the entire meal.

The whip finished first and stomped out of the room. His shotgun rider followed.

To Maria's surprise, Ford rose from his chair and walked around the table. As he reached her chair, she stood and held out her arms for McKenna. She wasn't sure what Ford had in mind but he had a purposeful look about him.

Maria and the other ladies finished before the men. While Jessie and Candida sat chatting quietly, the spinster twisted and untwisted the worn linen napkin in her lap. Maria stood and carried McKenna to the porch.

Ford and the whip faced each other at the boot of the coach, arguing.

"You'll never make the next stop," she heard Ford say grimly. "Not with what's headed this way."

"I'll have a fresh team and its mostly flat ground between here and there."

"I can't risk that with my daughter. Look at the sky, man!"

The whip didn't so much as turn his head but Maria did. Grey sky had given way to angry, roiling clouds of purple. They were some distance away, still on the horizon, but she had no doubt of the speed with which they were moving closer.

"You'll forfeit your fare if you get off here."

"I'll take my chances on that." Ford wheeled about and started toward the boarding house. When he saw Maria, his steps slowed.

He crossed to her, studying her face. "You heard."

She nodded, not sure what to say or do.

"That fool is going to kill every person on that coach for the sake of the mail. This is his third trip on this route. He's never seen winter on the plains much less a northern storm." Again, she nodded and Ford sighed. "Let me get your bags off. Please."

A dozen thoughts went through her head before she took a deep breath and lifted her chin. She handed McKenna to her father then crossed to where the whip stood waiting. "Mr. Bellamy will remove my bags along with his. I think you're unwise to move forward and I won't risk my life going with you into that storm."

When she turned back to Ford, she saw the other passengers all standing on the porch watching the exchange.

Candida had linked arms with one of the new male passengers, her full bodice pressed to his forearm, and she gave Maria a wink as she walked by. "Mr. Bellamy, is it?"

Maria said nothing.

Jessie rolled her eyes at Candida's back and turned to Maria. "Good luck to you."

"And to you," Maria whispered against the knot in her throat. The passengers would need far more than good luck to survive what lay ahead of them.

The spinster vacillated the longest, with the whip nearly shouting at her to get aboard or he'd throw her bags on the ground. She looked at the canaries who huddled in the bottom of their cage then looked at Maria. Abruptly she walked back to the porch without answering the man. Ford helped the whip remove her bag along with his and Maria's.

At the last moment, Maria remembered the firearm that had been Lem's. "My gun!" she shouted to Ford. He nodded and stepped into the coach to retrieve the shotgun from under the seat that had been hers.

When the coach lurched forward with its fresh team, Ford looked at the pile of their bags in the road then at the back of the coach. "God help them."

Chapter Twenty-two

Dressed as warmly as practicality allowed, Slade led his horse from the barn behind Jeb. Most of the men already waited between the house and the barn, their horses snorting and sidling, trampling the fresh snow beneath. All three of their wagons, two with flatbeds and one with slatted sides, were hitched to mule teams and loaded with hay and grain.

The storm had struck with a vengeance Slade had not foreseen. He'd experienced a number of northers in Texas and even one since moving to the Territory but this one had been a killer. And that was what he feared, that they would find cattle who'd been caught in the open and failed to make it to some kind of protection. Those that had sheltered against hillsides away from the wind or within a solid stand of trees would need the food the wagons carried.

Katherine and Hannah watched from the porch. He couldn't see the worry upon their faces but he knew it was there. The cattle were their livelihood but—even more—the animals depended upon them for food and couldn't be left to suffer starvation.

Slade forced his attention back to the men waiting patiently while the last of them gathered. The warmth of the morning sun was welcome in more ways than one. The sooner the snow melted, the less of their precious winter forage would have to be used. It was early yet and spring had proven more deadly than autumn of the previous year. He and Jeb would use every bit that was needed now but save every bit that they could for what was to come.

Jeb stepped closer to the men. "You men know what to do and how to do it. Just be sure to stay within sight and sound of each other. If you lose contact with anyone, you stop where you are until that man is found. And every man of you is to return here at midday. Understood?"

Jeb waited and Slade watched with him to ensure every man was paying attention and every man took that seriously. A horse could take a wrong step into a gully or off a hill without warning of any kind and man and horse would disappear silently, engulfed by the deadly snow. There was no room for a single mistake by anyone.

He and Jeb had debated splitting into teams and sending half out in the morning and half in the afternoon. In the long run, it made more sense to reach as many areas as possible as quickly as possible. But they couldn't afford to exhaust their men or subject them to frozen limbs or eyes blinded by the snow with too long of an exposure.

When Jeb turned to look at Slade, he nodded. They'd said all that needed to be said when talking through their plans with the lead vaqueros. Those plans had been communicated by the leads to their teams with either Jeb or Slade standing quietly and just listening to ensure complete understanding on all sides. Their cattle were important. Their men even more so.

Slade waited as they rode out in differing directions. As the last man passed, he fell in with Antonio's vaqueros. Jeb and a few of their more solid hands would remain close to the ranch house. If any of their men returned needing assistance or direction, Jeb would handle that.

There was a prickling along Slade's spine that was more worrisome than Slade liked, mostly because he couldn't explain it. Other than the bitter cold and the normal hazards of trying to maneuver where snow had drifted into piles or into crevices that couldn't be seen, there was nothing unnatural about the day. The surface of the snow was already yielding to the rays of the sun. It was possible they had lost a few cattle during the storm's swift passage but he'd found the range-bred creatures to be cunning when it came to their own survival. Yet the prickling remained.

Katherine stepped outside yet again to scan the horizon. Snow, melting from the morning sun, dripped steadily from the roof of the long porch. No sign of any of the men returning but they would soon. The bunkhouse cook would have something warm and hearty ready for the men when they returned. She would have the same for Slade and Jeb.

Hannah sat in the front room mending shirts, a task Katherine despised but Hannah didn't mind. She took a deep breath of unexpected contentment. This wasn't an easy life she and Slade had chosen but it was a good one. In New Braunfels, they could have called upon a dozen neighbors to help them raise a barn or overcome a disaster. Here they had vaqueros whose hands were willing and skillful but who were, at the same time, another responsibility for as long as they chose to stay at the ranch, theirs to keep safe and provide for.

"Katherine?"

Katherine's heart lurched at the odd sound in Hannah's voice as she called to her from the house behind her. She turned, her skirts suddenly heavy and tangling around her legs.

Hannah stood by the chair, the garment she'd been mending clutched in one hand, a pool of water drenching the hem of her skirt. Her sky-blue eyes held bewilderment and a hint of terror. "It's too soon."

Katherine took a steadying breath and forced a smile. "Apparently not. Let's get you comfortable and I'll get Jeb."

"I'm afraid," Hannah admitted.

Katherine gave her a fierce look. "We are *not* going to lose this child."

Hannah studied her face for a moment then nodded, the tension easing from her features. "Help me change my gown."

Katherine smiled and nodded, sending a silent plea heavenward as she followed Hannah to her room. The Comanche women relied on several herbs to help prevent miscarriages and early labor. Some were made into tisanes, some ground and placed in pipes for the woman to breathe in the smoke. One, she recalled, the women would chew, swallowing the juice but not the twig. But Katherine had none here nor the knowledge to prepare and use them if she did have.

She helped Hannah remove her gown, quickly taking the hand Hannah held out to her as the first birth pain swept her. Hannah's belly looked unexpectedly huge without the gathers of her gown around it. Seeing the spasm move across the tightly stretched skin, Katherine knew this baby would come even if she had every one of those herbs at hand. Whether they willed it or not, Hannah's time was here. The other woman bore the pain in silence, gripping Katherine's hand until it passed. Afterward, she raised her anxious gaze to Katherine.

Katherine gave her a nod of reassurance. "Looks like you're going to hold that baby sooner rather than later. I'd best get Jeb."

Hannah sighed as the pain ended. She lifted her arms for Katherine to slip a nightshift over her head, then eased down to the bed. "Not yet. Wait a bit. He'll just fret."

But if Katherine didn't get him, she knew he'd be furious. Especially if anything happened to Hannah. But Katherine wouldn't let that thought take hold. She watched as Hannah closed her eyes, waiting for the next pain. Hannah was as strong and stoic a woman as any Comanche mother Katherine had known. She just didn't look it. Her bones were fragile looking beneath skin pale as cream.

"Rest as much as you can," she whispered. "I'm going to get water heating and make sure we've plenty of linens close by." And get Jeb, but she didn't say it.

She stopped at the door, feeling more helpless than she had in a very long time. "I'll bring some water for you to sip when I return."

Hannah didn't answer and Katherine wondered if she were already asleep or simply bracing herself for the next birth pain. Katherine hoped she slept. Hannah was going to need all the strength she had.

Walking quickly along the breezeway back to the kitchen, she checked to be sure the cauldron was full of water, then swung it across the fire that burned low in the hearth. She stepped out on the porch and her breath caught in her throat at the sight of Slade riding away, slapping his reins against the hip of his horse with Jeb close behind.

Accepting that something unforeseen had happened, unforeseen and likely not good, she straightened her spine. Hannah got her wish. Jeb would be spared the anxious waiting and floor-walking that was all a man could do. And she and Hannah were on their own.

Jeb stared down at the body the vaqueros had unearthed from a snowdrift. He looked across at Slade, bewildered. "What the hell?"

Señor Arellano stared up at them with sightless eyes. An arrow centered his chest, but no blood stained his shirt.

"How did you find him?" Jeb asked finally.

"By chance," Slade said. "He wasn't deep. One of the men saw a young wolf pawing at the snow covering him. Thought it might be one of our herd and came to check it out."

Jeb forced his stare from the dead man and glanced around. He could see where Slade and their men had searched the snow around the body looking for something that could tell them what had happened. "That stand of trees marks our boundary, doesn't it?" The body lay just beyond their property line. The Spaniard lay on his own land, not theirs.

"That one and the next," Slade agreed. The trees grew along the creek bank just inside the line between their land and Arellano's.

"So, what in the hell was he doing so far from home in a winter storm?" Alone. No horse. Jeb didn't like anything he was thinking.

"Well, one thing's for sure. He can't tell us."

"And the arrow?" The point hadn't drawn blood. He'd been dead before it hit his body. Just like with Carlos.

"More of the same and none of it makes any sense. I'll send word to Kit but there's not much he can do."

Jeb agreed. This was trouble but it wasn't Indian trouble. "We need to get the body home. His household is likely out looking for him now."

"I'll take care of it. Let Katherine know I'll be home before daylight."

They stepped back and watched as their men brushed the snow from the still figure and readied him to return home as best they could.

Slade had been out in the cold and the snow all morning. Jeb knew he should offer to take Arellano's body home but something pulled at him, some inexplicable urge to get back to Hannah, to see her and know she was safe.

The property in front of Arellano's barn was filled with vaqueros, either mounted or holding their saddled horses, waiting for direction, much as their own men had done that morning. Judging by the weariness on the men's faces, they'd already been out and searching for the rancher for more than a few hours. They watched as Slade and Lorenzo drew near then shifted their stares to the burden tied awkwardly across the young mule's back. Expressions changed from weariness to despair and regret. It wasn't hard to guess that Arellano had managed to earn the respect, if not the affection, of these men during his brief time in America.

An older man, dressed a little less warmly than those

on horseback, turned and walked hurriedly toward the hacienda, pushing the door wide without knocking.

Slade and Lorenzo dismounted and nodded at the vaqueros who watched them uneasily. None made a move in their direction. When the door to the hacienda reopened, Arellano's young kinsman crossed the porch and came down the few steps. He was garbed for riding and his face looked gray with fatigue. He glanced into Slade's eyes as he walked toward him, then his gaze traveled to the mule's burden. He stopped, features grim, as he reached a hand out to touch the edge of the blanket shrouding the body.

For a moment, there was no movement, no sound. Slade felt the warmth of the sun, the crispness of the air, and the death under that blanket. Arellano's nephew took a deep breath and looked back at Slade. "My uncle?"

Slade nodded. "I'm sorry."

Javier dropped his hand and his head and Slade gave him the silence he needed to gather his thoughts. When he looked up again, his eyes glittered in the strong rays of the winter sun. "What about the men who traveled with him?"

"There was no one."

Javier's brows drew together. "I don't understand."

Slade waited in the silence that followed the statement. It wasn't a question and he couldn't have provided any answers if it had been.

"His horse?"

Slade shook his head. He'd wondered the same. Arellano had been too far from home to have walked.

Javier frowned. "My uncle came to me after the noon meal yesterday. He had papers regarding the operation of the ranch he wished for me to study. He spoke of two men who had come from the government with a request to look at our herd."

"Your herd?" Slade frowned. "Were they looking to buy?"

"They suggested to my uncle that a war between the states would begin in the months to come. Troops will need to be fed good beef." Javier shook his head. "I realized this morning that he had not returned, but hoped to find the three of them safe in one of the small buildings along the boundaries of the property. We looked there first, but all they held was the grain stored for times of need."

Slade couldn't imagine lying down to sleep knowing Jeb was missing while a winter storm swept toward them.

Something in his expression caught the young Spaniard's attention and Javier stiffened. "Our rooms are in different wings. We both prefer our privacy and frequently dine alone."

Since Slade hadn't made any accusation, he didn't respond to the comments. Instead, he glanced around at the ranch hands who'd ridden out all morning looking for the man. They'd backed away as Javier had approached. Perhaps in deference. Perhaps not. Slade could read nothing from their faces. He wondered that Arellano had ridden out with two strangers unaccompanied.

Javier's lips thinned, as if still sensing the criticism in Slade's silence. "My vaqueros will assist with my uncle's body. I must travel immediately to Taos to report his death and bring a priest to see to his burial."

Turning on his heels, he shouted orders to the men around him in swift Spanish. He'd slipped easily into his new role, Slade noticed. My vaqueros, he'd said. Not, my uncle's.

Before he entered the hacienda, he stopped and glanced back, asking the question, Slade could not answer. "How did my uncle die?"

"I didn't examine the body," Slade spoke carefully. "There was an arrow in his chest, one with feathers or marking, but that's not what killed him."

"How can you know this?" Javier's tone was haughty.

"There was no blood. A wound doesn't bleed after death. My thought is that it was left by someone who wished the Indians to be blamed."

"Or," Javier countered quickly, "as a warning of what is to come. My uncle's death may not have happened intentionally but could have been viewed as fortuitous."

Slade held his peace. Now wasn't the time for an argument. The Spaniard disappeared into the hacienda and the men around Slade and Lorenzo dispersed. Only one came forward. He was taller than those around him with lean muscles rather than bulk. Though he looked no more than Slade's age, his hair was snowy white.

"I am Raul. I will take Señor Arellano now," he said quietly.

Slade saw more sorrow in the servant's face than he had in the nephew's. "Raul, I am sorrow for this loss."

"He was fair, a good man." Face expressionless, Raul shot a look at the closed door of the hacienda and shook his head.

Slade took a gamble. "Did you see Señor Arellano yesterday afternoon?"

Raul lifted one shoulder then glanced at Lorenzo before looking away.

"Lorenzo, please take our horses to the trough to drink. Raul and I will take care of Señor Arellano."

Following Raul's lead, Slade turned toward the barn. "I saw the Señor early in the day. Not after that."

"And the two men who came to see the beef?"

"I saw no one." Raul's answer was firm.

"Perhaps Señor Arellano met them someplace."

Raul looked straight ahead. "I am the master of horse here. I, alone, saddle for Señor Arellano. No one else."

"And you didn't saddle his horse."

"His horse slept peacefully in the barn last night. The Señor did not ride from here."

Slade didn't say anything else until they reached the barn. "At some point, his nephew will figure out the knowledge you have. You won't be safe here."

Raul nodded but said nothing.

"Do you have family, Raul? Someplace to go?"

"I left Mexico when I was a child. My wife is dead many years. There is no one else."

"It's best you come with me. I've got enough work, but not enough help."

Raul stopped and looked him in the eye. "I am a hard worker, but I own no horse to go with you."

"Can you ride a mule?"

Raul smiled very faintly. "I can ride a panther, Señor."

By the time they reached the barn, planks had been hastily arranged at the back of the barn. They placed the body upon the planks and the men there began wrapping it more securely in heavy canvas.

Slade and Lorenzo waited at the rear of the barn while Raul gathered his few belongings. The men who remained paid little attention to the fact that Raul rode away with the American and his vaquero.

Chapter Twenty-three

Ford was pensive as he navigated his way from the livery stable back to the boarding house. Thoughts of the whip and passengers who had pushed on had never been far from his mind as he listened to the howling wind through the long hours. Snowdrifts were deep in the shadows near the sides of the buildings, but the layer of ice in the hardpacked road between was slick and treacherous. Fortunately, the sun blazed in a cloudless sky and would soon wear away even that reminder of the storm that had swept mercilessly and swiftly through the valley.

The livery owner had proved to be a woman which surprised him at first but her brisk, no-nonsense manner reminded him of Aunt Dee. Not as pretty, but strong and attractive and competent. She'd been more than willing to sell him what he wanted, and she shared knowledge with him just as readily.

He'd learned more than he expected about the remainder of their journey. Maria had trusted him to keep her safe—and he would—but the next decision would have to be hers.

She and McKenna were in the rocking chair on the front porch. McKenna sat on Maria's lap, facing her, both feet planted on the wood slats of the chair on either side of Maria's hips. Maria's hands were firmly against McKenna's back supporting his daughter as she bounced hard in her excitement over the game they played. The child laughed out loud and Maria smiled, her heart in her eyes as she looked at McKenna. At his daughter.

Ford's steps slowed as he reached the boarding house. And his heart stilled. He hadn't expected this. Hadn't expected to feel the way he did as they huddled in bed through the night, McKenna safely between them, talking while the storm raged. Never expected to feel what he did in this moment. Hadn't even wanted to feel this way. He'd learned to deal with his lust, knew it wasn't wrong to need a woman. But this wasn't lust. Or it was, but it was so much more than that. This was a feeling as strong and deep as the love he'd had—and had still—for Elizabeth. It was no less passionate, no less abiding. But, as different as the two women were, so was his love for them just as different. He didn't know how that was even possible but he knew, now, that it was.

The hell of it was, this woman belonged to, and soon would wed, another man. His gut clenched at the realization.

She looked up unexpectedly and her smile stopped his heart even as that smile faltered. Her complexion colored faintly and she dropped her gaze to McKenna. "Papa's here," he heard her whisper.

McKenna twisted and wriggled trying to see him and he scooped her up. He smiled down at Maria. "Can we talk?"

She looked suddenly uncertain at his tone but nodded. He took the chair beside her and McKenna snuggled against his chest.

"I walked to the livery stable to get a horse for you."

His admission brought her gaze to his quickly. "For me?"

"I thought it would be good if we both could ride outside the coach when it was safe to do that. I can easily carry McKenna." He hesitated. "They had a nice palomino mare. She's tiny, but a little fiery. You'll need both hands to keep her in check." The livery owner had been honest about the abilities and flaws of each of her horses. She'd pointed out the ones that were pricier for their flashy looks and the ones that were steady and safe. For all of her love of speed, the little mare had been one she deemed sure-footed and least likely to deliberately unseat a rider.

Maria smiled at his words, then said, "You bought her? For me?"

He felt a moment of uncertainty. "I hope you don't mind. I guess I should have let you look at her first. She was the one I thought would suit you."

"No, truly, it's fine. I'm … I'm grateful and happy."

He felt a moment's relief but there was more he had to tell her. "The livery owner says we're less than a day's ride from Taos."

She studied his expression. "But … that's a good thing, is it not?"

"I suppose. But it's more than two days by coach, because of the gullies and steep rock hills to get around."

"And?"

"And the next coach isn't due to arrive for another three days."

To Ford's relief, she looked more thoughtful than distressed.

"You're considering not waiting for the coach." It wasn't a question.

"It occurred to me as a possibility," he admitted.

"But you're uncertain?"

Only because of Maria, but he wouldn't say so. "The livery owner has made the trip to Taos by herself plenty of times, even ridden the palomino there and back. She says it's safe enough and the landmarks are easy to follow."

"She? A woman owns the stables?" Maria sounded intrigued

"Owns the stables and sells horses to the army." It was the latter that had surprised Ford the most and the reason she had the quality of stock she did in such a small settlement. "We'd both be where we're going days before the coach would have us there."

"It is what you'd rather do."

He realized she didn't voice it as a question. He didn't want her to feel pressured regardless of his preference.

"The decision has to be yours, Maria. The coach has some conveniences for you that the open trail won't but you'd be home sooner." And with her fiancé sooner. The realization cut as sharp as a blade.

"What would be best for McKenna?"

The question was one he'd already asked himself and answered. Still, he gave it some thought before answering. "Every single day she's on this journey is a risk. I knew that starting out. And the shorter the journey, the less opportunity for danger. But there's also the truth that

there's a certain safety in having extra people around her."
He hesitated. "To be honest, though, the only two people
I'd trust with her are you and me."

Maria looked pleased at the compliment, but the
pleasure faded and her expression turned pensive. He
watched her face, wishing he could hear her thoughts,
wishing he could kiss her as if she belonged to him, and
already missing her as he knew he would.

"I think," she said softly, "that we—all three of us—
have had enough of the stage line."

And he still didn't know what she was thinking.

Maria awakened in the pre-dawn hours with the weight
of loss already pressing down upon her. She would miss
Ford and McKenna horribly.

They'd lain down with McKenna cradled between
them with Ford on the mattress but fully dressed and on
top of the covers as he'd been the night before. They'd
talked long into the night, about her childhood and her
years in Boston, about the loss of Ford's parents and the
aunt who had mothered Ford and his sister, about his sister
and all that she had endured. They'd fallen asleep holding
hands, fingers entwined.

For a long while, Maria had lain still, listening to Ford's
even breathing in the early dawn hours. She knew she'd
fallen in love with him. She knew it was wrong. A man
waited for her, waited to marry her. A man her father had
chosen. A man who trusted she would come to him with
an open and willing heart, not one bonded to a man who'd
left his own in a grave far away.

But then, as light edged its way into the room, Ford

opened his eyes and smiled at her and she couldn't regret one moment of their time together nor would she mourn for what she could never have. She had today and she wouldn't waste a moment of it on sadness. The sadness would come soon enough.

They broke their fast on hot cakes and fried pork before Maria returned to their room to wash McKenna and dress her in clean clothing. The little girl played tug of war with the warm cloth Maria used to wipe her and each tug on the cloth was a tug on Maria's heart.

She looked up from McKenna's giggles to find Ford standing in the doorway, an unfathomable look upon his face. Maria felt unaccountably clumsy as she dressed McKenna.

And then they were ready to go. They'd sorted through their bags before they slept, taking the little that might be needed during the day. The rest would arrive in Taos where Ford would meet the coach and bring her belongings to her. So, she would see him at least one more time. She clung to that thought as they walked out into the street, she carrying McKenna, Ford carrying his saddle bag with what they'd need for their ride.

She stopped still at her first sight of the palomino hitched to the rail beside his grullo. "Oh, Ford, she's beautiful."

"Let's hope she's as pretty on the inside as she is on the outside," Ford said with a smile, clearly enjoying her reaction.

"And my gun!" Maria said with pleasure. He'd already placed it in the scabbard at the back of the saddle, a saddle he had to have bought for her along with the mare. She turned to him, touched but suddenly anxious. "My father will pay you for the mare and for the saddle."

For a moment, he didn't answer, just stood looking down at her as if he were memorizing her face as she kept hoping to memorize his. The thought stole her breath.

"They're gifts," he said at last, softly.

"Thank you," she whispered against the tears that threatened, turning her face slightly before he saw more than she wanted.

He fastened his saddlebag in place before taking McKenna from her and swinging easily into the saddle, despite the weight of his daughter in his arms. His strength always fascinated Maria. He wasn't bulky, his muscles were smooth and lean beneath his clothing and she'd noticed more than she should have.

She stroked the mare's nose then stepped her foot into the stirrup. The small palomino mare felt perfect beneath her. The morning was crisp and bright and her mood was suddenly lighter than she'd hoped. She had today with Ford and a pretty little mare and saddle that would bring him to mind in the years to come. She would think of him and say a prayer for his safety and his happiness. His and McKenna's.

The morning passed pleasantly with Ford pointing out things he wished her to see. She tried to soak up as much as possible of his words, his gestures, the tone of his voice as he pointed to a hawk circling above, then a silver-coated coyote on a rocky ridge above them.

There were places where the snow still lay heavily banked against outcroppings from the hills around them and places where the ground showed not a trace as the sun climbed steadily in the sky.

They stopped often to stretch their legs and give the horses a break. McKenna enjoyed those moments of holding her father's hand and balancing on unsteady legs.

She'd be walking on her own soon, Maria thought, wishing she would be there to see, while she tried not to wonder what woman might be a part of Ford's life when that day came. Who would raise McKenna with Ford? Would the woman love the little girl enough? As much as Maria already did?

It was with those thoughts already clouding her mind that they came upon the over-turned coach. It lay against a rocky precipice, wheels skyward as if some giant hand had cast it carelessly aside. Ford saw the circling of vultures first but Maria's gaze quickly followed his skyward then to the area below the scavengers and her breath caught in her throat.

Ford stepped down and she did the same, reaching her arms for McKenna, knowing he had to see, to be sure. It took him a few minutes to climb to where the coach lay. Maria fought the urge to call to him, to tell him to be careful, as if someone or something could spring suddenly from the debris.

The silence seemed absolute. She no longer saw the vultures, no longer heard the soft whisper of the wind against the rocks. The blast of Ford's gun both shocked and sickened her.

When he returned, his face was grim. He took McKenna and said, "one of the mules," but she knew he lied. To protect her from the horror of what he had seen and been forced to do, he had lied.

She thought of Jessie and of Candida and her heart wept.

They reached Taos before nightfall. Mindful of Maria's reputation, Ford was careful to arrange separate rooms, leaving McKenna in her care while he ensured the safety of the horses. During the night, he spent more time staring at the ceiling than he did resting. Tomorrow would be the last time he saw Maria. He couldn't think beyond that reality.

They struck out again at first light, both of them quieter than they'd been the previous day.

Ford's first glimpse of Maria's home solidified what he'd already known. Maria was a young woman with the world at her feet. She came from wealth and would doubtless marry into wealth. He had more than enough to be comfortable, more than enough to provide for his daughter and a wife and any children to come, but he would always be a man who needed to work hard to keep what he had. There would never be an endless supply of gold at his fingertips.

He wanted to be happy for her. He tried. But he couldn't help but wonder would *she* be happy, would wealth be enough or would she long for things that money could not buy? And he wondered if she would think of him in the years to come as she lay in another man's arms, as she lay in childbed giving birth to another man's children.

The smile on Maria's face as she slid from her saddle told its own story. She was happy and relieved to be home, no doubt grateful to Ford for seeing her there in safety but her thoughts were on things to come.

Ford could accept that. As long as Maria was happy, he could accept that.

Within moments they were surrounded by servants and then the front door was flung wide and a man Ford suspected was her father stood in disbelief, then rushed forward to catch Maria in an enthusiastic embrace.

Maria was at once laughing and crying. Ford could barely follow the swiftness of their speech or their language, but it was clear this was her father and she loved him dearly. Moments later, they both turned to Ford and Maria made introductions.

"Were it not for this man, Señor Bellamy," Maria said shakily, "I would be in an over-turned coach with ice and snow for my graveclothes."

"My gratitude to you, Señor Bellamy."

"Your daughter was a blessing to me, Señor Cordova. To me and to my daughter. I am forever in her debt."

"You must come. You must meet Maria's mother and dine with us. She will be equally grateful to you."

"I would be honored, but my family awaits news of me as well." Ford doubted that was true because he'd been deliberately vague about the date of his departure or when he would arrive, but he knew he needed to be gone from here. Leaving Maria would be difficult. He did not want her parents to see or discern just how difficult. It would, in fact, be hell.

He saw the hurt in Maria's eyes, but it was best. And he could not have borne her pity.

Stoically, he watched as she hugged and kissed McKenna in farewell even as he ached for the feel of her against his chest, the touch of her hand in his. Those moments had passed. It was time for him to acknowledge the fact and move on.

At the last moment, she held out her hand to him. Conscious of her father's eyes on them, he took it and smiled. "I am grateful for your care of my daughter, Señorita. I wish you joy in your wedding. If you ever have need of me, I will come in gratitude for all you have done for McKenna."

The sudden tears in Maria's eyes nearly unmanned him, but all she said was, "Go with God, Señor Bellamy, and know the same is true. If you ever have need of me, I will come in gratitude for all you have done for me."

Ford shook her father's hand yet again before remounting and turning his horse to the west of the Cordova property, to what would be his home with his sister and Slade until he and McKenna had a place of their own.

Chapter Twenty-four

As Slade rode out with Arellano's body, Jeb finished redirecting the men before focusing on the care of his horse. He unsaddled then rubbed him down, making sure the sweat had dried where the saddle pad had been before giving him fresh hay and water. Only then did he allow his thoughts to turn to Hannah. She and Katherine wouldn't appreciate him bringing his concerns, his fears—he admitted to himself—for his wife's safety. Yet, whenever everything that needed doing was done, he could no more have stopped himself from heading up to the house to check on her than he could still the sun from rising or setting.

There were times Jeb and Hannah still laughed together at how hard he'd tried to rid himself of her in those days after he'd come upon her, dutifully trying to bury a husband who'd heaped emotional abuse on her. Now, the thought of losing her was his single fear in life.

His stride lengthened as he saw the back door open, then slowed as he recognized Katherine's willowy figure. Likely she had Hannah inside resting. The women were good together. He often heard them laughing as they worked and he knew he and Hannah had done well to hook their future with Slade and Katherine's.

When Katherine lowered herself to the chair beside the door, Jeb's heart stilled. She held a baby in her arms. His baby and Hannah's. She lifted her eyes at the sound of his boots on the porch steps. He saw the weariness, the glitter of tears threatening to spill, and his world caved around him.

The pressure on his chest stopped his breath. "Hannah?" He stumbled forward, her name a whisper, then a roar. "Hannah!"

Katherine stood quickly, calling his name and lifting the child to him, but all he wanted was his wife. The baby wailed and the sound merged with the sound of Katherine's voice as he stepped around her and reached for the door.

"Hannah's sleeping," Katherine called to his back. "Jeb, she sleeps."

Her words pierced the dread wrapped around him but he kept walking until he reached their wing of the house, their room, not quite believing even after he touched her cheek, felt the warmth of the hand that rested upon the quilt tucked around her. Not until then did a gut-deep sob of relief leave him.

He heard Katherine behind him and stiffened, still fearful of what she might have to say.

"It was hard, but Hannah's strong, stronger than I ever knew. It's good your son came early. He's already an armful." He turned to look at her and she held that armful out to him. "Sit. She'll want to see both of you as soon as she wakes."

Jeb sank to the chair beside the bed and raised his gaze to Katherine, unashamed of the tears that burned his eyes. She placed the baby gently into his arms.

Katherine smiled. "Hannah got her way. You have a strong, healthy son. You'll have to try for a girl next time."

When Jeb said, "I don't think I can do this again," her smile turned to laughter.

"I don't think you'll be able to stop it. Hannah wants a houseful and she rarely takes no for an answer."

Jeb couldn't argue the point and didn't try. For now, all he cared was that his wife was safe and his child healthy. Later he'd ask Katherine why the hell she hadn't called him to come in as his son was being born.

He barely heard Katherine as she told him, "I'll leave you to get to know your son. I've got some broth simmering for Hannah when she wants it."

He stared down at the eyes that were open, but seemed not to see him. His son. Jeb hadn't expected to feel like this. Hell, he wasn't even sure he knew *how* he felt. Fiercely protective, for sure. Filled with pride. Humbled by his good fortune. All of that and more. His thoughts whirled along with those emotions. They'd need to add a room. Not too soon, but maybe in a year or two. He couldn't imagine sleeping with his son out of reach, much less out of sight.

Hannah stirred, then awakened. Her eyes fluttered as they opened and she turned her head as if sensing Jeb at her side. When she saw him holding the baby and watching her, she smiled.

"I love you, Hannah." The words didn't seem enough, not nearly enough, but they were all he had.

"We have a son and he looks like you."

Jeb lifted his brow and studied their son's face. He couldn't see it yet but it wouldn't be a bad thing if it were so. A boy shouldn't carry features as delicate as Hannah's. "Where's my daughter?" he teased gently.

"Next time." His smile faded and Hannah sighed. "Jeb, I'm fine. I want lots of children."

"I'm afraid, Hannah," he admitted quietly. "I can't lose you. I couldn't bear it."

"You'll never lose me. One day, one of us will go on, but we'll be waiting up ahead for the other and we'll live on in our children and our children's children." She grinned. "For now, help me out of this bed. I want to be part of what's going on."

Katherine stepped quietly from the room and took a deep and shuddering breath. She wouldn't tell Jeb, not now, maybe never. There had been a moment in time, a real and physical moment, when she thought she was losing Hannah. With her pains at their worst, Hannah's pulse had become uneven and weak. Katherine had feared having not only to tell Jeb that she'd failed to keep Hannah safe but having to live without her best friend for the rest of her life.

The tears Jeb had seen, the tears she'd hadn't allowed to fall, had been tears of relief. With Jeb at Hannah's side and the baby securely in his arms, she walked back out to the porch and sat on the steps and let them come. As they fell, they carried away the long hours of the morning and her own horrible fear that nothing she did would be enough to save Hannah and her child.

She was still sitting on the porch, her face damp, when Slade returned, riding straight to the porch as soon as he saw her, just as he always did. He frowned when he was near enough to see her face. "What's wrong?"

"I hope you aren't hungry," she said, smiling at him tiredly. "There's no food ready yet, but we have a baby." She looked beyond him to the two men headed for the barn. "Who is that with Lorenzo? On the mule." She couldn't picture any of their vaqueros riding a mule. Their pride would never permit it.

"He was Arellano's master of horse. There's a lot to tell and some decisions we'll need to make. I'll be in soon." His voice was grim, and Katherine knew whatever news he had to share wouldn't be good. "Kit may come as well. I sent a rider with a message to him this morning."

"I'll make coffee and get Jeb." As her gaze swept the horizon again, she stilled. Another horse and rider approached. The Indian agent, perhaps. But, there seemed something odd about the silhouette as if the rider carried a bundle of something before him. Or a child, perhaps. She stepped to the edge of the porch and shaded her eyes against the afternoon sun. A bubble of joy swept through her as she leaped from the porch and started to run, calling Ford's name.

Katherine was enchanted with her niece. As she made sure Hannah and her son were comfortable in a rocker near the hearth and that the stew bubbled gently in a large kettle, her eyes went again and again to the little girl who looked so much like Elizabeth. And having Ford sit at their table with Jeb and Slade filled her heart in a way she hadn't known she needed. She'd missed him with an ache she'd accepted as part of moving on with her life. She felt whole again, anxious still about what Slade had to tell them, but ready to take on whatever battle lay ahead.

Ford's arrival, followed by Kit's, had delayed that discussion until after dinner but she knew it weighed heavily on Slade. She could see it in his eyes even as he smiled at her flurry of questions to her brother about Dee and Doyle and Shea.

Kit just sat, patient and quiet in the midst of the reunion, enjoying the coffee Katherine had poured for him. He was a family man, first and foremost, Slade always said. She could see that in him as his steady gaze traveled from Hannah on one side, holding her son, and Ford on the other, his daughter nestled sleepily against his broad chest.

Not until after dinner was served and enjoyed, and not until after Kit helped Slade clear the table insisting Katherine take those moments to visit with her brother, did Kit look at Slade and nod.

It was time, Katherine knew, time to know what faced them, what must be handled. She took a seat on the far side of Ford and held out her arms to McKenna who came to her readily. Ford gave her a grateful smile and leaned in to listen.

He was one of them, with a daughter to protect. He wouldn't back away from a fight. He never had, but Katherine hoped he never had reason to regret the choice he'd made in coming.

Kit's gaze took in Ford, then Jeb, then fixed on Slade. "Let's hear it then."

"You and Jeb know most of it," Slade said, "but Ford

doesn't so I'll start at the beginning."

The telling of it took a while. Slade was concise but so much had happened. Too much, Katherine thought. She looked at Hannah when he recounted the arrow that had taken her mare, but Hannah's attention stayed fixed on her son. Katherine knew she listened and heard, knew she remembered by the way her fingers pleated the soft knitted blanket that wrapped her son.

The loss of Carlos—hearing it told again so starkly—returned Katherine to that horror. Their bulls, the Warrens'. Then Señor Arellano's body so close to their property line.

Ford shifted in his chair, drawing Slade's gaze to him. Slade nodded. Katherine knew he'd listen with a fair mind to whatever opinion her brother voiced.

"I understand your respect for this chief, but how can you be so confident it isn't him or one of his braves?"

"I can give you a few reasons. First, we've been here two years, not once has there been a problem with the band. Second, Jishnu and I have talked many times. He knows I'll not see them go hungry. They've killed a cow or two for food when forced to it and always left something in exchange on our porch for the taking. Mostly, though, they're self-sufficient and damned proud. Third, you ever seen an arrow let fly from any Indian with no markings or the markings, the feathers, removed?"

Ford shook his head. "Can't say as I have. Even so, are you sure he's got the younger braves in check? Sometimes young men can do stupid things."

Despite the gravity of the moment, Slade smiled at him. Katherine's first glimpse of Slade had been of a man come to hunt her brother down. "As sure as I am of anything," Slade said. "All Jishnu wants is to keep his small tribe safe. He won't jeopardize that."

"And I'll give you another reason," Kit said after that. "Jishnu and his band are within easy reach of four ranchers. Only this place and the Warrens' have been attacked, not Arellano's and not Cordova's."

"Because they're Spaniards?" Jeb looked surprised.

"No," Slade said softly, "because one of them is guilty."

"But ... why?" Katherine shook her head. "What is their purpose? And who?"

"I suspect I can answer the who," Slade said, "maybe even the why. Not Cordova. He's been our neighbor as long as Jishnu and no more a problem than the Jicarilla. Arellano is more newly come, as is his nephew, and their arrival is close to the start of the trouble. Too close."

"I can add to that," Kit said. "I checked. One family has opposed the claim you've filed for Ford."

"Arellano," Slade said and Kit nodded.

"And now the uncle is dead," Jeb said. "Which leaves Javier."

"Which is why Arellano's master of horse is here with us. He may be the only one who can say for sure that Javier lied about his uncle leaving with two government agents trying to secure a cattle contract."

"Cattle agents?" Kit shook his head. "I would have heard something."

Slade gave a nod. "Which confirms the lie along with the fact that Raul never saddled Arellano's horse for him. Arellano didn't ride out on his own, alone or with anyone else."

"I suspect you're right," Jeb said, "but why? What does Javier gain by his uncle's death? Arellano was leaving and leaving his nephew in charge, likely to be his heir, particularly once he marries Cordova's daughter. Their marriage could be considered the beginning of a dynasty for both families."

Katherine noted the sudden tension in Ford's shoulders as he leaned forward. "Cordova? The neighbor you believe killed his uncle is the man who is to wed Maria?"

A flood of questions and possibilities followed Ford's questions but Javier, alone, knew the motives for all he'd done. And the men intended to have answers and retribution.

They made their plans before everyone lay down to sleep. They would go to Cordova's first, hopefully to convince him not to wed his daughter to a man they believed to be a murderer. From there, they would go to confront Javier Arellano. None of them had the authority to arrest the man, but none of them shied from the thought of taking him forcibly to authorities in Taos with their accusations.

Ford was on a bedroll in the kitchen. Kit had chosen the barn. Katherine had taken McKenna to sleep between her and Slade.

Ford was still awake when his sister slipped back into the room with him. She sat on the edge of his bedroll and he could see her expression by the light of the fire burning low in the hearth.

"You care for her, this Maria."

He'd told them just enough, that she'd helped him care for McKenna during the trip, that he'd seen her safely to her father's before finishing his own journey. As he'd talked, he could tell by Katherine's expression that she'd seen far more than that in his words. Hell, maybe they all had. He didn't care, not now, not when all he could think about was the danger that Maria would be in if she married a man who had no qualms about murdering, not just strangers, but his own blood kin.

"I love her. I'd marry her."

"Does she know?"

He shook his head. "I didn't say anything. She was promised to another."

But that wasn't quite true. He'd likely said too much in their time together, let her see too much, especially those last days when they'd been on their own. But he hadn't said what he should have, what was most important. He hadn't told Maria what he'd just told Katherine.

He sighed. "I guess you don't like hearing that. It's only been a year since Elizabeth died."

"Ford, Elizabeth was the dearest friend I had in New Braunfels. I was happy when you wed, but I'd never want you to go on alone forever. A year can be short when filled with joy; a lifetime if there's only sorrow. Don't waste another if you have the chance to be happy."

"I love you, Kate."

"And I love you, Ford. Please be safe tomorrow and keep your woman safe."

Ford clenched his hands in the dark. "I plan to."

Chapter Twenty-five

The horses stamped their feet impatiently as the four men rechecked their weapons, leaving nothing to chance. Perhaps Javier Arellano had acted alone, perhaps he had men who followed his orders. They needed to be prepared for either eventuality.

Ford was grateful for the men who rode with him. He didn't know what they would face in the hours ahead. One devious man or a small army led by that man. The thought of death didn't frighten him but he was damned afraid of harm coming to Maria.

The snow had melted entirely in some places and their ride was effortless. On hilltops, the snow had melted during the day then refrozen through the night to a treacherous sheet of glass. They allowed their horses to set the pace, picking their way carefully. As impatient as Ford was to know for sure that Maria had come to no harm, he knew the risks of pushing the animals where the footing was uncertain. Still the delay was maddening.

Then, almost unexpectedly, the Cordova Hacienda loomed ahead.

Maria stood behind her father, confused yet intuitively anxious. Even frightened. Her betrothed, a man she did not know and instinctively disliked, paced the floor before them.

Her father shook his head. "I'm sorry for your loss, Señor, but I do not understand your haste to wed my daughter."

"It is for the best. I must secure our inheritance, mine and therefore my wife's. This is a match of wisdom not emotion. There is no need to delay. We will journey to Taos, the three of us and see this done."

"Papa, I don't wish for my wedding day to be in haste." Maria had steeled herself to speak her piece, yet the fury in the glittering eyes of her betrothed nearly took her breath. Even worse, it seemed to her, was the benign expression he presented to her father, a sharp contrast to what he allowed her to see. But she refused to be intimidated by his anger. "I want to be married here, in our chapel, by our own priest and with you and mama beside me and our friends around us."

Her father studied her eyes, then turned to Javier. "My daughter's wish is reasonable and so it will be done."

Maria gave a sigh of relief only to catch her breath as Javier Arellano wheeled about and pulled a gun from his vest. "It will be done as I say."

Her father cast a telling look her way then nodded at

her affianced. "Very well. I will need a moment or two. We must change our clothing for the ride. I will send word to the stables to prepare our horses." His voice hardened. "But, harm my daughter—now or later—and you will die by my hand."

"Papa…" he squeezed her hand and she fell silent. She would not wed this man, but she trusted her father. She would say no more until she found herself with no choice but to refuse him.

"Change your clothes, my heart, and let your mother know all is well and we will return soon."

With her heart beating hard in her chest, she did as her father bade. But the gown she donned was black and she tucked the small pistol her father had given her into the hidden pocket of her skirts. She'd kill this man before she wed him. Her heart longed for Ford Bellamy, but she knew she had only herself to rely upon. Indeed, she must keep not only herself safe but her father as well. Javier Arellano would pay attention to her father's actions but he surely thought too little of any female to search for a weapon.

She stepped into her mother's room and gave her a kiss upon the cheek. "Papa and I would ride with my intended. We will return soon."

Her mother, who always saw the good in people and circumstances, nodded. "Dress warmly, Maria, there is ice upon the ground. I saw it from my window earlier." Then she returned her attention to her embroidery.

Taking a deep breath, Maria joined her father at the front entrance to await their horses, saddled and brought to them. Javier Arellano had resumed pacing, this time in the dirty snow that still littered the grassy area that fronted their home. Despite her stress and confusion at what was happening, Maria did not miss the four riders who topped the crest of the hill that fronted their home. She turned quickly away so as not to draw Javier's attention to them. She couldn't know if they were friend or foe. Perhaps Javier awaited their arrival as accomplices to this abduction. Still, she sent a prayer heavenward and hoped even as she steeled herself to take advantage of whatever opportunity came her way.

Kit held up a hand and said softly. "Hold up."

Ford looked beyond him to the Cordova home. Even from this distance, he'd know her anywhere, anytime. Maria stood with a man he thought he recognized as her father, even though they'd only met the previous day and spoken for a few, too brief minutes. He didn't recognize the man who strode back and forth in front of them, but his heart knew him and anger burned deep in his chest.

He wasn't surprised when Jeb cursed and said, "That's Arellano's nephew."

Ford had steeled himself for this, that it would not be so easy as to go in with a warning for Maria's father and spirit Maria away to safety.

With a nod to Slade, Ford did what they'd discussed and prepared for and faded to one side while the others continued toward the main entrance and the confrontation to come.

Comforted by the pistol in her pocket, knowing she would shoot to kill the man before she let him touch her, Maria stood calmly by her father. This was not how she had expected her betrothed to present himself but she'd learned much during her journey home and her time with

Ford. She could protect herself when need be, herself and her father who had never been anything but good to her.

She didn't fear taking a life to protect a life, not after what she'd seen. Not when that life was as dear to her as her papa's.

As the riders approached, she realized the four had become three but she didn't react to that, or to anything. The closer the three could come before Javier noticed them, the better for her. If they would not help her, she could at least use them as a distraction. If they were foe, then so be it.

The first man to catch her eyes, however, gave her a nod and the nod gave courage. She didn't know him but he didn't call out to Javier and his glance in her intended's direction was grim.

Javier froze as he saw them, then he cursed. Maria felt a surge of hope as the three riders drew near. Javier's hand curled hard around her wrist as he jerked her in front of him and tried to back her toward the door of the hacienda. But she resisted as much as she dared. She could not let him get her inside, away from the men.

Her father stepped forward at her struggle. "Back away," Javier told him tersely without turning his face from the three on horseback.

Her father looked into her eyes and she nodded, frightened of what Javier might do to him if he refused.

One of the men nudged his horse a step forward and Javier's grip on her arm tightened painfully.

"Why, boy?" he asked calmly, "What's all this been about?"

"Who are you?" Javier's tone remained belligerent, but she heard the faint thread of uncertainty that had not been there before.

"Name's Carson. Kit Carson."

"I've heard of you. My uncle praised your work with the natives." He almost spat the last word.

"The uncle you killed?" The man, Carson, kept his tone even and his gaze fixed on Javier as first the rider on his left, and then the rider on his right, dismounted.

"I killed no one." Javier tried to force her another step backward but they were at the door. "But I'm not sorry for his death. He brought me here to take his place then judged me not worthy. His property is now mine and your laws cannot touch me. I am of noble Spanish blood not some ill-bred cowhand."

"We'll see what the hangman says to that," Carson said evenly.

"Bastard," Javier said, sounding less certain.

Because she was watching the men closely, she saw when the gaze of the man on Carson's right flickered to a point behind her, then away. She stilled, no longer pulling against Javier's grip, not wanting him to turn to look at her and realize there was a fourth man, the one who had disappeared from view.

She cast a quick glance at her father and knew he had seen as well but he, too, kept his gaze on the men in front of him. As her heart thudded in her chest, she felt the warmth of a hand on the small of her back, watched as the short barrel of a pistol eased forward over her shoulder to press against the back of Javier's neck.

"Don't make me spill your blood on my woman's gown," Ford said quietly. "I won't like it."

With a howl of rage, Javier dropped his grip on her arm, whirling with both hands on his pistol. Instinctively, Maria dropped to the ground as shots rang out with deafening nearness.

She heard her father cry her name as Ford pulled her up into his arms, turning her face from what she knew was the carnage of multiple bullets entering Javier's body.

Maria leaned into Ford's strength and lifted her eyes to the mountains and to the hills they'd crossed together. My woman, he'd said. And, for the first time, since returning to New Mexico, she felt as if she'd truly come home.

Before he released her from his arms, he whispered, "Maria Cordova, will you marry me?"

She drew back slightly so that she could see his eyes. "Elizabeth?"

"I thought I'd buried my heart in that grave with her. I didn't. I love you, Maria. I need you. Will you be my wife?"

"Now and forever," she said, softly but clearly. "For all the days of my life."

Susan Yawn Tanner is a bestselling author in both romance and mystery. She lives in Mississippi with her menagerie of cats and horses.

Visit Susan's website to discover more about the author and her books. Sign up for her newsletter where she announces new books and exciting giveaways.

susanytanner.com